LIES AND LULLABIES

LIES & Lullabies

by **SARINA BOWEN**

TUXBURY PUBLISHING LLC

ONE

JONAS

Pine boughs scraped against the windows of the forty-five-foot tour bus as it crept along the last half mile of the dirt road. By the time the driver came to a stop outside the Nest Lake Lodge, I was already on my feet. And when the door swung open, I jumped out to taste the Maine air.

This was the moment of truth. I inhaled deeply, taking in the summery scent of lake water and lilacs.

Yes! It still smelled the same. That was a good sign.

Slowly, others began to trickle off the bus behind me. First came Quinn, our drummer. She stretched her legs without comment. But then Nixon, our lead guitar, stepped down and began to laugh. "No shit, man. Really? We drove a hundred miles out of our way for this?"

"Hey! Trust me." I smiled at my two best friends. "Nest Lake is magic." At least it had been once upon a time. And that was why we were here. This detour was supposed to help me remember the last time I'd been truly happy. Before I wrote another album, I needed to convince myself that happiness wasn't impossible.

"Christ." Nixon pulled his T-shirt down over his tattooed abs. "Where's the bar? Where are the women?"

I took a moment to examine my oldest friend, and I didn't like what I saw. A pale, tired face with dark circles under the eyes. 'Twas the season to worry about Nixon.

Most people looked forward to the summertime, but not him. Summer was when Quinn and I watched Nix for signs of a breakdown. From June till September—usually in the midst of a grueling tour—Nixon would trade his beer for whiskey. He would sleep too much and brood too long.

It was only Memorial Day Weekend, and already the man looked hollow. Not good.

I put a hand on Nixon's shoulder. "Think of this as a couple of days off, okay? There's nothing here but trees and the lake. You can thank me later."

He eyed the lodge's low-slung roofline with suspicion. "Have we fallen on hard times? Should I be worried?"

They both stared at me, but I didn't give a damn. "Forty-eight hours," I told them. "No TV, no cell phone service. Just put on a pair of trunks and jump in the lake."

"Shit, I lost my suit in Toronto," Nixon complained. "That sick night in the hot tub with those triplets? I'm lucky I still have both of my balls. Things got hairy."

"Enough about your hairy balls," I quipped. "No suit, no problem. Jump in naked. Or read in the hammock. When the weekend is over, you're going to beg me to stay."

Nix twitched, and then slapped at his neck. "Mosquitoes? Fuck. This is going to be the longest two days of my life."

I'd already begun to walk away, but I turned around to say one more thing to my two best friends. "Listen, team. I wrote seven of the songs off *Summer Nights* about a half a mile from where you're standing. If it weren't for this lake, the words 'one-hit wonder' would appear in each of our Wikipedia entries. So quit bitching about my favorite place in the world."

At that, I turned away. Walking toward the lake, I spotted two canoes parked on the bank, with life jackets and paddles at the ready. I walked past these and out onto the lodge's private dock. The green scent of Maine was strong on the breeze.

"I only have one beef with Maine," said a voice from behind me. "But it's legit."

I didn't need to turn around to identify the speaker. Our tour manager—and my good friend—was the only one who could cast such a huge, bald, muscular shadow on the dock boards. "What's that, Ethan?"

"There aren't any other black dudes in Maine."

I chuckled. "I'll give you that. But it's just a visit. We aren't moving in."

"Color me relieved. You need anything? I'm going inside to divvy up the rooms."

"I'm good. Really good, actually."

"Glad to hear it. Dinner's at seven."

* * *

AN HOUR LATER, I convinced Quinn to row across the lake with me. "You don't even have to row. I'll do all the work."

"Hey, I'm game." She picked up a paddle and strapped on a life vest.

She tried to hand me the other vest, but I held up a hand, refusing it. "The summer I was here, I swam across this lake most days." I squinted against the glare off the water. "In the morning I'd write. And if I made some good progress, I'd swim and lie in the sun in the afternoon. Otherwise, it was back to the grind after lunch."

"Sounds very disciplined," Quinn said with a sigh. "Maybe I should try it."

"Totally worked!"

Five years ago I'd used that summer to regain control of my life. Secluding myself in the woods had served a couple of purposes. First, it got me away from the crazy Seattle scene. Then, with no distractions and nothing to occupy myself in my room at the tiny bed and breakfast but my favorite acoustic guitar and several empty notebooks, I'd finally written the band's overdue album.

Not only had that album eventually gone double platinum, I'd had the best summer of my life. Because for once, I'd proved to myself that I could get the job done. I didn't have to be just another blip on the music scene—a chump who got lucky with two hit songs before fading into oblivion. I didn't have to be a fuckup. Not all the time, anyway.

Now I steadied the canoe at the edge of the water. "Hop in," I instructed. "You sit up front."

After Quinn was settled on the seat, I shoved off, then stepped carefully into the rear of the boat. Sitting down, I dug my paddle into the water and headed toward the western shore and the tiny town of Nest Lake. After only a few minutes of paddling, the little public dock and the B&B where I'd rented a room that summer came into view.

It had all happened *right* here. The narrow door at the back of Mrs. Wetzle's house had been my private entrance. After a day spent writing, I used to slip on my flip-flops and shuffle down to the dock for a swim. On the Fourth of July, I'd gone skinny-dipping here with my only Nest Lake friend.

Just remembering that night made my chest ache. No wonder songwriters made so much of summertime memories. If I closed my eyes, I could still conjure the potent, warm air and bright stars.

And beautiful Kira. She was the best part of that memory.

"Turn around so I can get undressed," Kira had said that night, her fingers poised on the hem of her T-shirt. I remembered precisely how she'd looked, her cheeks pink from embarrassment, her sweet curves framed against the dusky sky.

Even though I'd been sorely tempted to peek, I'd turned around, obeying her request. Kira was gorgeous in the same way that Maine was—fresh and unspoiled. But she'd been off limits. It had been a rare instance of me staying "just friends" with a girl. And staying "just friends" had been another of my summertime goals.

At the time, I was freshly dumped by my supermodel girlfriend. We'd had the worst kind of pathological relationship, and

I'd needed to prove to myself that I could go twelve weeks without relying on a hookup to feel better.

I'd *almost* succeeded.

Funny, but now I couldn't even picture that ex-girlfriend's face. But Kira's was seared into my memory. Her tanned legs and sunny energy had tempted me from the minute I'd blown into town.

But I'd stayed strong. I hadn't watched her strip down that night on the dock. In fact, I hadn't made a move all summer long. Not once. Every time my gaze had strayed from her sparkling silver eyes to the swell of her breasts under her T-shirt, I'd kept my urges to myself.

Of course, *looking* wasn't really against my rules. So after we'd slipped naked into the dark water of the lake, I'd admired Kira's shoulders shimmering in the moonlight and the place where the water dripped down between her breasts. She'd held herself low at the surface, preventing me from seeing much. The mystery had made my attraction that much more potent. I'd floated there, close enough to touch her, while the gentle current caressed my bare skin.

Submerged in the water, we'd watched the fireworks shoot up from the other end of the lake, their bright explosions mirrored in the water's surface. When it was finally time to get out of the water—and after my brain had invented several dozen fantastic ways to appreciate Kira's naked body—I'd asked *her* to turn around while I climbed out on the dock.

Usually, I'm a hundred percent comfortable with nudity. But I couldn't let Kira see the effect she had on me. I didn't want her to know that my mind had been in the gutter the whole evening. Pulling my dry briefs and khaki shorts over my dripping wet body had been difficult with a rock-hard cock in the way.

"Jonas, it really is a beautiful lake," Quinn said, interrupting the movie reel of my memories. "I can see why you'd come back."

"It was the best three months of my life. No lie."

She was quiet for a moment, and I thought the conversation

was over. But then Quinn asked a question. "So... Why did you wait five years to come back?"

I rolled my neck, trying to shake the last of the tour-bus tension from my neck. "Because I'm a goddamned idiot," I said, rowing toward the little beach. It was the truth, too. If Maine had lost its magic, it wasn't the Pine Tree State's fault. It was *my* fault. I'd been too stupid to see what was right in front of me.

* * *

WHEN WE REACHED the water's edge, I dragged the canoe up onto the gravelly sand. "We can leave the boat right here. Nobody will bother it."

"Really?"

"Really. That's how it's done here in Outer Bumfuck."

Quinn laughed. "Are you going to show me the town?"

"Of course I am. But it will take about ten seconds."

I admired Quinn's shapely legs as she leaned over to stash her oar in the boat. It took surprising body strength to play the drums, and the muscle looked good on her, especially in her bathing suit and Daisy Dukes.

My drummer and I were truly just friends. We'd met eight years ago at work in a Seattle bar. Years ago—when I was hammered on Jack Daniel's—I once kissed Quinn, in just the kind of dumbass move that can ruin a good friendship as well as a good band.

Luckily, after about five seconds of stupidity, we pulled back and sort of stared at each other. I'd said, "Okay, nope" at exactly the same time she'd said, "Ewww." Then we'd burst out laughing, and never tried that again.

Thank goodness, because I was usually too impulsive for my own good. Quinn and I would've never worked as a couple, anyway. Two moody artists? That's just a bad idea.

Besides, Quinn shied away from romantic relationships. She was happiest when she was scribbling music into her notebook or tapping out a rhythm with the drumsticks that she never seemed to put down.

From the public beach, we made a left toward Main Street. "So..." I gestured like a tour guide. "Here you see downtown metropolitan Nest Lake."

The only living being in sight was a golden retriever sleeping on the sidewalk. As I began to talk, he opened one lazy eye to look at us.

"You have your post office, which is open about a half an hour a day, but don't bother trying to figure out when, because they haven't updated the sign on the door since 1986. And there's the soft-serve ice cream place, the Kreemy Kone. Open until nine. The crown jewel is here—Lake Nest General Store—where I ate dinner every single night for an entire summer, even though it isn't actually a restaurant. And that's it. You've seen the whole town."

Quinn raised a finger, counting the cars. "Four."

"This is busy, actually. A big crowd for Memorial Day weekend."

"Wow." She smiled. "And your fans are about to rush you, I can feel it."

Right on cue, a woman came out of the general store with a gallon of milk. She dismounted the wooden stairs, turning away without giving us a second glance. Then she tucked herself into one of the cars and drove away.

"And then there were three," I said under my breath.

Seeing Main Street brought me into a strange reverie. In spite of the sunshine, I felt as if I was having a very vivid dream. I'd thought about this place so often, and now I was here for real.

Crazy.

"I can see why you came here to write," Quinn said. "But how did you find it?"

"My mom used to come here when she was a little girl. One of the few pictures I have of her is on the porch of the general store."

"Ah," Quinn said. And because she knew I didn't like to talk about my parents, she left it at that.

I'd lost both my parents when I was seven. Coming back here five years ago was a way to try to remember my life before everything had gone wrong.

Did it work? I guess. But the cure was only temporary. Lately I'd been feeling just as lost.

Five years ago I'd come here when my band's new album was overdue. The record label was pissed off at me, so Maine seemed like a good place to hide from their nagging. And my glamorous girlfriend had just dumped me. A tabloid had just run a story about how I'd cheated on her. They used pictures of me with a woman that I slept with the night *after* we broke up.

I was twenty-five years old and already in a slump. So I'd come to this place my mother used to tell me about. It was one of the only details I could remember about her.

I'd needed some magic, and that's what I'd found here in Maine.

"God, it's hard to believe places like this still exist," Quinn said. "Can we go into the general store? And then I want ice cream."

"Lead on." I followed her up the store's wooden steps, through the screened porch and into the shop itself. What hit me first was the scent. It smelled *exactly* the same inside—musky and rich, like pickles, salami, and sawdust. And it looked mostly the same, lit by old soda lamps hanging from the ceiling on chains, with half an inch of dust on each one.

What's more, Kira's father stood behind the cash register, looking just as grumpy as he had five years ago. The old man proceeded to ignore us both, because he always ignored the summer people. And yet he'd been in business forever, because there weren't any other stores for ten miles.

Two or three years ago, drunk and in a melancholy mood, I had finally picked up the phone to call this very store. It was a call that I'd waited too long to make, and I'd known it was hopeless even before that surly old man answered the phone in his gravelly voice.

"Is Kira there?" I'd asked, knowing it was a long shot. No girl waits two years to hear from the asshole who'd rejected her. Besides—Kira had always said that she was going back to college after our magical summer.

"They moved to Boston," the old man had told me.

Right. That's what I'd expected. They'd moved to Boston. *They.*

Hell, I'd expected that too. Kira wasn't single anymore. Why would she be?

Thousands of miles away, in a Texas hotel room, I'd hung up the phone and poured myself another two fingers of scotch. But I'd never stopped thinking about Kira. And I probably never would.

Only one thing in the store looked truly different now. And although I'd expected this, it still made me sad. Her sign was missing. Above one of the back counters, a carved wooden plaque had once hung. KIRA'S CAFE. Her homemade specialty had been a quirky little meat pie, about five inches across. Under an artfully cut-out crust lay curried chicken, or sausage and peppers. There'd been a ham and egg version I'd particularly liked. My first week in Maine, I'd tried a different one each night. My second week, I'd repeated the cycle.

That's how we'd become friends. After I'd eaten her savory pastries nine nights in a row, Kira began feeling sorry for me. So she'd surprised me with some new dishes. I walked in one night to find that she'd made me a big square of lasagna. The next night, she'd grilled up a bacon cheeseburger while I waited.

As the summer progressed, she'd gotten even more creative. The pan-fried lake trout had tasted so fresh I'd almost cried.

"You are the most loyal customer I've ever had," she'd said. By then, I'd memorized the shape of her smile and the flush of her cheek when I complimented the food.

But I didn't hit on her. Not once.

At the beginning, restraint had been easy. I'd come to Nest

Lake to be alone and to stop chasing women. I was still bitter about the tabloid article. I didn't need any distractions. I was going to finish that album or die trying.

But by midsummer, my vow of chastity had gotten a lot harder. Literally. The time I'd spent with Kira had evolved from a simple nightly transaction to a real friendship. And every night I went to bed hearing her laughter echo in my head and wondering how her skin would feel sliding against mine.

But I was young and dumb. At the time, I'd written it off as mere horniness. Five years later, I knew better.

Well before Labor Day, Kira's bright smile and intelligent eyes had stolen my heart. And her curvy body turned up in all my dreams. But I never slipped up and made a pass. Not just because I'd been feeling stubborn, but there was something vulnerable about Kira. I couldn't have told you exactly what, but still it held me back. Banging her like one of my fans would have felt wrong.

Besides, if I'd talked Kira into my bed, there'd been a risk that she wouldn't make me dinner anymore. And then I would have been stuck with the miserable fare that my B&B landlady referred to as "food."

Somehow it had all been enough to keep even a dedicated horn dog in check.

"Earth to Jonas," Quinn teased. "Let's pick up a magazine or two, and then I want some soft serve."

I'd been staring at Kira's old counter, memories flooding through me. But where her delicacies once sat, there were now only scary-looking danishes wrapped in cellophane. It was no better than gas-station food.

It was true what people said. You can never go back.

I turned toward the magazine rack, shaking off my disappointment.

TWO

KIRA

I pulled up in front of the general store, putting the car in park. After the three-hour drive from Boston, both my companions were asleep. In the passenger seat, my older brother's head rested against his bicep, which he'd curled against the window. And when I swiveled to see my daughter in her car seat, her eyelids fluttered, then settled closed again.

As I rolled down my window, Adam woke up with a shake of his head. "Ugh. We're here," my brother grumbled.

"It's only two days. You always survive somehow."

"I suppose." He rolled his neck.

I studied him. "You look beat, Adam. Are you okay?" He'd told me that there was something he needed to discuss with me this weekend, and now I wondered what it was.

"I'm fine. Just tired." He removed his seatbelt.

"Dad will have the baseball game turned up good and loud. You'll keep the beer flowing. We'll be fine."

"I know." He sighed. "But how do you stand it? All the jabs at your choices. And mine."

"I just remind myself that he's a sourpuss to us, but he's good to Vivi. Do you want to tell him we're here, or should I do it?"

Adam turned to look up at the store, considering. "I'll get it over with." He opened the passenger door. "Plus, I can buy my first six-pack."

"Good plan."

"I want to go in!" Vivi yelled from the backseat.

"Oh, you're awake!" I swiveled around again. My daughter fiddled with her car seat straps, trying to spring herself free.

Adam opened Vivi's door. "Come on, princess. Let's go see grumpy."

"You mean Grandpa!" my little girl corrected.

"Right. Just like I said." He swung her out and onto his hip.

"I'll unload our things and then come back for you?" I suggested. The house was barely a quarter mile away.

"We'll walk it," Adam countered. "She's a big girl now."

"Okay. See you there."

I watched Adam carry my daughter up the wooden steps and onto the store's screened porch, then I turned the car around in the post office driveway. Idling past the Kreemy Kone, I happened to glance at the couple seated at the picnic table. The woman was watching me, but the guy was reading a magazine. Then, maybe because he sensed my gaze, he looked up, smiling. His mouth fell open in surprise.

And my heart absolutely stopped.

Jonas Smith was sitting right there on the bench. After five years, he barely seemed real. In my mind, he'd become a mythical figure. Back when I'd known him, he'd called himself John Smith. He'd given me a fake name. A fake name, and thus a fake friendship for an entire summer.

And on the very last night, he'd given me a baby.

Then John Smith had left town, and I'd never spoken to him again, had never seen his face. Not in person, anyway. It wasn't until a year and a half later that I'd spotted him on my computer screen, looking out at me from an ad for a new album called *Summer Nights*.

And now he sat casually on the picnic table bench in shorts and a T-shirt. Like a specter from my past.

Stunned, I pressed the gas pedal. But in my rearview mirror I saw that he'd stood up, his eyes following my car.

The woman he was with called to him. "Jonas?" He didn't respond. Instead, he took off, trotting after me.

Go home was all I could think to do. But of course, John, or *Jonas*, knew where my father's house was. Adam would be on his way there too. With Vivi.

Oh God.

I had driven maybe fifty yards, to the place where the road veered left and curved around the lake. But I didn't make the turn. Instead, I stopped the car in front of the beach. I got out and closed the door. I could hear the slap of flip-flops coming my way.

"Kira," his voice begged.

With my heart beating wildly, I walked away from him, down the little slope and out onto the town dock. My throat went dry. I knew I wasn't behaving rationally. The dock was a dead end, unless I planned to *swim* away from him.

But there was no escape anyway. The sensible part of my brain knew I would have to deal with the fallout. If he was here in Maine, I was going to have to tell him the truth even if he'd broken my heart.

"Kira."

I closed my eyes at the sound of his voice. The water lapped gently under the dock. If I turned around, he might not truly be standing there. I held my breath.

That's when he began to whistle softly. The first four bars of "You Are My Sunshine."

Goosebumps rose on my arms.

"You remember," I gasped, whirling around. Five years later, and he still knew to warn me. He hadn't forgotten that I used to startle if he—or anyone else—approached me from behind.

He walked towards me slowly, his hands spread wide, muscular arms on display. His hair was shorter now, but still the most beautiful shade of sandy blond. "Of *course* I remember, sweetness. Never sneak up on Kira."

At that, my eyes filled with tears.

"Hey, now," he said gently. He'd made it all the way out on the dock, so close I could almost touch him. His blue-green eyes regarded me warmly. "I'm sorry to take you by surprise. Don't I get a hug?"

Lord, I needed to get a grip. I took a step towards him, and he folded me in. He smelled the same, like sunshine and soap. It hurt so much to see him again. It was *excruciating* to be wrapped in his hug.

"God, I've missed you," he said.

And I had absolutely no reply to that. My heart urged me to hold on tightly and never let go. To confess that I thought of him every single day.

But I didn't do it. Because I was still so angry, too.

Drawing off that anger, I summoned a little willpower, stepping backward, freeing myself. "If I ask how you've been, which name should I use? Jonas or John?"

A look of dismay creased his handsome face, his eyes closing for a moment, before opening again to pin me with a turquoise gaze. "Kira, I'm so sorry about that. That summer I was just trying to get away from it all."

I swallowed. "Really? But I told you all *my* secrets. You must have thought that was pretty funny."

He blinked, his face as stunned as if I'd slapped him. "Jesus, Kira. *Never.*"

That wasn't the reaction I'd been expecting. And it was suddenly very hard to hold his gaze. I'd spent the last few years shaping my idea of him to match the pictures I saw in *Us Weekly*. The problem was that the guy standing in front of me on the dock did not look like the frivolous celebrity in those articles. This was the same man I'd met all those years ago. His face was open and youthful, his voice rich and mellow. His gaze seemed to touch me everywhere at once, making me feel flushed and confused.

He stepped forward again and wrapped his arms around me. And I let him. I took a deep breath of him, and my heart began to gallop again. When I put my arms around his back, I felt his lips press against my hairline. It was a chaste kiss between old friends.

Or rather, it should have been. But the feel of his lips on my skin sent a charge through my body. Tipping my face to meet his wasn't even a conscious act. It was more like the inevitable result of a five-year absence and Earth's gravitational pull.

When I moved my chin, his lips slid softly down my cheek-bone. Still, it might have ended there. He might have released me, but he didn't. "Sweetness," he whispered.

And then? His kiss slid to the corner of my mouth, pausing there, hovering. Torturing us both.

I couldn't resist. I leaned forward an immeasurably small distance. At that, he made a low sound in the back of his throat. He melded his mouth onto mine, his hands curving around my lower back. With a sigh, he teased my lips apart until his warm tongue met mine.

The next moments were lost to me. I melted against his body, knowing nothing except the stroke of his tongue against my own and the feel of his breath against my face. His strong arms held me in their grasp. It was the sound of my own gasp that finally brought me back down to earth. And I became aware that someone was standing on the little beach nearby, watching us.

"Oh my God, your..." Horror stopped me from finishing the sentence.

He looked over his shoulder without releasing me from his grasp. "My drummer," he said quickly. "We're old friends."

I pushed on his chest until he took a step backwards. I was hot and confused. I needed oxygen and time to think. "Look... we need to talk." I couldn't tell him my secret now. Not with an audience. And not without a little rehearsal. "Tomorrow," I added.

"Okay," he said, his voice low and even. "I'd like that."

"Um, lunch?" I asked, my eyes on my shoes. I couldn't quite

catch my breath. There wasn't enough oxygen in the atmosphere anymore. There might never be again.

"I could meet you on the porch at the store," he suggested.

That's where we'd always sat together. But that place was way too public for the conversation I needed to have. "No... Where are you staying? At the B&B?" The very mention of the place made my cheeks flush.

His eyes flared, too. "No. My whole band is at the Nest Lake Lodge for the weekend. I made them come here with me."

"Okay." I swallowed. "Can I find you there at noon?"

"I'll make us a picnic," he said, a grin blooming on his face.

God, he was beautiful. *A picnic with John.* There had been so many days during the past few years when just the promise of spending an hour with him would have seen me through any trial. But our reunion would truly be a trial. For both of us. I needed to keep my head. "That would be fine."

"Tomorrow, sweetness," he said.

I stepped past him and forced myself to walk away, my heart racing, my face hot. "I'll be there."

As I stepped off the dock, I felt the eyes of the other woman tracking me. I should have given her a wave or a smile, or even introduced myself. But at that moment, I couldn't manage politeness. I just went back to my car and, with shaking hands, turned the key in the ignition. I drove away without another look toward the beach.

With unseeing eyes, I parked the car in my father's weedy gravel driveway. Leaving the keys on the seat, I heaved myself out of the car and up the creaky wooden steps of my childhood home. When I opened the door to the screened porch, Vivi and Adam looked up from the rocking chairs.

"Mommy's home!" my brother said.

"We got cheese," Vivi said. "And crackers."

"Thank you, Uncle Adam," I managed. My brother was my bedrock. Without him, the last few years would have been impossible.

"What's wrong?" he asked quickly.

I just gave a little shake of my head. "Later."

"You didn't beat us here," he pressed.

"I know. I ran into someone. I'll get our stuff now." I ran back outside toward the car, still feeling unsteady. Out of sight of my family again, I parked my backside against the car and bent to brace my shaking hands on my knees.

Breathe, I coached myself. It had been several years since I'd had a panic attack, but one threatened now. I straightened up again, drawing a slow breath. The trick was to lower my heart rate, which would break the cycle.

A rapid heartbeat convinces your brain that something is wrong, a therapist had explained to me years ago. *And in turn, your brain tells your heart to get ready to flee. Which elevates your heart rate even more.* Fear begets fear, in other words.

At twenty, I'd needed someone to help me learn to control my panic. At the time, the worst mistake I'd ever made was simply to walk through the wrong parking lot at the wrong hour of the night. I'd paid for that mistake.

But now, at twenty-five, I had quite a few more mistakes under my belt.

And now I would pay for those, too.

To calm myself, I counted the pine trees across the road. There were nine of them. Between their straight trunks, flashes of Nest Lake sparkled in the distance.

I'd grown up here in this house, where only glimpses of the water were visible. If my father had purchased a house on the other side of the road, with lake access, his property value would have risen tenfold.

But that's just how life worked. Sometimes the distance between wealth and scraping by was as thin as a country road.

After a few minutes, I was breathing more easily. I lifted our overnight bags out of the car and pulled them into the house. I would need to put my game face back on so I could make it through the family ritual here in my father's house. Even though my mind would be a quarter mile away at the general store. Everything had begun there.

The first night he'd come into the store, it had been right before closing time, and I'd been working alone. And since John had worn soft sneakers, and was kind enough to prevent the door from slamming, I hadn't heard him approach. When he'd greeted me, it had startled me so badly that I'd dropped a full mason jar of pickled onions, breaking it on the floor.

"I'm so sorry," he'd said before helping me clean up the mess.

I'd been so flustered that I hadn't gotten a good look at him that first night. I'd sold him his first meat pie and a soda to go with it, my heart pounding with unnecessary fear.

Even if I had gotten a good look at him, I wouldn't have recognized him. I wasn't the kind of girl who paid a lot of attention to rock songs on the radio, or the people responsible for them.

But after that disaster, he'd always whistled on his way into the store. Whenever I'd heard the first part of "You Are My Sunshine" drifting down the street, I'd known he was on his way over for supper.

After a week, I'd felt comfortable enough to tell him I appreciated the warning. "You have no idea how much that helps. Last fall I was mugged. And even though it's been almost a year, every time someone walks up behind me, I jump."

His turquoise eyes went wide with surprise. "Shit, I'm sorry. You got mugged *here*, in Nest Lake?"

I laughed. "Can you imagine? No—this was in Boston, in a parking lot at the university."

John rubbed his whiskers with the knuckles of one hand, his chiseled face still full of concern. "That sucks."

"It really, really did." I changed the topic. "I made whoopie pies today. Do you want one for dessert?"

"Hell, yes. Whatever that is. It sounds naughty."

That made me blush, because my crush on him was already blooming. "You don't know whoopie pies? The official treat of Maine? They're everywhere. Mostly, they're dreadful, but you didn't hear it from me."

"You want me to eat something dreadful?" Those bright eyes twinkled.

"I said they were *mostly* dreadful. Mine are exquisite, naturally. You should know this." I surprised myself by flirting with him. It had been so long since I'd felt flirty with anyone.

When I handed the bag with his food over the counter, he reached right in and plucked the whoopie pie off the top. "Mmm," he said after taking a big bite. "Sweetness."

"It's not *too* sweet, though," I argued. "Most of them are, but mine have dark cocoa and cream cheese in the frosting. For tang."

He licked his lips. "It's perfect. *You're* the sweetness." He winked at me as he walked out.

And that naughty wink did funny things to my insides.

After that, he called me "sweetness" from time to time. The man was a charmer. I looked forward to his visits so much that I soon found a way to prolong them. A trip to our dusty attic at home produced an old card table and two chairs. I set these up on the screened porch at the front of the store.

I was too shy to let on that I'd put the table there just for him, but he figured it out right away. From then on, he ate his meals sitting on the porch, instead of carrying his food back to his room at Mrs. Wetzle's. After I locked up the store at eight, he would often be sitting there, staring out into the darkness and listening to the crickets.

"Can I ask you a favor?" I said the third time I found him relaxing on the porch an hour after he'd eaten his dinner.

"Shoot."

"If you're walking back to the B&B, can we walk together?" I'd been nervous to ask, so all my words tumbled out in a rush. "There hasn't been a... mugging here for years. But I'm creeped out anyway. And I asked the guy at Kreemy Kone to walk me home a couple of times, but he thinks I'm hitting on him."

John laughed. "The teenager who wears that Metallica T-shirt with the arms cut off? He ought to know better than to think you're hitting on him."

"You'd think." I smiled at him to cover my own embarrassment.

"Happy to help," he said, rising to go.

And that's how our friendship began. Never mind that he was devilishly handsome, with wind-tossed hair and a sinful mouth. Even though he let his beard grow out all summer, that brilliant level of attractiveness could not easily be dimmed.

I'd begun to worship him even before June turned into July. But we remained strictly friendly, even as our chats grew longer, night by night. Instead of walking home after the store closed, I began sitting with him at the table. Sometimes he bought a six-pack of beer and we'd drink it on the porch after I locked up. We spent hours just shooting the breeze and talking about our lives.

Of course, John/Jonas left out some very crucial details. In the beginning, I left out a few doozies, too.

Even so, we never lacked for conversation. I told him that I was majoring in hospitality. "Although I hate that word," I said with a giggle. A giggle! Like a school girl. But it was hard to keep my head when he was nearby. "I want to open a restaurant someday."

"If you're opening a restaurant, I'm eating there," he promised.

He told me he was a composer in Seattle. That explained the strains of the guitar that I often heard drifting into my window in the morning. Or late into the night. He had the most beautiful hands, with long, supple fingers. I was dying to watch him play the guitar, but he never volunteered, and I was too chicken to ask.

Even if I'd managed to gather enough courage to ask for a private concert, I still wouldn't have figured out the man playing the guitar had already been nicknamed "the golden kid," by *Rolling Stone*. Or that his first album had been compared to early work by U2.

He was just a guy named John, who I was crushing on.

One evening, he bought a Maine souvenir pack of playing cards. That's when we started playing rummy and canasta on the rickety little porch table. The card games somehow made my secrets flow faster. I told him that my on-again off-again high school boyfriend would soon be back from a two-year deployment in Afghanistan, and that I wasn't sure I wanted to get back together. But I was considering it.

And John confessed that he'd just been dumped by his girlfriend.

"She... left you?" I asked, disbelieving. Even then, when I had no idea that the man sitting in front of me was a rock star, it was impossible for me to imagine a woman rejecting him. Not only was he outrageously sexy, but there was a light in his eyes that I knew was special. He was smart, as well as warm and funny. How could any girl turn that away?

"Well, I was a rat bastard," he admitted, his voice low.

"Maybe you just slipped up once?" I asked, embarrassed for him.

"Nope. Honestly, I've been going through a dark time. I would have dumped me, too. I don't even know if she ever loved me."

I was dumbfounded. "Then why are you...?"

"Thinking about her?" He smiled ruefully. "I don't know. Maybe I don't want to be the jerk she's accused me of being. Maybe I want to call her when I get back, just to let her know that I'm not the thoughtless whore she thinks I am."

"Maybe she'll take you back," I said. And he just shrugged, like it didn't matter.

But after that, I was careful to keep the discussion away from girlfriends or sex. Because I didn't want him to read my raging crush right off my face.

Each night, after our card game, or a stroll by the moonlit lake, he walked me fifty yards past the B&B, to my front door. Sometimes we'd pass Mrs. Wetzle sitting on the front porch of the B&B. I didn't appreciate the way the old woman stared at us as we walked by. It made me feel oddly guilty. Like I was a teenager again, and out past curfew.

"She doesn't like me," John whispered under his breath. "She actually said, 'If I'd known you were a musician, I wouldn't have rented you the room.'"

"That's weird."

"Yeah. I mean… it's not like I'm practicing drum solos, you know? It's just a little strumming here and there."

I stopped myself from saying how much I enjoyed hearing the sound of his guitar on the nighttime breeze. I had my pride to maintain. "She's a little judgmental," I whispered instead.

And it was true. I'd already experienced Mrs. Wetzle's judgment firsthand.

When I'd decided to take a semester off after being attacked in Boston, I'd begun helping my father with the grocery deliveries. My ugly little story got around town awfully fast, as these things always do. The first time I brought a delivery to Mrs. Wetzle's house, the old woman had grabbed my wrist. "You have to learn to be more careful in the big city."

I'd felt all kinds of shame that I didn't even have a name for.

"I think she makes me bad lunches on purpose," John had complained. "She hopes I'll leave."

That made me laugh. "It's not personal. She's a famously bad cook, with one exception."

"Really? What's the exception?"

We'd arrived at my screen porch already, which meant that it was time to go into the sleepy house alone. But we paused for a last bit of conversation. "She makes really good homemade popcorn balls with molasses. She delivers them to the neighbors at Christmastime."

John crossed his arms over his muscular chest and smiled at me. "Maybe she'll make me one when I leave in September. But I won't hold my breath."

I thanked him for walking me home. He gave me a friendly wave and walked away as I climbed the porch steps.

He did that every night except for the one that changed my life.

And what happened that night hadn't even been his decision. This whole scandal was all on me.

THREE

JONAS

After those precious minutes on the dock with Kira, I herded Quinn back into the canoe, and then launched it, feeling great. I was in the best kind of shock. Not only was Kira in Nest Lake, I could still taste her on my tongue.

I *never* thought I'd see her again. But some kind of wish-granting goddess had smiled down on me, offering me another chance to reconnect. I wouldn't let it go to waste.

My elation lasted about four minutes.

"So..." Quinn started from the front of the canoe. There were questions in her voice.

"So." I repeated flatly. There was no way I felt like sharing. Quinn and I were close, but the hope I was feeling was too fragile for friendly dishing.

"An old friend?" she pressed.

"Yeah." *Please let it go.*

"She's your sweetness, huh? Just like in the new song?"

Fuck. Leave it to a female to overhear that and make the connection. "Quinn, I'm not talking about it, okay? Just let me be. And if you say anything to anyone else, I'll kill you dead."

"It's just that..." She bit her lip. "Did you see her *before* she turned her car around?"

"What do you mean?"

"You were reading your magazine. Which I brought back with me." She patted her back pocket. "You can thank me later. But anyway, first she pulled up in front of the general store, and a guy with a baby got out of the car."

My whole body went cold. "What?"

"You heard me, Jonas. They went into the store together. And then your girl turned her car around and passed us."

The earth lurched beneath me. "She wasn't wearing any rings," I said stupidly. It was the first thing I'd checked when I walked out onto the dock.

"Not everybody likes jewelry, Jonas." She said it in a perfectly gentle voice, but it shredded my heart anyway. Because she was right. And Kira didn't go out for bling. She was beautiful in a completely natural, unadorned way.

Fuck.

Chewing on this revelation, I paddled the canoe back across the lake in silence until the front of the lodge came into view. So did Ethan and Nix. My guitar player was lying in a hammock in front of the lodge, and Ethan was doing some pushups on the lawn.

But I didn't even greet them. I shoved the canoe onto the bank and went inside, looking for someplace to think. I'd rented out the whole place for the weekend, so nobody would bother us. Poking my head into a couple of rooms, I found my luggage beside a quaint double bed. I shut the bedroom door and dropped myself onto the quilt.

Someone—probably Ethan—had opened the windows already, so sounds of my friends' voices drifted in. The afternoon ticked by slowly. Tomorrow I'd be able to see Kira again. But tomorrow seemed like a long way away. As the light began to fade, the voices on the deck grew louder and more raucous. The smell of burgers on the grill eventually wafted through the window, but I did not get up to join the others.

My mind was too full of memories of that other summer— the one when I'd pulled myself together. All day I'd worked on songwriting, pausing only for Mrs. Wetzle's lousy lunch offerings and a quick dip in the lake. Then, feeling good about myself, I'd eaten some of Kira's excellent cooking, and smiled across the table at her for a couple of hours over a beer or four.

I'd kept my head down, filling the pages of my notebooks with lyrics and chord progressions. My phone remained powered down and stashed in a drawer. No producer nagged me, and there were no conference calls with the record label. I grew the most outrageously ugly beard, and didn't get a haircut all summer. By Labor Day weekend, I'd been shaggier than I'd ever looked in my life, but I'd felt so much better about myself that it wasn't even funny.

On the second-to-last night I was in Maine, Kira asked me if I wanted to go to the county fair. "Sure," I'd answered. I would have followed her anywhere.

Preserving my last moments of anonymity with a baseball cap pulled down over my eyes, I went to the fair with Kira in her father's car. The whole evening was silly and glorious. First I talked Kira onto the Himalayan ride. And as it spun us senseless, I held Kira's wrist in a death grip. She just laughed and threw her head back, thrilled with the motion.

Then, as the sun set, we ate corn dogs and caramel apples. We attempted to pop balloons with darts. I was a terrible shot, but after a dozen tries, and probably fifty bucks, I won a purple stuffed cat. We laughed at how ugly it was, but Kira tucked it under her arm anyway, and we got in line for the Ferris wheel. The queue inched forward as couples boarded.

"How about that view?" I joked when we were finally aloft.

"It's killer," Kira whispered from her side of our little metal bench. In the daylight, we could have seen for miles. But Maine was so rural that all we could see beyond the fairgrounds was the blackness of distant valleys and lakes.

Perhaps it was the novelty of seeing Kira away from the general store. But as we went whirling through the night air, hip to hip, I felt a new kind of electricity between us. Turning, I studied Kira's wide-eyed profile. And it suddenly became very difficult not to kiss her. I'd be leaving in less than thirty-six hours, and I wasn't happy about it at all.

Do it, my subconscious begged. *You know you want to.* I was pretty sure that she wouldn't mind at all. The way she held my gaze a little too long when we laughed, and the way she blushed when I complimented her? Those were signs. Reading girls was one of my talents.

Somehow I had resisted, held our attraction at bay. But just when I was complimenting myself on my self-control, she opened her mouth and broke my heart.

"John?" she said softly. "I just want to tell you that hanging around with you this summer was a great help to me."

"Yeah?" I croaked.

"This year was really terrible, and you helped me forget about it. You took me out of my own head. Because you..."

"I what?"

"It's too weird. Too hard to say out loud."

"Well, now I'm desperately curious. But no biggie."

She'd laughed, but it held a nervous edge. "Okay, fine. I needed to have a guy friend, one who didn't hit on me. Because..." She swallowed. "Last year. It wasn't my pocketbook that was stolen that night in that parking lot."

My body went cold, and I stared at her for two beats of my heart. "Kira, are you trying to tell me that you were..."

She nodded, eyes wet. The lights from the Ferris wheel were reflected in her tears. "See? You can't even say the word."

"Forced?"

"Raped," she said, her voice flat.

"Come here." I'd spent the summer trying not to touch her, but now I wrapped an arm around her shoulders and pulled her against my body. There was nothing sexual about it. I buried my nose in her hair. "I'm so sorry, sweetness." I tipped her head to rest on my shoulder and took a shaky breath. "Goddamn it, Kira. I would do anything to make that not be true."

Miraculously, I kept my voice gentle, but my insides were tight with anger and helplessness. I'd felt a surge of blood in my ears, like nothing I'd ever experienced. I thought of myself as a rational man, but at that moment I would have killed the guy who hurt her. No question.

My free hand curled into a fist in my lap, but Kira picked it up, softening my fingers. "I didn't mean to freak you out. I just wanted you to know how much you helped. You made me feel safe. And you reminded me that men aren't terrifying."

Her words did nothing to lessen my uneasiness. I was hit by the same sort of shock that comes after swerving to narrowly avoid a car accident. Because every time I'd restrained my desire for Kira, it had been at my own whim. Holding back was something I'd done for my own selfish reasons. I'd had no way of knowing that my actions—or lack of them—were important to her.

It was just incredible luck that I hadn't fucked it up.

I felt dizzy as the old Ferris wheel spun us through the darkness. I held her tightly, privately sick with the idea that anyone could do that to sunny Kira. "I don't know what to say. I could blather on about how nobody has the right to hurt you. But you know that already. Please tell me this bastard is in jail."

"He is. But not because of me. The guy got caught a month later, when he tried it on someone else. But that girl's boyfriend heard her screaming. John? You're kind of squeezing me..."

I eased my grip. "Shit. Sorry. Not what you need."

She shook her head before resting it on my shoulder again. "No, I'm not afraid of you. That's what I've been trying to tell you."

We sat quietly for the rest of the ride. No more words were necessary. I stroked her hair, and tried to breathe through the tension in my chest. When our turn on the Ferris wheel ended, the carnies opened the car's door. We disembarked, our evening over. I held Kira's hand as we walked back to the car. It wasn't a conscious act. I could barely let go to allow her to drive home. And when we pulled into her driveway, it was all I could do not to follow her into the house.

I'd fallen for her, but I'd been too stupid to realize it. As we reached her door, I wished I could spend my last thirty-six hours in Maine holding her. Instead, I gave her a single, tight hug goodnight. "I'll see you tomorrow," I said, my voice raw. "We need to play one more hand of cards before I go."

She nodded against my chest. "I hope I didn't freak you out."

"You could never." I kissed the top of her head. "Goodnight, Kira."

* * *

ON MY LAST day in Maine, I spent an hour trimming and then shaving off my beard. My newly smooth face had unattractive tan lines striped down it, but it was nothing that a few sunny days in Seattle couldn't fix.

When I whistled my way into the general store for the very last time, Kira gasped. "Oh my God, you look so different!" She ran out from behind the counter to put her palms on my cheeks, and my eyes fell shut from the warmth of her touch. I would have happily stayed right there forever, but she darted away.

"I made you a lobster roll for dinner," she said. "I know we're not on the ocean, but it's something you're supposed to eat when you come to Maine."

"Awesome." I smiled at her and accepted my dinner plate. "And there are whoopie pies, right? I can't leave without one more of those."

"Do you even have to ask?" She gave me an eye-roll. "This is your last meal in Maine. I'd get kicked out of hospitality school if I didn't throw in a whoopie pie."

"We can't have that," I said, carrying my plate toward the front porch.

"I made myself one, too. I'll be right out," she called.

I took my seat at the table, feeling sad. A limousine was coming before dawn to whisk me away to the airport. And by the end of tomorrow, I'd be back in my Seattle apartment. Back to the demands of a record label. The recording dates, the business meals, the A-list parties, and exclusive restaurants that had almost begun to seem ordinary.

My life in Seattle was never dull. But it never felt like *mine*. The end of a work day never brought the promise of a warm glance from a familiar face, and a meal thoughtfully prepared by someone who'd been expecting me.

Back in June, I'd wandered into this store in search of food. But truly, it was a different kind of sustenance that Kira gave me. God, I knew I was going to miss it.

We ate together that night. The lobster rolls she'd made were delicious, and we washed the food down with my favorite Maine beer. But our walk home later was sad and strained.

"Stop here a second, would you?" I asked when we approached my door at Mrs. Wetzle's. "I want to give you my phone number." I unlocked my door for the last time and stepped into my little room.

Kira followed me, closing the door against mosquitoes.

"Here." I grabbed a fine-tipped sharpie off the desk, the kind I often carried in my pockets in Seattle, for signing autographs. "Give me your hand."

She raised it, and I wrote my cell phone number on the edge of her palm.

"Oh my God, that tickles," she said, just the same way the groupies always did.

Carefully, I wrote out the digits of my number. On groupies' hands, I always signed my name. If the girl was especially hot, I might add my hotel room number. I shoved these thoughts out of my head and capped my pen. "It will be weird having cell phone service again."

"Yeah," she agreed. Then she stared at me, and we endured our only awkward silence of the entire summer.

"What?" I finally whispered.

Her gaze became shifty. "Actually, I have the weirdest favor to ask." She cleared her throat, and then began speaking rapidly. "You can totally say no. I won't be even a little bit offended. Actually, I feel bad asking, because I know you were staying away from women as, like, a personal challenge. And you might decide to ask your ex to take you back..."

Even with that clue, I had no idea what she was about to say.

"...and you may not be attracted to me at all. But since you're leaving anyway, I thought I'd ask, so here goes. I wondered if you would..." She lost some of her nerve, and asked the rest of the question to her shoes. "...make love to me? Just as a favor. Because I've read that after a—" She cleared her throat. "Well, to try it again, you're supposed to be with someone who makes you feel really safe."

To say that her request blew my mind was a serious understatement. I was so startled that I had to replay her words in my head just to make sure I hadn't misunderstood.

Kira wanted to have sex with me?

Before I could answer, a new shower of mortified words began to rush out. "I'm sorry. This is totally embarrassing," she gasped. "That's why I waited this long to ask you. And you haven't ever tried... But that's part of the reason I asked, honestly. I trust you. You haven't spent the summer trying to get into my pants. I'm sorry. I'm so sorry."

"Kira..."

"God, you must think I'm insane."

"Kira..."

"I'm *so* sorry."

"Kira," I repeated, my mind reeling. "Stop apologizing."

"Okay. I'm going to go now." She bolted toward the door.

"Wait!" I lunged, catching her hand. "Come here," I choked out. She was still leaning toward the door, so I stepped in front of her and wrapped her into a hug. "You can be sure that I wanted to."

"What?" she asked against my shoulder.

"I wanted to get you out of your clothes. But I didn't try."

"Why?"

"Because I was using self-control for the first time in my whole damned life." And after last night's revelation, I was ridiculously glad. Any other time in my life, I would have tried to get her naked right away. But I hadn't done that, and by happen-stance, I'd helped an amazing person feel a little bit better.

"So you won't do it?" Her voice cracked. "I should never have asked. I just made everything weird, didn't I?"

I stood very still, wracked by indecision. And—let's face it—lust. Merely holding her against me was making me crazy. It was all too easy to picture myself removing Kira's clothes item by item. And then laying her down on the bed—

Jesus. Too tempting by half. But I'd spent the whole summer trying not to think with my dick, and I didn't want to start now.

I sighed. "I don't know, sweetness. You might regret it. Your high school guy is coming back from the army. He should be your safe person."

She pulled out of my embrace. "You'd think. But I haven't seen him in two years, so it's not business as usual. And I'm afraid he's going to come back with his own set of issues. All of the guys returning from the Middle East do. And then if I *also* have issues..." She swallowed. "Before I potentially get into that position with him, I want to know if it's something I can actually do. I've thought about all of this. So many times. And you and I... It's just so *easy* between us. That's how I got this crazy idea in the first place."

"It's not crazy," I whispered, reaching for her again. God knows I'd indulged in the fantasy a few times already. I'd always felt vaguely guilty afterwards.

She cleared her throat. "It was wrong of me, though, to ask you to stomach it. Maybe touching someone who's been..." She shuddered. "I mean, I went to the hospital... He wore a condom. They got no DNA. I got tested, too. But it was an icky thing to ask you to do."

"Hey." My gut gave a twist, and I reached up to take her face in my hands. "That is *not* true." I kissed her forehead. "You are dead sexy. And I practically had to duct tape my hands together all summer to stop myself from showing you how true that is."

Her eyes were sad when she looked up at me. "I wish I believed you."

"Hell." My pulse already felt thready, and my head spun with uncertainty. "Kira, are you *sure* you're ready to try? Because if you're not... It won't be fun for you." And it wouldn't be fun for me, either. No matter that I'd spent the summer staring at those long, tanned legs. If she cried in my bed, I would feel terrible.

Her gaze was level. "Everybody is different. But it's been almost a year. And sometimes when I can hear your guitar at night, I can't sleep."

"Oh." I grinned to cover up the pain she'd just inflicted in me. "So you're attracted to my guitar playing." *Didn't that just figure.*

"No. I can hardly hear it. But I know you're awake, and I can picture your hands on the strings. And then I picture them on me. That's how I know I'm finally feeling better. Because the idea of it makes me want to..."

My groin tightened. "What?"

"Touch you, too." She turned her head away, embarrassed.

I tipped my head back, letting out a hot breath. *Fucking hell.* There was no way I would turn her down. Seriously. All I could hope for now was that I wouldn't fuck everything up somehow.

Catching Kira's downcast chin in my palm, I eased her pretty face closer to mine. Tonight her eyes were the color of a stormy sky. "Let's try something," I whispered. And I finally did the thing I'd spent the entire summer avoiding—I leaned down and skimmed my lips gently across hers.

For a moment, I froze there at the corner of her sweet mouth, still hampered by uncertainty. Believe it or not, it was difficult to cross the line I'd worked so hard to maintain.

But then Kira made a soft sound of yearning, and I couldn't hold back anymore. I tilted my head to perfect our connection, taking the softness of her mouth against my own.

Mmm. Our kiss was sweeter and slower than I usually went for. But no less hot. Before I knew it, I was tracing her lips with my tongue—the same lips I'd been staring at for three months— and a low groan escaped from my throat.

She opened for me, and I was a goner, tasting her for the first time. She tasted of summer, and of good beer and happy times. With a whimper, she leaned even closer, bringing her breasts against my chest. And all my reservations flew away on the cool evening breeze. Locking my arms around her, I took my time tasting her, our lips sliding together, our tongues slow-dancing. I wove my fingers into her hair, only to find that the texture was even softer than I'd imagined. As I stroked her delicate jaw with my thumb, our kiss went on and on.

And Kira was right there with me, her hands wandering, her body warm and hungry against mine.

All right. Those were good signs, although my awareness was dialed up to eleven. My cock had its own ideas, straining against my shorts. I ached to slide my hands down her body, cup her ass, pull her even more tightly against me. I wanted to hurry her out of her clothes.

But I kept myself in check. The sad reason behind this tryst filtered through my lust-filled haze, and I found the will to ease up.

Go slow, I coached myself. *Slower than you've ever gone.* I stepped back, breaking our kiss. I left my forehead tipped against Kira's. "Never thought I'd get to do that," I rasped.

"Me neither."

I took a deep, slow breath, reining myself in. And then I took her hand in mine, slowly guiding it down to the thickening bulge in my shorts. I placed her palm over my erection, then watched her reaction.

If I was expecting fear, there wasn't any. In fact, her eyes burned brighter. "Really? Is that a yes?" She sucked in a breath but didn't take away her hand. "The flip side is, if it doesn't work, I'll leave you like this."

Hell, that wasn't anywhere near the top of the list of reasons why this was a bad idea. "I don't care about that. But Kira, if you're not ready..." *Shit.* "I *really* don't want to be the guy who scares you. That's selfish, but it's true."

Nose to nose, she studied me. And while she did that, she

moved her palm slowly up my fly, and then down again. I had to bite the inside of my cheek to avoid groaning.

"Please?" she asked. "I think it will be okay."

I caught her exploring hand in my own. It was almost impossible to believe that this was really happening. I studied her eyes one more time, and they were just as clear and warm as every other time I'd gazed at her.

"Okay." Of course I said yes. "How do you want this to go down? You need to tell me exactly what you want to happen." I smoothed her hair away from her cheek.

Her face was already flushed from all that kissing, and she stumbled on her words. "I didn't... I hadn't thought that far ahead. We just need to go slow."

"Sure. But..." I looked around. "Lights on or off? You need to be comfortable."

"So do you."

I gave her a quick kiss. "I'm easy." She really had no idea. With a beautiful girl in my room, I found it much harder to stay clothed than to get naked.

"Well..." She walked over to the lamp on the bedside table and turned it on, then she went back to the wall switch, shutting off the overhead. "As long as I can see your face, I don't think I'll be scared."

That was a sobering statement, and my heart gave a squeeze. Was I a good enough man to be somebody's safe person? *Me?* I wasn't exactly short-listed for any humanitarian awards.

With an even tighter rein on my libido, I sat down on the bed. "This is going to work best if you make all the first moves. And we need a safe word. When you need a break, what are you going to say?"

"Stop?" She walked over to stand right in front of me.

I shook my head and smiled up at her. "Too easy to confuse with *don't* stop. So 'oh God' is no good either."

Her flush deepened. "How about 'wait'?"

"'Wait,'" I repeated. "Alright. Now come and get me." I

guided one of her hands to my shirt buttons. "Go on. You're making this happen."

I looked down to watch as she tentatively fingered the first button. "This is weird for me," she whispered. "It's been a long time."

"Hey." I reached around to give her a playful little pinch on the bottom. "Whose idea was this? Keep going. You need to be the one in control." Not only would that keep me from rushing her, it just made good sense. If she initiated every move, there was no way I could accidentally freak her out.

And truly, I'd rather have third-degree blue balls than frighten Kira. If she ended up having a panic attack in my arms, it would slay me.

Her eyes flickered to mine again. Then she glanced down at her work, a sly smile on her lips. Her fingers fumbled on the buttons, and my heart squeezed again. There was a sweet awkwardness here that was unfamiliar to me. But I guess that was to be expected when you already cared for someone you'd never been naked with. So this was normal, right?

But... bloody hell, had I *never* been in this situation? It had been years, anyway, since I'd waited longer than a few drinks to sleep with someone.

Wow. How was that even possible?

"Do I have to do all the work here?" she asked as my shirt finally slipped off my shoulders. She was standing over me, her gaze caressing my bare chest.

In answer, I gathered the hem of her T-shirt, and with a glance into her eyes to be sure that it was okay, I lifted it cautiously over her head. She wore a plain white bra underneath, and in my opinion it hid too much of her. Slowly, I leaned forward to put my lips on her sternum. With gentle fingers, I reached around to unclasp her bra in the back.

It fell away, and her beautiful breasts were right there at eye level. I'd been picturing them all summer long, and now here they were, rosy nipples hardening in the night air. I eased her body closer to mine, my chin between her breasts. I tilted back, looking up into her face. "Are we still good?" I whispered.

"Very good." Her eyes were wide, looking down at me with something like wonder.

This is a privilege. I formed that thought even as I cupped one of her breasts in my hand, turning my face to flick my tongue across her nipple. "I'm glad I shaved," I said into the soft swell of her breast.

"Oh," she said quietly, her body tipping towards mine. Her hand fisted my too-long hair as I slowly kissed her breast. She wasn't afraid of me. I could tell by the way she melted into my body.

Her skin was velvet to my touch. I slid one palm down to her belly, pausing to admire the pretty taper of her waist. When I rested my fingers on the button of her shorts, she didn't flinch. "Is it time to remove these?" I whispered, tracing a lazy circle over her tummy.

"Okay," she answered. "But then you have to take yours off. I can't be the only one undressed."

"That's really not a problem for me." I chuckled. Then I dropped Kira's shorts to the floor, and her panties with them.

Damn. Kira naked. This was the one beautiful Maine view that I never thought I'd see.

For a moment, I could only stare at the sleek curve of her hips, and the trim little triangle of hair between her tan legs.

It was too overwhelming to stay there, eye level with her chest. So I stood, popping the button on my shorts, pushing them down. I dropped them onto the floor, along with my boxer briefs. Naked myself now, my arousal kicked up another notch.

Easy, I coached myself. *Slow*.

Lying down, I positioned myself on my back. For a long moment, Kira only stared at my body. I saw her swallow roughly, and just as I began to wonder if she was going to back out, she moved quickly, sliding onto the bed beside me. Instinctively, I rolled closer.

She stiffened. "Wait. I'm not ready."

Jonas, you asshole. As quickly as if I'd been stung, I rolled away, lying beside her again on the bed. I made sure to put a few inches between us, not touching her at all. Then I took one of her smooth hands in mine, drawing it up to my lips to kiss her knuckles. "I know that, sweetness. We're just warming up, here, okay?"

"Okay," she breathed.

"In fact, there's not going to be *any* sex until the moment you say so. Got it?"

"Yeah."

I closed my eyes and counted silently to ten. I opened them again, taking measure of her gaze. Those beautiful gray eyes were steady. "For now, we're only going to make out. So come here and kiss me." I smiled at her as calmly as I could manage, even as my heart rate soared. I wanted to make her happy. I wanted that so damned badly it hurt.

As commanded, Kira scooted closer. I cupped her sweet jaw in one hand and kissed her. When I felt her tongue probe my mouth again, and her body relax into my kisses, I pulled back once more, squeezing her hand. "Now, you put my hand wherever I'm allowed to touch you."

Kira blew out a little nervous breath, and then brought my fingertips onto her breast.

"Mmm..." I said against her tongue as my palm cupped the soft swell. I slid my thumb over her nipple, and it pebbled under my touch. We kissed, and I let my hand stroke her smooth breast. I'd waited so long for this moment, and I hadn't even allowed myself to hope that it would arrive.

With a small sigh, Kira gave my hand a little shove farther down her body. I let my palm rest precisely where she'd put it— right over her belly button. I did not even spread my fingers. Instead, I only deepened our kiss, sliding my tongue over hers until Kira purred with delight.

She gave my hand another push. Again, I applied a strict interpretation of the law, smoothing my fingers over her hips, dusting just past the top of her mound. When I did it again, not quite touching the good stuff, she gave a little huff of frustration.

"Is this okay now?" I asked, smiling against her lips, sliding one finger slowly between the petals of her body.

Her answer was to moan into my mouth, which made me chuckle. She was so responsive. Already slippery with desire. When I touched her, she arched in for more. *Sweetness.* My heart rate kicked up a notch. And when I eased her onto her back, it was with hands that had begun to shake with anticipation.

Go slow, I reminded myself again. But it sure wasn't easy. Bending over her body, I skimmed my lips down her neck and chest. Pausing at her breast, I flattened my tongue against her nipple. That earned me a gasp of delight, and I worshipped her breasts as my fingers stroked between her legs. She gave a happy moan as I slid down to begin kissing and nibbling on her hip. Slowly, I nosed towards her sex.

"Oh," she panted. "You really don't have to do that."

I paused, stroking her with my thumb. "But I want to taste you," I said quietly. I dipped my chin to give her a single lick up the center of her sex, and she gasped with excitement. "This will relax you. And if it doesn't, say 'wait.'"

Spoiler: Kira never said "wait."

I kissed her senseless, my tongue stirring lazily over her pussy. There was nothing better than this. I had a beautiful girl writhing against my lips, arching her back with a low, sexy moan. And I had the perfect view up her sleek body, the curves undulating like waves in the Pacific. And the sounds she made were a richer melody than I could ever write.

"Oh, John. Oh my God, I never... *ohhh*..." She didn't finish the sentence. She quivered instead. I felt a surge of victory as her body trembled beneath me. She came on a moan, and I swear I'd never felt such satisfaction at making anyone happy. Ever.

As soon as she fell back onto the pillow, relaxing again, I hiked myself up to hold her. "Kira," I whispered into her ear. "I don't want to hear you talk about being icky again. Because you are delicious."

Her eyes flickered to mine, and I saw a small flash of disbelief, followed by a smile. Her obvious pleasure made me feel like a hero.

And wasn't that just laughable? Some people built houses for the homeless, or raised money to cure cancer. All I'd done was give a nice girl an orgasm.

But hey, I was the right man for the job.

"That wasn't part of my agenda," she said finally.

"No?" I gave her my best lady-killer smile. "It should be. Because you'll be putty in my hands now. Unless that's all you can take for one night?"

"No sir." Her face was grave. "It only counts if we do the deed."

I groaned appreciatively. My dick was hard as a board. "Please tell me you have birth control. Because I don't have a thing." That had been part of my chastity strategy. Even though I was quick to get naked, I never went without protection. Leaving the condoms behind in Seattle meant one more obstacle to slipping up.

"I brought it," Kira said.

"Let me have it, then."

"It's for me, not you." Kira's cheeks flushed the telltale pink of a woman who had just been satisfied. Hell, she was more beautiful now than I'd ever seen her. She got up and went to her purse. She took a package out, and I heard the tear and crinkle of paper and plastic as her naked body passed by on her way into the bathroom.

I sat up against the headboard, trying not to get too excited. I hadn't had sex in three months, except with my palm. Without a doubt, the dry spell was a personal record.

But when Kira emerged with a nervous expression on her sweet face, it wasn't too difficult to dial back my expectations. "It's never too late to change your mind." Though I hoped she wouldn't. I held my arms out in what I hoped was a nonthreatening way, and she climbed into them.

I kissed her again, testing the waters. And she pressed those gorgeous breasts to my chest and gave as good as she got. "I don't want to change my mind," she whispered, giving my shoulders a tug, trying to pull me down on top of her.

But I reminded myself once again to take things very, very slowly. "Actually, let's stay up here." I tucked a pillow between my back and the headboard.

"Could I, um..." She hesitated.

"What, sweetness?"

The way her forehead crinkled when she frowned was endearing. "It's sort of embarrassing. I want to touch you... You know, to remind myself that it's not an instrument of torture."

Jesus Christ. The things this girl had been through broke my heart. The wrongness of it might have wilted me, except for the fact that she had just asked if she could get a really close look at my dick.

I tipped my head back. "Play all you want. I don't embarrass."

Biting her lip, she reached over, brushing a hand tentatively over my cock.

After a moment, I blew out a breath of pure desire. "Come even closer." I tugged her elbows, drawing her over my lap to straddle me. With wide eyes, she maneuvered her bare ass onto my thighs. I cupped her hand in mine and brought it to my shaft, curling her fingers around it. *Jesus.* I held my breath as she stroked me. And when she brushed her thumb over my cock head, a single drop of liquid glistened there.

She inhaled sharply. "God, you're gorgeous. I can't believe you're really letting this happen."

Letting it? I wanted to shout with joy. Kira wanted me, and it didn't have a fucking thing to do with Hush Note or rock and roll. Instead, I was about to get laid just for being John Smith, A Good Listener.

There was a big fat lesson in there somewhere. But I'd have to find it later, because all the blood had left my brain and was currently pulsing in my cock. Kira's fingertips dragged over me again. I was going to disgrace myself if she didn't stop that soon.

I slipped a hand onto her belly, then smoothed it down, my

thumb grazing her mound. When I dipped even lower, she closed her eyes. "Okay." Her voice was shaky. "I'm ready."

"Come here," I rasped, tugging her hips closer. "I want you to ride me. Can you do that?"

For a second she looked startled. But then she nodded. She rose up on her knees, and I held my breath again. She leaned forward, trapping my cock underneath her body. Slowly, she sank down on me, and this time I couldn't help myself. I let out a monstrous groan. "You feel so fucking good."

She was tight and hot, a wet heaven. Without a condom, I could feel every delicious particle of her body against mine.

Hold back, I reminded myself for the hundredth time. *Wayyy back.*

With her hands on my shoulders and her face pensive, she rose up, sinking slowly down on me the same way again. God in heaven, I was panting already. No moment in my life had ever required so much restraint. I wanted to jack my hips off the bed. But I allowed myself only the slightest roll of my pelvis to meet her. Instead of grabbing her hips like I wanted to, I rested my fingertips lightly on her waist, my hands barely skimming the velvet swell of her ass.

Slowly she moved against me as the cool lake breeze blew through the curtains, bringing the scent of late summer with it. I took a deep breath of that perfect air and focused on Kira's serious face. I had never paid so much attention to a lover during sex, to the blush of her cheeks and the set of her mouth. For the first time, I knew what it was like to really give myself to someone, like a gift. And holy hell. The result was the sexiest thing I'd ever seen.

And I'd seen some pretty crazy shit.

As she rode me, Kira shifted around, unconsciously seeking her pleasure. And when she found it, something exquisite seemed to bloom across her face. Squeezing my shoulders, her movements quickened. Her eyes opened wide, her gaze locking onto mine.

Usually during sex I shut off my brain. Because wasn't that

the point? But not this time. I was witnessing something beautiful, and I didn't want to miss a second of it. Carefully, I slid down the sheet, laying us both down, giving Kira more room to maneuver. Her soft tits rubbed my chest as she moved, making me groan. Suddenly, I had to have my mouth on hers. Craning my neck, I reached up, kissing her hungrily while she fucked me. Still, I listened carefully to every breathy exhalation, to every noise she made. But there were no signs of trouble, just the sounds of a woman rediscovering all the joy that two bodies could bring one another.

Her breathy moans increased in pitch, her hair sliding over my nipples like silk.

"That's it, baby," I gasped, my own voice cracking. And then she groaned in ecstasy, throwing her head back. The erotic look on her face nearly did me in. "Sweet Jesus," I hissed.

And finally—wrenching my hips off the bed for relief—I came in three long, hard bursts. It was the best fucking orgasm of my life, with Kira's sweet body milking mine.

Afterward, I flopped onto the pillow, feeling as if I'd just run a marathon. Who knew that holding back would be twice as potent as lunging for it?

When I opened my eyes again, there were tears running down Kira's face.

"Don't cry now," I whispered, reaching up to wipe them away. "That was perfect."

"I'm just so happy. For a long time I thought..." She gulped in air, and then leaned her cheek against my palm. "He took something from me, and now I feel as though it's possible to get it back. Thank you."

Fuck, my own eyes began to feel misty. Kira laid her head in my chest, and I stroked her hair until her tears stopped. Even as I wiped them away, her body was still hugging my cock, torturing me with the small aftershocks of her climax.

Everything about the moment was perfect.

Five years later, I hadn't forgotten a second of it. No night had ever topped it, nor even come close. If I was a smarter man, I would have realized how much it all meant before it was too late.

I hadn't, and I'd always regretted it.

Today, though, Kira had kissed me again. She'd kissed me like our night together was as fresh in her memory as it was in mine. That had really happened.

If she was happily married now, would she have done that?

The weird thing was that I'd always *wanted* a happy ending for her. These past few years I'd been picturing her with a husband and a couple of cute little kids. In my head, that's how things ended up, and I had been okay with it.

Until today. All of a sudden it wasn't okay. Because seeing Kira again made me wish for things that an asshole like me wouldn't know what to do with. I wanted to hold her in my arms and kiss her again. And never stop.

I groaned aloud, flipping onto my stomach, pressing my erection into the quilt on my lonely bed.

We have to talk, she'd said. What the hell did that even mean?

FOUR

KIRA

"Let's play with all the old toys," Vivi demanded. "And then I want to catch fireflies. Where is my jar?"

"One thing at a time, toots," I told my daughter. "And I don't think we'll spot fireflies this early in the season."

"But maybe," she argued.

I gave her a vague nod, but my mind was elsewhere. Somehow, I was going to have to stumble through the next eighteen hours with my family, even though I was consumed with fear. Telling John—no, *Jonas*—that he was the father of my child?

Terrifying.

I wished I'd just blurted it out today on the dock. Then it would at least be over with. But that hadn't happened, because I'd been blindsided. Escaping from him had seemed like a fine idea at the time.

It didn't anymore. Until tomorrow at noon, I would have a clenched stomach and a bad case of the shakes.

For once, my brother wasn't much help. Adam had withdrawn to the porch with a beer and a magazine. He didn't emerge until suppertime when our father came home. The heavy sound of his feet on the porch steps was as familiar as breathing.

"How's my princess?" he boomed as the screen door slammed shut.

Vivi came running, leaping into my dad's arms.

I watched my gray-haired father swing my daughter around with the same surprise I always felt when the two of them were together. Because he'd never once called me "his princess." Becoming a grandpa had softened this man.

And thank goodness. My whole life, he'd been pretty hard to take.

We'd never had an easy relationship, and on the day I'd told him I'd been raped, it became even more strained. Maybe he was just worried, or maybe he blamed me. I'll never know. But he became even more silent and brittle than usual.

It didn't help that we were trapped in this house together for months afterward, the cold Maine winter keeping me in sight of his grim expression for weeks at a time. And with Adam away at law school, I'd been lonely. It was the longest winter of my life.

When summer finally arrived, everything got easier. My father and I were both busy at the store, since summer was our high season.

And then John had turned up to distract me. He'd been a charming diversion with enormous consequences. I'd gone back to college right on schedule after Labor Day, thinking that my life was back on track, but six weeks into the semester, I began to feel utterly exhausted and caught a cold that wouldn't go away. Eventually, I wandered into the student health building and asked if maybe mono was going around.

A very astute doctor asked me a whole battery of questions. The final one was, "When did you last have a menstrual period?"

That's when I understood just how badly I'd messed up.

The first person I'd told about my pregnancy was Adam. He'd held me while we both cried on each other. Then I'd summoned the nerve to tell my father over Thanksgiving, when Adam was around to back me up.

My father had turned white, and then red. "You're moving home immediately," he'd said, slamming a fist onto the table.

"She's going to finish the semester," Adam had argued. "Obviously."

"You're out of control. Both of you," he'd raged. The ranting went on for hours, until I ended up in my bedroom sobbing, while my brother handed me tissues, one after another.

As it happened, I did not move back to Maine at all. I couldn't spend another winter with my father's constant reminders of his disappointment.

"Honestly," I'd told Adam, "I don't think I can do it."

"You'll move in with me," he'd offered without hesitating. "In Boston."

I'd cried some more after that, but they'd been tears of gratitude.

Now, four years later, my father had a completely different attitude. Vivi was his favorite person in the world. And the minute he came home from the store, Vivi began to pepper him with her demands. "I didn't get to go in the rowboat yet," she complained to her grandfather, climbing into his lap.

He stood up, lifting her with him. "Is that so? I think it's time to light the grill right now. Come outside with me." He gave me and Adam barely a nod of greeting before taking his princess outside.

Luckily, Adam's mood rallied. Setting aside his magazine, he opened a bottle of white wine, pouring three glasses. Humming to himself, he cooked up the sausages, grilling onions and peppers on the side.

At some point he noticed my long silences and began shooting worried glances in my direction. And when that failed to lighten me up, he tried another tactic—making cracks about how much he *lurved* sausages.

"So plump and juicy," Adam deadpanned, rolling the food on the grill with a set of tongs. "They're my *favorite.*"

Our father gave him a dark look after the third or fourth sausage joke. Then he slunk around the corner of the house to smoke a cigarette away from Vivi. After all these years, he was still dismayed by Adam's sexual orientation. I'd never understood it. Adam was a successful lawyer who took good care of his friends and family. What more could a father want?

My contribution to dinner was a salad, which I served with forced cheer at the appointed time. But I didn't fool anyone. During dinner, my brother's concern radiated across the table.

Later, after the glacial movement of the mantel clock finally brought about Vivi's bedtime, we three adults spent a polite half hour in the living room. After enduring thirty minutes of Dad's baseball game on TV, Adam popped off the sofa. "Kira, take a walk with me? You'll listen for the little skeeter, won't you, Pop?"

He gave us a stoic nod. "Could you wheel Mrs. Wetzle's groceries over to her door? She didn't answer when I rang earlier. I parked them behind your car."

"Sure thing," Adam said, pulling me off the sofa.

Together, we went outside, where the last of the day's light was just a stripe in the western sky. My father had left an old red wagon in the driveway, with three bags of groceries tucked inside. Wordlessly, Adam caught the handle and pulled it down the drive.

A minute later we approached Mrs. Wetzle's place, and I tried not to stare at the room in the back. He wasn't there, of course, but the ghosts from five years ago were all around me. They always swarmed when I came to Maine for a summertime visit.

Adam stopped beside the kitchen entrance, knocking twice on the old metal door.

Mrs. Wetzle appeared a minute later. "Could you carry those inside?" she asked.

Adam met my eyes, and we exchanged a moment of silent irritation that the old lady did not even say *please*.

While Mrs. Wetzle held the door open, I grabbed a bag filled with hamburger buns and condiments and ran it into the house, leaving it on the first available kitchen surface I could find. Then I turned tail and got the heck out, then waited for Adam a few yards away under a big pine tree.

The winter I'd been pregnant, and totally starting to show,

the whispers about me grew loud in town. Even though I'd been mortified to ask, I had knocked on Mrs. Wetzle's door one afternoon to inquire as to whether she might have a phone number for John Smith who had spent the summer there.

I didn't tell Mrs. Wetzle why I'd wanted it, but the old lady had known. A long and terrible moment of silence had passed between us, while I'd squirmed under her dismayed gaze. "I never should have rented to a musician," she'd said, while I'd wished that the frozen earth would open up and swallow me.

"Did you save his number?" I'd had to ask a second time.

Mrs. Wetzle shook her head. "He pre-paid. I didn't need to even ask for it."

"Thank you anyway," I'd mumbled, making my escape.

I'd been avoiding Mrs. Wetzle's gaze ever since. And when the Christmas popcorn balls arrived each year, I gave mine to Adam.

Adam abandoned the wagon under the tree, because nobody would bother stealing it. "Come on," he said, grabbing my hand. "Spill it, sis. You look destroyed. Like Sarah Conner at the end of Terminator 2."

"That's an apt comparison. Because the crud is about to hit the fan," I said.

Adam giggled. "Just say 'shit,' Kira, like everyone else does. Or pick a different metaphor. Flying bits of crud just aren't scary."

"In this case they really are." Before we could reach Main Street, I steered my brother toward the lonely dock, instead of the ice cream place.

"Damn. If we're not even going for soft serve, this must be really serious."

Oh, you have no idea. I dragged Adam out to the end of the dock and sat down cross-legged. He flopped down next to me. And then I blurted it out. "He's back in town."

My brother was silent for a long moment. "No shit?" he said, finally. "I assume we're talking about Vivi's daddy."

"Right after you guys got out of the car, I saw him. And we

spoke for a minute." I edited out the kissing, not because Adam would disapprove, but because I wasn't quite sure how it had happened, or what to think about it. "We're having lunch tomorrow."

"Jesus! So how's that discussion going to go? 'These sandwiches are fantastic. And by the way, our kid turns four next month.'"

"I'm going to tell him."

"Of *course* you're going to tell him! That's the right thing to do."

I flinched. "Adam," I put a hand on his wrist. "I haven't done the right thing. Not at all."

"Not true!" He rubbed my back with one hand. "You've done all the right things, Kiki. It hasn't been easy, but you're doing well."

"No. You don't understand." I took a deep breath. "I never told you that I found out who he was."

"Wait... What? He's some guy named John Smith who spent the summer in Mrs. Wetzle's place. Are you saying that wasn't true?"

"It was, and it wasn't," I whispered.

"*Kiki.*" His voice held a warning. "There's enough soap opera in our lives already. What's the story?"

Right. If it was this hard to explain it to Adam, how was I ever going to tell John? Or Jonas. Whoever. I sighed. "Okay, when Vivi was nine months old, I saw his face on an album cover."

Adam whistled. "A *good* album cover?"

"Do you know the band Hush Note?"

I watched Adam's eyes bug out. "Oh my god, Kiki! You got knocked up by a rock star? What's his name?" Adam dug his phone out of his back pocket.

"He's Jonas—"

"—Smith!" he yelled. He spoke to his phone: "Siri, show me if Jonas Smith has a hot body!" He squinted at the screen. "Hey —Hush Note is releasing a new single this weekend. Wait—

what I really need is YouTube." He tapped feverishly on the screen.

It was just my luck that cell phone service had arrived at Nest Lake. In no time, my brother pulled up a video clip of Jonas Smith in concert. I leaned over Adam's shoulder to see. I'd done this before, though, peering at clips of him, trying to understand who he really was.

On Adam's screen, Jonas sang hard, one sculpted arm clutching the microphone, torqueing his body as if to squeeze the sound out. The stage lighting had an orange hue, lending him an otherworldly appearance.

After a moment, I had to look away. Whenever I saw one of those videos, it brought him further away from me, not closer. It was like watching a stranger.

Today on the dock, though, I'd found the real man. And tomorrow we would meet again, and I would spill my secret.

But then what? He'd probably freak out and disappear. And that was actually the *best* scenario. The scarier one was that he'd sue me for custody. Not that John was mean. But living with Adam—a lawyer—had been an unwelcome education on the topic of interpersonal disasters. The cases passing through my brother's office showcased every kind of crazy thing people did to hurt one another.

I dreaded telling him.

"That is one hot piece of man," my brother said, still squinting at his phone. "A burning hunk of love." He clicked the phone off and stuffed it into his pocket. "But Kira, you knew who he was, and you never told him? That's so wrong."

"I *know*, Adam. I should have tried harder to contact him."

"Did you try at all?"

I was silent, because the answer to that question was somewhat complicated. But he mistook it for denial. "Tsk, tsk," he said. "You *are* a bad girl."

"What do you think will happen?" I raised my eyes to him, and the sight of my thoughtful big brother was a balm on my soul. Without Adam, these last few years would have been unsurvivable.

He leaned back on his elbows. "Well, really that depends on him. If he wants to acknowledge the child, the court will grant him visitation, if he asks for it. And you'll get a shitload of money in child support. Actually, you can get the money whether he wants to acknowledge Vivi or not."

"I never cared about his money."

"God, Kiki, why not? If you took a full course load, you could graduate in a year. Seriously, why wouldn't you take the help that's coming to you?"

This was another difficult topic, because I'd been sponging off Adam for years. Any child support I'd failed to collect had cost my brother more than it had cost me. But I *did* have a reason for not telling Jonas Smith about Vivi. Actually two reasons.

Just after he'd left Maine, I'd reached out to him, and he had ignored me. That had hurt very badly. I told him how much he meant to me. And in return, he said nothing.

And then there was the guilt. "The pregnancy was my fault, Adam. I told him we were covered, but..." I cleared my throat. I would tell my brother anything, but it was hard to say it out loud. The birth control gel I'd brought with me that night had been purchased during happier times. It was past its expiration date, which I hadn't checked.

Also, you were supposed to reapply it in between uses. But I hadn't done that, either.

So I'd born a child with a man who never wanted to hear from me again. And while I knew he deserved to know—and that Vivi deserved to someday meet her father—I hadn't told him. Yet. I knew I needed to. I just hadn't made it happen.

"It doesn't matter," Adam said. "The law doesn't care which of you forgot to put the goalie in front of the net. Even if you flat-out lied, any guy who has sex is still responsible for the results."

"I didn't flat-out lie."

He covered one of my hands with his own. "I believe you, Kira. But I'd still love you no matter what."

I let out a big breath and said a silent prayer of gratitude for my brother. In the silence, I heard the distant thump of a bass line echoing across the lake. "Do you hear that? His band is staying at the lodge. I'm supposed to meet him there tomorrow."

"Do you want me to come with you?"

Honestly, it was tempting. "No. I'll need you to babysit. Dad will be at the store." My phone buzzed. "I'm not used to having cell service here." I checked the screen, and it was a text message. "Oh, jeez. I forgot about Luke. I was supposed to see him this weekend."

"Did you stand him up?"

"No, it's nothing like that." That high school boyfriend who'd enlisted overseas? We were still in touch. We'd blown up as a couple, of course, when he came back from his tour in Afghanistan to find me pregnant with another man's child. He'd gone back for another tour after that. But we'd stayed in touch, occasionally seeing each other when I came to Maine.

During our most recent phone conversation a few weeks ago, he'd said he wanted to see me and talk to me about something. I'd been curious at first, but now my head was spinning in other directions.

My brother chuckled. "You're booked for lunch tomorrow. But I guess dinner is still available."

I fingered my phone. "The message says he wants to take Vivi and me on a bike ride. He borrowed a seat for her."

"Interesting. That sounds romantic, actually. But now I realize you were holding out for a rock star."

"Adam, you know that's not true."

He grinned. "So, what's the deal with Luke? I'm pretty sure he's still into you."

"He hinted that he's looking at jobs in Boston." Luke was a solid guy. He'd managed to come back from overseas with a clear head, and now he was finishing up an engineering degree at the University of Maine. Unfortunately, he'd let me down at the very moment I'd been most vulnerable. I didn't know if I could ever get past that.

"Please tell me you don't have any more bombshell secrets," my brother said. "I enjoy drama, of course, but the fallout is just so messy."

"Now you know all of my secrets, Adam."

"Uh-huh. Weren't you the one telling me earlier that coming up here to visit Dad was really no big deal?"

I laughed. The sound echoed over the water. I heard a fish jump and the gentle lap of the lake beneath us.

"Kira, was he awesome in bed?"

The question took me by surprise. "It was one night, Adam."

"Oh, honey! Just the *once* and you got pregnant?"

"Well... twice. But one night."

He laughed. "You still didn't answer the question."

"I thought big brothers didn't want to hear that stuff."

"You're not sixteen. And there's a serious lack of men in both our lives, Kiki. Just tell me one hot thing about him."

"I can't," I whispered. "I can't pick one thing. Because everything about that man is hot."

Adam collapsed onto the deck with an exaggerated groan. "Wow."

Even if I wasn't willing to talk about it, I still thought about that night all the time. It had been hot, but also sweet. After John and I had made love the first time, we'd held each other for hours.

Strangely, it hadn't been the least bit awkward. We lay in the same comfortable silence we'd often enjoyed, only without clothes. Occasionally he'd kissed my cheek, or stroked my hip. He was a hands-on guy, and I had the vague idea that he'd been nearly as starved for affection as I'd been.

He held me in silence until eventually saying: "If you end up getting together with your high-school sweetheart, I hope he realizes how lucky he is."

"Do you think I'll have to tell him about my... terrible night a year ago?" I'd asked.

That's when his hand went still on my back. "He doesn't *know?*"

I shook my head. "It didn't seem like the kind of news you email. Also, I didn't want to distract him. It's dangerous over there."

"Well, yeah. You have to tell him. He needs to understand that you might still get scared. Some little thing he does could trigger your fear. What if he gets a little rough, thinking that's fun for both of you?"

I raised my head to look at him. "Like what? Show me."

He gave a nervous chuckle. "No way."

Propping myself on an elbow, I looked him in the eye. "Why?"

When he looked back at me, it was with an expression that I couldn't read. "Someday I hope you can have deliciously rough sex without a second thought. If you feel like it. But not tonight, and not from me."

"You don't like it that way?" I asked.

"I thought I did. Right now I barely remember my own name." He gave me a sexy grin. "God, Kira, you look... triumphant."

"Do I? That's because I am."

"That's because you conquered me, and had your way with me." His silly smile reappeared, and we both laughed.

And—Lord—he was so attractive, stretched out naked beside me. Like a work of art. High on my own bravery, I allowed myself to brazenly admire his body while I still had the chance.

The intensity of my gaze must have been contagious, because his grin faded, too. He rolled closer to me, propping himself on an elbow, dropping his head to kiss me.

The kiss was another scorcher. I opened my mouth and took him in. Before too long, he was on top of me, and I found myself shifting my hips around with pleasure. "Oh," I gasped. "You feel good up there."

"I really do," he panted. "Is this okay?" He bore down with

his hips.

God, yes. I could only moan my approval. He worked his mouth down my jaw and onto my neck. I let my hands wander the beautiful muscles on his chest until I felt myself flood with desire all over again. It was as if he'd flipped a switch, and it couldn't be shut off again.

"Look at me, sweetness." I raised my eyes to his serious ones. "Before this gets too far, tell me what not to do up here. I don't want to walk into any tripwires, if I can help it."

I cupped my hands on that chiseled, movie-star chin. "Don't worry. As long as you don't sneak up on me from behind and smash my face into a dumpster, we'll probably be fine."

His face slackened with dismay. Without another word, he pivoted, collapsing onto the bed by my side. His arms wrapped around me. "Please tell me this guy got put away for a really long time."

"He did. You're shaking."

"I'm just so sorry."

"You're holding me awfully tightly."

"Is it scaring you?"

"No."

"Then deal with it."

I laughed. "I ruined the mood, didn't I?"

"Pretty much. I can't climb on top of you with that image in my head."

"See? This is why it's tempting not to tell the ex-boyfriend when he comes back. He might not be able to handle it."

"That would be his loss." He held me close, but his grip relaxed, and after a time I realized he'd drifted off. His face was serene, his chin against my shoulder.

The light was still on, and I knew I should probably switch it off. But as I sat up, I just couldn't stop admiring him. I knew he was out of my league—five years older, not to mention incredibly handsome. The glow of the lamp made his skin even more golden than it was in the daylight. And the tan line at his waist invited exploration. I dropped my head and began to trace his skin with my lips, dropping kisses down his belly.

"Mmm," he murmured sleepily.

I'd honestly never been so bold in my life, but I did not want to stop touching him. His tight abs changed color from bronze to pale gold as they plunged past a set of trim hips. A strip of sandy hair wandered down the center of his lower belly, and I followed it. Feeling very, very brave, I pressed soft lips against him. *Everywhere.*

Later I would wonder—if I'd just let him sleep, would I have gotten pregnant? Probably not, I'd eventually decided.

But I wasn't thinking at all, back then. I'd teased him until he was thoroughly awake. He'd made a comical growl, low in his throat. And then he pulled me down onto his chest for a kiss. I had never been kissed like that before—as if I were vital to someone's continued survival. Drunk on my own lust, I allowed myself to be rolled over.

John shifted his body over mine again. At first, the weight of him felt wonderful. He kissed my neck, my ear, my collarbone. But then somehow I began to feel a little bit trapped, and too warm. I forgot to think about how sexy he was and focused only on my growing anxiety. "Wait!" I cried out.

He went still immediately, rolling to the side. "Kira..." He was breathing hard, but his eyes were full of compassion. He propped his head in one hand. "Do you trust me?"

I did, but that was beside the point. And it wasn't easy to explain. "I trust you. I do. But sometimes I just panic, and it doesn't matter that I know you wouldn't hurt me."

He'd looked thoughtful. "Okay. I know a thing or two about triggers."

"Really?" I tried to focus on his face and words and relax my body.

"When I was a kid, I saw a horrible car accident. For years, the squeal of a truck's brakes made me crazy. It still does. But also, the sound of feedback from a microphone sometimes reminds me of it. Sometimes I have to stop and remind myself out loud which sound I'm hearing and *order* myself to remember that it isn't dangerous. I'll be standing up there in front of..." He let the sentence die.

"What?"

He shook his head. "I just talk to myself, that's all. And sometimes people stare. But it calms me down."

I looked into his kind eyes and smiled. "Whatever works, right?"

"Right. The trick is to convince your body to listen to what your heart already knows. You try it. Say out loud what we were going to do."

"We were going to make love."

A slow smile crept across his face. Just then, I would have done anything to keep it there. "And how's that going to feel, Kira?"

"Awesome."

"Be specific. Tell your body *exactly* what good things will happen."

This little game was far, far outside my comfort zone. But I'd brought the two of us here by my own design, and he was trying so hard to be good for me. So I took a deep breath, and said, "You're going to... fill me up."

He turned his chin to face me, a devilish smile in his eyes. "Go on."

"Oh good grief!" I complained. Dirty talk wasn't something I was used to.

"But I'm a details man." He chuckled.

"Fine." I rolled, putting my mouth beside his ear, so I could whisper. "You're going to stretch out on top of me and slide inside." His sexy little grunt of approval gave me courage. "Then, we'll make out like the Apocalypse is near. Until we both..." I finished on a hot whisper. "...*come*."

He took a deep, shaky breath. "Mother of God. I don't know if that's working for *you*. But I, for one, am *convinced*."

At that, I laughed out loud. The aroused grimace on his face was hysterical. And ultimately, that's what relaxed me—the laughter. He was amazingly sexy, lying naked just inches away from me. But he was still the same man I'd talked to every night that summer, with the same warm eyes and quick smile. It made my heart sing to be near him—clothed or naked.

I let myself laugh, and he laughed too. He came closer again. "Mmm..." he said, prowling my sensitive neck. I felt the flush of desire return. And when he kissed me again, I opened to him with a sigh. He deepened the kiss, making sweet love to my mouth. But still, he didn't attack. Supporting his weight on his elbows over me, his eyes flashed with humor and warmth. Just as on our many walks home in the dark, it was impossible to stay scared when he was nearby.

"I want to touch you now," he whispered, his eyes dropping down to look at my body. When he looked up again, the heat in his expression had risen to a slow burn.

"Do it," I breathed.

He used his knees to spread mine apart, and when his fingers slid between my legs, I couldn't keep still. I had to shift my hips with every sweet stroke. He put his lips over my breast and sucked gently.

"Okay." I took a breath. "Please. *Now.*"

On a groan, he looked down between our bodies. "Use your hand. You're still in charge."

So I wrapped my fingers around the base of his cock and tugged him down between my legs until the thick head of him grazed me. It felt amazing.

"Now let me see your eyes." He smiled at me, and our bodies slowly connected. With one smooth push, he was inside. His face took on a more serious expression. I wiggled a little under him, wanting to revel in the beautiful fullness. But he held perfectly still. "Sweet Jesus, you are sexy, Kira. Don't let anyone tell you otherwise."

"Move, will you?" He felt so good, and things were going so well.

He smiled down at me again. Then he pulled back at a speed

so slow it was almost imperceptible. When he'd almost left me entirely, I grabbed his bottom and tried to bring him back.

"Patience, sweetness." Again, he eased forward, almost so slowly that it didn't count.

"The gentle treatment is nice, but I can take more."

He gave me a grin, still warm but also wicked, and picked up the pace from glacial to merely dragging. With long, languid thrusts he worked deeper inside me. His lips grazed mine, and I leapt for his mouth, pressing my tongue against his. I kissed him hard, trying to show him what I needed. "You're making me desperate."

His chuckle sent shivers down my spine. "That's the point." He sat up a little, lifting my hips. Then, rising to his knees, he slung my calves onto his shoulders.

"Oh my God," I panted. I felt odd this way, my body half inverted. It was dirty somehow. But I forgot that thought as he began thrusting in earnest. The only sounds were our gasps and the slap of his taut body against mine.

His hand crept around my hip, his thumb reaching down to stroke me. It was just like I'd imagined—his fingers working me like the fretboard of his guitar. And as he strained through each thrust, every perfect muscle in his chest and arms flexed too. With each forceful push of his hips, he bit out a breathy word of praise. "So. Hot. Baby," he said. "Beautiful. Girl." We were both slicked with sweat. And then he seemed to lose the capacity for words. His breathing became ragged, and the sounds falling from his lips were exquisitely unformed.

I focused on his heavy-lidded eyes and on the sweet agony I saw there. It was then when I understood I was not the only vulnerable person in the room. Above me, he was coming apart bit by bit.

And he was beautiful. *This* was beautiful. This was how it was supposed to feel.

The start of his low groan vibrated through me. Then it grew, the sound of his climax thrilling us both. My own body pulsed in reply, gripping him as he shuddered above me. Waves of sweet sensation took me under, and I saw fireworks inside my eyelids.

"*Fuck.*" Dropping my hips, he slid over my body. His hips jumped one more time and then were still. He buried his face in my hair, and I wrapped my arms around him, feeling the rapid rise and fall of his chest against mine.

Our two hearts thumped together. There weren't even words for the way I felt.

For a long while after, we lay tangled and salty together, silent and speechless in the cool night air. I drifted in and out of sleep, too happy and emotional to completely let go of the night.

But nothing lasts forever. A few hours later, a hired car pulled up in the predawn darkness to take him on the two-hour trip to the airport.

Our goodbyes were necessarily hasty. He threw his clothes on, remembering to grab his toiletry bag from the bathroom and his suitcase from beside the door.

Before he left, and even as the limo driver made a quick bump on his horn, he sat on the bed beside me. "Be well," he said. His face was sad.

I'd sat up, putting my arms around him, and he'd pulled me close. "I don't like to say goodbye."

"Then we won't," he agreed. "I'll just say this." He pressed his lips to mine one more time, his tongue making a last slide against mine. When I responded in kind, he made a little sad sound in the back of his throat. He'd gentled the kiss, finishing it with a sigh against my lips.

Then, he'd gotten up, opened the door and disappeared for five long years.

It wasn't until my own departure at dawn that I'd discovered his guitar sitting there, forlorn.

And it wasn't until two months later that I'd discovered I was pregnant.

* * *

THE MOON HAD RISEN, lighting the dock and the little beach beside us. In the distance, a loon made its mournful cry.

"Why do you think he didn't tell you his real name?" my brother asked me suddenly.

For years I had pondered this question. "I have no idea. Probably it's just something rock stars do." Although he'd had plenty of chances after getting to know me to come clean about it. That small betrayal still stung. But now there were more terrifying questions in my heart. "What's going to happen, Adam?"

My brother squeezed my hand. "Nothing we can't handle, Kira. I mean that. No matter what scary shit comes our way this week, we're going to be okay."

"You believe me, don't you?" he prodded. "I wouldn't lie. We'll get through this."

"Okay," I agreed, my voice only trembling a little.

FIVE

JONAS

"You look like shit, boy," Ethan said as we stretched out after our five-mile run.

"Thanks, Ethan. I love you, too." I lifted my right foot, catching it behind myself and tugging upwards to stretch out my right quad.

It was a beautiful, blue-skied morning, and we were completely alone. Most places the tour bus stopped, we couldn't run anywhere except on a hotel treadmill. And even then, getting in a peaceful workout was a crapshoot. Fans interrupted me in the damnedest places. They chased me down the sidewalk. They followed me into the locker room at the gym—even the women. *Especially* the women.

Maine was my idea of heaven.

"Seriously, did you sleep at all? Those bags under your eyes are as big as my grandmother's. Let's do some abs." Ethan dropped to his back on the lawn, his knees bent.

I knelt, holding down Ethan's feet with one of my knees. "I slept some. And it's nothing that a little coffee won't fix." As Ethan began a set of oblique curls, I eyed the lodge, which was still quiet. "What do you think it would take to get Nixon out here with us?" I asked.

Ethan grunted. "Don't know." He did twenty more curls before his set was over. "Whatever that guy is going through, it would take a hell of a lot more than a workout to fix."

"Couldn't hurt, though," I muttered. I couldn't tell how much Nixon was drinking this week, but he didn't *look* good. And he hadn't for quite a while. He didn't write music anymore, either. "Nixon needs a whole summer in Maine. This shit can cure anything." It was my turn to curl. I assumed the position and prepared to torture my midsection according to Ethan's ambitious specifications. I crossed my arms on my chest, engaged my stomach muscles, and began to crunch.

Above me, Ethan shook his giant head. "See, that's what I don't get."

"What?" I huffed.

"You talk about this place like it's the best thing that ever happened to you. And I gotta think that girl you saw yesterday had something to do with it..."

Shit. Obviously Quinn hadn't kept her big mouth shut. I gritted my teeth and kept on, determined to make it through the set.

"...And yet, you haven't come back here in five years. Instead, I gotta listen to you moan about what a lonely fuck you are. I'm startin' to think you like it that way."

I had three more curls to do, and it just about killed me. One... Two... I wondered if anyone's stomach ever broke right in half? Three... *done*. I draped my arms over my knees, breathing hard. "Why are you trying to piss me off?"

"I'm not." Ethan lay back, readying himself for another set. "I'm just telling you what I see."

I brought my weight down on Ethan's feet with a little more force than was strictly necessary. "Well, thanks for that. I'm not a masochist, Ethan. But sometimes a summer is just a summer. That's all you get."

"What, did the girl turn into a pumpkin at midnight?" Ethan asked this question while banging out a serious of whip-fast curls.

I felt tired just watching him. "Something like that."

"Sounds like bullshit," Ethan said.

"Sounds like you don't know a thing about it."

"So *tell* me. You loved this girl, and she turned you down?" Hell—the big man could do a set of sit-ups and still have enough breath left to break my balls.

"Not exactly," I said before I could think better of it.

"So what happened?" Ethan put one of his giant hands on my shoes, and we switched positions again.

I began my second set of abdominal agonies, thankful for once that it wasn't possible to speak. To convince my body to finish the set, I promised myself a skinny-dip in the lake after this. Swimming, and then coffee. That was something worth living for.

"Nicely done," Ethan said when I finished. "That will keep them screaming your name when you rip your shirt off during the set."

I flopped onto the grass. "At least I have that."

"So what happened with the girl?" The dude would not let it rest.

I studied the impossibly blue sky. "She was meant to be somebody else's girl, that's all."

"Seriously? You threw down for this girl, and she said, 'No thanks, I'm with this other schmo?' Now I can't *wait* to meet her."

Of course the truth was more complicated. When I'd met Kira, I'd been a very immature twenty-five. After my best summer ever, I'd returned to Seattle, and things had gone well for me almost immediately. The record label had loved the lyrics I'd written in Maine, and they'd set up a brisk production schedule for *Summer Nights*.

I'd had to lay down a couple of the electric tracks first, because I'd left my favorite acoustic guitar in Maine. Ethan had called Mrs. Wetzle and asked her to ship it to the address on its luggage tag—my management company's address in L.A. But when the guitar finally made its way back to me, the name on the return address had been Kira's, not the innkeeper's.

Inside the case, I'd found a letter tucked under the strings, right over the sound hole. *John*, she'd printed on the envelope, and the name had already looked strange to me. The summer had begun slipping away before the jet had touched down at SeaTac.

The letter inside the envelope had been short, and it had caused my chest to tighten.

JOHN,

You've only been gone a few days, but it feels like months. Maybe you won't want to hear this, but I miss you terribly. I hope we're still friends? Did I wreck that?

I'd call you to say this if I could, but I no longer have your phone number. (Apparently indelible ink will smudge.) But here goes nothing: I love you, and I wish you hadn't left.

When you get this, I hope you'll call me, if only to tell me that the guitar made it unscathed. And I'd love to hear your voice. If I don't hear from you, I guess I'll know I've overstepped. But I couldn't not say it.

Thank you for being the best guy I've met in a long, long time.

Love always, Kira

PS: the store phone is 207.663.2774. I close on weeknights until mid-September. It's just a lot quieter now that you're gone.

* * *

I HAD READ the letter several times in a row. It seemed impossible that someone like Kira could love me. I didn't trust it. After all, a night of really excellent sex could scramble anyone's brains.

Hindsight made me wish I'd reached for the phone immediately. But I didn't call. I wasn't sure I deserved that kind of love.

She'd only seen the best parts of me. Not the drunk, insecure nights, or the sleazy things I'd done.

So I'd tucked the letter back into its envelope, and then folded it in half. I'd put it into my wallet. It went everywhere with me—on visits to the record label, to jam sessions with Nixon and Quinn. Sometimes, during a quiet moment, I'd take it out and read a portion. *Love always.* Or *Thank you for being the best guy I've met in a long, long time.*

I wanted to call. I wanted more. But I was so sure I'd fuck it up somehow. If I didn't call, it was still perfect. Someone loved me just for me. That had never happened in Seattle. That had never happened anywhere.

And then I'd become busy. Producing the album had been a grind. I'd promised myself I'd call Kira when things settled down. But a week passed, and then another. At some point I'd looked up and it had already become November. She would have gone back to college in Boston. I'd missed my chance.

Still, I could have gotten her Boston number from her father. I didn't try to track her down, though. I just... didn't. At the time, I'd known it was a mistake, but we were three-thousand miles apart, and I didn't know what I could possibly offer Kira from that distance. At the time, I'd felt letting Kira go was probably the right decision for both of us. That girl did not need to hitch her wagon to a fuckup like me.

And anyway, my great big life had been distracting enough that I didn't have time to sit around and wonder what might have been. The album I'd written went big, which felt good.

It hadn't felt as good as winning Kira's love, although it would take me years to realize it. I'd carried her letter in my pocket until the corners of the envelope began to wear off. Then I'd tucked it into a safe place at home.

I'd met other women, of course. But not one of them had made the same impression on me. I'd gone on the dates my publicist set up for me, always with actresses or models—people with their own publicists, and their own need to be Seen (with a capital S). The occasions were often awards ceremonies, or A-list parties. The girls had always been very beautiful, but compared to Kira, they'd been plastic—styled and painted and perfected within an inch of their lives.

And even if they'd been awesome people underneath, I would have never known. It had been impossible for any real spark to penetrate the charade of an A-list date. The women who'd walked the red carpets with me were on the job, the same as I was. They'd needed their photographs taken with the right celebrities, and they'd needed those pictures to appear in just the right gossip rags.

The encounters had left nothing to chance. They'd been almost entirely empty and rarely led to sex.

For sex, I could always count on the fan girls trying to shove their way past the security staff backstage at my concerts. During the earliest years of my career, unfettered access to a quick fuck had been just as exciting as most red-blooded American men imagined it would be. All I had to do was scan the backstage crowd for the most appealing face. A nod to the bouncers would bring the girl—and often one or two of her friends—ducking under the ropes to party with me. For the next several hours, I would be fawned over, admired and fucked to my liking. There was no need to seduce these women, or even to be too interested in them.

And that got boring fast. I'd discovered that sex lost something when you didn't have to do anything other than show up. Most nights I'd found my pillow more appealing than a hookup, and I began to put less and less effort into my increasingly infrequent sweaty encounters.

The low point had been when I discovered that even the most casual conversation was unnecessary to get a woman to undress me. One night, in San Francisco, I'd been drinking with a woman after the show, sucking back my rum and Coke, staring into space, and thinking of other things. When our drinks were empty, she'd stood up and taken my hand, silently offering to move the night along to the next stage.

Amid the glitter and booze, the problem had become clear:

once you'd looked into the passionate eyes of someone who loved you just for you, nothing else would do.

But by then it had been too late. On a lonely night, I'd finally called the store. "They moved to Boston," the old man had said when I asked for Kira.

They.

Kira had gone back to her army man. Of course she had. She'd moved on, and I would never get that perfect summer back.

Even so, seeing Kira yesterday had caused my heart to spasm. I was dying to talk to her, and I'd been counting the hours ever since.

Nothing will come of it, I reminded myself every few minutes. She'd probably tell me just how far she'd moved on. Married. With kids. And that was going to hurt. Big time.

The best I could probably hope for was to get another song out of it. A nice ballad of heartbreak and loss. And then what?

More sex with strangers, probably.

ONE NIGHT last year I'd ground through the motions with another hookup after a show. Afterward, the band had climbed onto the bus for a six-hour drive. I had taken a couple of hits off of Nixon's bong—which was something I never did, because drugs just weren't my thing. High for the first time in years, I'd tried to have a conversation with Ethan about my sex life. I remembered it clearly, even though the voices in my memory sounded like a conversation from the bottom of a barrel.

"Ethan," I'd complained, "these women are always there, and they're always ready. It's like, it's starting to seem normal."

"You're living the dream, Jojo. What's the problem?"

Ethan had put his giant hands on top of his own shaved head, looking for all the world like Buddha. The stoned-up me had to stare at him a second before continuing. "But, dude," I whined. "It's like... they're not *normal*. Who throws themselves at a complete stranger?"

"You do, Jojo. Once or twice a week."

"Yeah, but I do it because they make it seem, like, normal. And that shit is not normal!"

Ethan had laughed, shaking his big head. "See, Jonas, these women who throw their panties at you? They've been listening to you croon words of love directly into their brains, via their phones. They think they know you already, lover boy. It's just like my grandma talking back to *Good Morning America*."

"Fuck me." Ethan's explanation had made it even worse. If what he said was true, the girls were at least half deluded into thinking they knew me. So that made me the biggest skank of all.

"Jojo, don't take this the wrong way," Ethan had said, patting me on the knee. "But weed is not your friend."

After our conversation, I had eaten an entire sleeve of Pringles. The inside of my nose smelled like pot and dehydrated potato for a week. But at least the marijuana-induced wisdom stuck with me. The random hookups slowed to a trickle when I finally noticed that my "fuck the emptiness away" strategy wasn't working all that well.

Now, lying in the grass in Maine, smelling the lilacs and the lake water, I felt unsettled. No—it was worse than that. The idea of loading up on the bus and leaving Maine for another five years made me feel positively unhinged.

"Breakfast in forty-five," Ethan said. "And I'm still making you a picnic lunch for noon, right?"

"Right. Thanks," I said, peeling myself up off the grass. How was I even going to survive until noon?

SIX

KIRA

By ten o'clock in the morning, I'd already taken two walks with Vivi, read seven picture books, and made a beautiful quiche with a whole-wheat crust and caramelized onions.

Who knew a morning could last for five years?

And as I rolled out the crust for my quiche, I was reminded of all those summer afternoons when I'd cooked for Jonas Smith, aka John Smith, aka the man I could not stop thinking about.

Usually, I enjoyed my memories of him. But this morning they only made me want to throw up from stress.

"Looks good," my father grunted, passing through the kitchen.

"Hey, thanks." A two-word compliment from my father was rare. Money and enthusiasm had always been in short supply in this house.

"Mama?" Vivi tugged on the hem of my shorts.

I cleared my throat and tried to sound perky. "What's up, buttercup?"

"Hungry," she said simply.

"I'll bet." The kitchen smelled of onions browned in butter. You'd have to be comatose to resist that scent. "Ten more minutes. The crust isn't brown yet."

"I'll get a book," she said.

"Great idea."

When the quiche was finally ready, I sent Vivi to gather Adam and my father to the table. I cut a microscopic piece for myself, since my appetite was completely vanquished by the butterflies in my stomach. But Adam and Dad made loud noises of approval about my cooking, as they always did.

It was the one thing nobody ever argued about.

"Someday you'll have your own cafe," my father said, folding his napkin.

"Someday," I repeated.

My dad put down his fork. "Why not soon?"

This again? "Because running a small business with a preschooler is a bad combination. I love to cook for people. But I do not want the stress of dealing with the Boston health department, hiring workers, trying to get a decent price on real estate." I got tired just thinking about it.

"Open it here," my father said, waving his arm in the direction of either the driveway or Main Street.

Across the table, Adam snorted. "Seriously? You stay in business, Pop, because all seven people who live here would rather pay your prices for toilet paper and beer than make the forty-minute trek to the big box stores. There's not enough traffic for a restaurant, except in the summertime."

"It wouldn't have to earn all that much," my father pressed. "She and Vivi could live here."

"With the rowboat?" Vivi piped up, hope in her voice. She loved that freaking boat. And now I wanted to stab my father with a fork for bringing my daughter into this.

"Yeah," my father said, smiling at Vivi.

"Why not throw in a pony?" Adam quipped, helping himself to another slice of quiche. "Kira can't move to Maine, Dad. We don't want this claustrophobic town for her."

"*We?*" Dad growled. "What say do *you* have? And Maine is safer than that dirty city."

Oh yay. More tension. Whenever the four of us were together, it was always simmering just beneath the surface. And our arguments about where Vivi and I should live were never really about real estate.

"How would you know Maine is better?" Adam grumbled. "You never visit us. You never go *anywhere*."

"I can't leave. I run a small business."

"Every other seasonal business in New England closes for two weeks in March and two in November," Adam pointed out. "It's fine if you love it here and never want to leave, okay? But don't accuse Kira of being stubborn. That's hypocritical."

Dad glowered at Adam, but did not argue. That didn't mean that Adam won, of course. Rather, Dad had used up his entire allotment of conversation for the day.

"I like Maine," Vivi said in a small voice.

"We all do," I said quickly. "But Boston is where our friends live. We'd miss them if we moved away." I didn't have many friends, if I was honest with myself. I worked too hard to socialize. But I'd never bring Vivi to live in such seclusion, where the nearest preschool was probably fifteen miles away. Besides—I was just a few credits shy of graduating with a degree in primary education. I needed to live in a city, where there were jobs.

My father got up from the table, carrying his plate into the kitchen to rinse. Adam purposefully lingered at the table until my father left to check on the store. Only then did he get up to tidy up the kitchen.

At least the family drama had made me forget about my noontime meeting for a good ten minutes.

Yay.

* * *

AT A QUARTER TO TWELVE, I kissed Vivi goodbye, leaving her to play a hand of Go Fish with Adam. I climbed onto my old bike, first pedaling in the wrong direction to pick up a six-pack of beer at the store. "Adam shouldn't drink so much," my father said, writing down my purchase on our home tally.

"He's fine," I mumbled, feeling guilty for allowing my father to assume that the beer was for Adam. But I was too busy quaking from nerves to invent another explanation.

The stop at the store had used up a good solid two minutes. So I put the beer in the bike basket, then pedaled slowly back around the lake. I needed to get my head in the game. I'd sit Jonas down and calmly tell him what had happened. He'd listen. He'd be shocked, but then he'd be okay with it.

He just had to be.

I pedaled onward toward the Nest Lake Lodge, which was just a rustic, oversized house with beds for ten people and a big communal bathroom. Most of its customers were there for fishing weekends, or family reunions.

When I was a little girl, I'd thought of the lodge as a place that rich people rented. Now I knew better. Rich people didn't come to Nest Lake at all. They went to Kennebunkport and the coast.

Last night I'd slept very poorly, tossing and turning in my old bedroom, thinking about Jonas Smith and the bomb I was about to drop on him. The beer bottles gave a little rattle as I went over a rock. I'd bought Shipyard's Summer Ale, which had been Jonas's favorite all those years ago.

Now *there* was a clue that I'd missed. During our summer together, he'd drunk expensive local microbrews, which was not the stuff of starving composers. I'd been too much in awe of him to stop and wonder about things like that.

The other gift I'd brought for Jonas was the photograph of Vivi in my back pocket. Our one night together had totally changed my life. And now it would upset his.

I pulled up in front of the lodge and leaned my bike against the furrowed bark of a pine tree. The ride had taken barely any time at all.

Stalling, I stared at the giant tour bus parked twenty feet away. It was *purple*, and there was a picture of Jonas's face on the side.

"Ugly, isn't it?"

I whirled around to see him watching me from the steps up to the lodge's private dock.

"It's okay, you can say it." He smiled at me, crossing his arms. "When I complained, they told me that tasteful busses don't sell records."

I had absolutely nothing at all to say to that. In fact, I'd forgotten how to speak entirely. My mouth was bone dry, and my knees felt spongy. To hide my growing anxiety, I reached into the bike basket for the beer.

"Oh, yes!" he said when he saw the label. "I can't believe you remembered. I haven't had any of this in a long time. Thanks."

I smiled weakly as he crossed the gravel drive and took it out of my hands.

"You want this left open, Jonas?" another voice called out. I looked up to see a tall black man stepping down from the bus door, his arms around a pile of sheets and towels. "You can show her the bus," the man offered. "It's almost civilized again."

"No thanks, man," Jonas said. His chin dipped, as if he was embarrassed by the idea.

"Ethan, this is my friend Kira. Kira, Ethan is my boss."

Ethan laughed, as if Jonas had made a joke. He tucked the laundry under one arm so that he could hold out a hand to me, which I shook. "I'm the tour manager," he said. "It's a really thankless job, but somebody has to do it."

"It's so nice to meet you," I said, finding my rusty voice.

"Likewise." He gave me a big smile. "I'll find you both with lunch," the man said, before striding away.

"Thanks, Ethan." Jonas held a hand out to me and cleared his throat. "You okay, Kira?"

No, I sure wasn't. But I needed a little privacy to say my piece. "Is there somewhere we can talk?" I took his hand, and when his warm fingers clasped mine, I had to close my eyes for a moment. For five years I'd believed that I would never again feel his touch. And now having him so close to me was torture.

"Sure," he whispered.

Holding my hand, he led me up onto the deck. The dock

angled off in one direction, but we made a left turn around the front of the building, where two people were lazing on lounge chairs. Seated under an umbrella, the woman I'd seen on the beach yesterday was reading a book. She was unnervingly beautiful, with long, blond hair and a tiny silver ring in her cute nose.

A man—tattooed and scruffy-looking—lay back in the sun in the chair next to hers.

Jonas ignored them both, leading me across the deck without a word. As we approached the far end of the space, the guy called out to Jonas. "Whatcha got there? Aren't you going to share?"

"Fuck off, Nixon," Jonas said without a glance in his direction.

"I meant the beer." The guy laughed.

"With you, a guy can never be sure." Jonas stopped when we reached the end of the deck. He dropped my hand in order to take two striped towels from a neatly folded stack. "Kira, this is Nixon, our lead guitar. And Quinn, our drummer."

They both murmured greetings, while watching me with undisguised curiosity. "Nice to meet you," I repeated.

"Watch your step, Sweetness," Jonas said as we approached a ramp down to the grass below.

That's when I heard a sharp intake of breath from Nixon. "No shit," he whispered.

I looked up to find him staring at me. In fact, now everyone was staring. "Is something the matter?" I murmured.

"Not a damned thing," Jonas replied, reaching for my hand. He threw a glare to the guy, and then helped me down onto the grass below. There was a little beach and a lawn, and nobody nearby. "I thought we'd hang out down here," he said, his blue-green eyes studying me.

"Okay," I managed.

Jonas walked down toward the water's edge, and then spread out the two generous towels to make a picnic spot. My stomach flipped as I followed him. I kicked off my shoes and sat down.

"I couldn't wait to see this place again," he said, toeing off his sneakers and sitting down beside me. "I never thought I'd get to see you, too. You told me you were going back to Boston."

"I did." I knew two-word answers weren't going to cut it. But there was a lump in my throat the size of Maine, and I didn't know how I was going to be able to do this. And now he was staring at me. I turned my chin to meet his gaze, and when I did, my stomach dropped. There was so much warmth in his face that it hurt me to see it.

"It's *great* to see you, Kira," he said. "I need to know everything. Did you get back together with your army guy?"

"No," I breathed. "It didn't work out."

He frowned, looking almost afraid to continue. "So, do you live here again?" he asked. He glanced away, and I wondered why he looked a little unsteady himself. But then he put those beautiful eyes right back on mine. "Are you married?"

I shook my head to both questions. "I live in Boston. With my big brother."

As I watched, a parade of emotions flickered across his face, ending with another of his potent smiles. "Adam, right?"

"That's right," I whispered. It was startling how well he remembered these details about me. "How about you?" I heard myself ask. "You went back to your ex-girlfriend?" Having read a few tabloids, I knew he wasn't married. I never should have asked, but I was desperate to steer the conversation away from my life, in order to calm my fraying nerves.

Jonas flopped down on the towel, propping his face in his palm. "No, I was never doing that. But it's still a funny story. On my trip home from Maine, I bought a trashy magazine in the Boston airport, and her picture was on the cover. Guess who got engaged to a football player while I was away?"

"I'm sorry," I said quickly.

Jonas shook his head and smiled. "I'm not. I'm only telling you that story so you'd know that breaking my little vow of chastity wasn't a big deal."

My neck got hot almost immediately. Because it was a big deal to me.

"Anyway, I was pretty lonely after that and did a bunch of self-destructive shit I shouldn't have."

I cleared my throat. "You don't seem lonely now."

"Really?" His eyes fell to the towel. "I have the band, and as long as I keep writing hits, they love me. But I don't make new friends. Actually, Kira, you're the last new friend I ever made."

"What? Why?" That didn't make any sense to me. "A guy like you? You're surrounded by people who love you."

"That's not how it works. I'm surrounded by people who want a piece of me, so they can brag about it to their friends. Or who want money. I'm telling you this to explain why I gave you the name John Smith the summer I met you. It was the best summer of my life. And I think about you all the time." He raised his eyes to mine, and they were the color of a tropical sea.

I swallowed hard. *Then why didn't you answer my letter?* The question was on the tip of my tongue, but I knew I wouldn't ask. It would make me sound petty. Besides—ignoring my letter was *nothing* compared to my whopping sin of omission.

Just then, Ethan came around the corner of the lodge holding a picnic basket.

"Thanks, man," Jonas said, reaching for the basket.

"You guys need anything else, just holler."

Jonas opened the basket and peeked inside. "This looks great."

"Don't mention it. But..." Ethan pulled out his phone. "It's almost ten past the hour. Jonas, your single is going to debut in a minute. I told the local station you'd call them after they played it." He held up the phone.

Jonas shook his head. "No way, man. Not now. Besides, you can't get a connection out here."

Ethan squinted at the phone. "I've got four bars."

"Really?" Jonas met my eyes. "There's a signal here now? That's just plain wrong."

"Come on, dude," Ethan argued, folding strong arms across his stomach. "It's a two-minute phone call. They're making a big deal about the single, which you want, right? Quinn's setting up some speakers to blast it right now. I thought it would be fun. And then when the song ends, this phone is going to ring. It will be the producer."

"Quinn thought it would be *fun*," Jonas repeated, sitting up quickly. "Hell, Ethan. Don't play that shit right now. Tell Quinn that's not cool..."

Even as he said it, the sound of a radio station could be heard from up on the deck. The low, even tones of the DJ's voice floated on the breeze. "...brand new single from Hush Note, the first off their new album. And the title is *Sweetness*." A drumbeat faded in under the DJ's last words.

Jonas's jaw got tense. "Ethan, now is not the time. Please turn that shit off."

Ethan gave an exasperated sigh and lumbered off toward the deck.

The song continued to play, a guitar riff coming in on top of the drumbeat, and after a moment, Jonas' voice began to sing:

It was many years ago now
That summer was my saving grace
We were so much younger then
But I will not forget her face

GOOSEBUMPS BEGAN to crawl up my spine. And then the chorus made my heart absolutely stutter.

SWEETNESS...
I let the good one get away
Wherever she is, I pray she's okay
My only sweetness

SWEETNESS. That's what Jonas used to call *me*.

Suddenly there didn't seem to be enough oxygen on the beach. Maybe it was the song, or maybe it wasn't. All I knew was that there was pressure in my chest, and there was no way I could sit still anymore.

"Hey now," Jonas said as I struggled to my feet. "Kira, I'm sorry. I should have warned you about the song. Timing has never been good to us." He stood up to face me, his eyes clouded with an emotion I couldn't decipher. As if Jonas were the one with secrets.

Fighting the taste of bile low in my throat, I took a couple of steps away from him, towards the back of the lodge, away from the people and the music. A split second later, I could feel him following me.

Panicking now, I turned and said the only thing I could think of. "Wait!" I cried.

He froze, surprise on his face.

I still felt as if I couldn't breathe. "I'm..." How to explain? "I feel panicky." I turned my back to him and continued toward the trees. There was no path, but I crashed through the underbrush until I found my bike against the tree. I grasped it like a life boat, tossing a leg over and sliding onto the seat. My feet found the pedals, and I pushed off and sped away.

I didn't stop until I'd made it to my father's house. But, panting with anxiety, I couldn't go inside. Fighting for calm, I sat down on the porch steps and put my head in my hands.

SEVEN

JONAS

I watched Kira ride off, wondering what the hell had just happened. Sure, she probably guessed that I wrote that song about her. But she'd only heard the first few bars before sprinting away like I was the devil himself.

Spinning around, I located the lodge's bike shed. I rolled a bike out and hopped on. The seat was too low for me, so I had to stand up on the pedals.

But no matter. I rode off after Kira, my first time on a real bike in years.

The road curved around to the left, and Kira's house soon came into view. She was sitting on the front steps. She didn't look all that surprised to see me biking toward her, but the look of pain on her face was so vivid that I could feel it in my gut. Something was wrong, and I still didn't know what.

"Feel any better?"

She shook her head, and I thought I saw fear in her eyes.

"Kira," I said softly. "I know you want me to leave you alone right now, but I can't—our conversation isn't over. In twenty-four hours I'll be back on that bus. Honestly, you're scaring me. When I last saw you, things seemed like they were on the upswing for you. When I said I think about you all the time, I didn't mean to be a creeper. I meant that I was picturing a happy ever after for you."

"Mama!" a little voice called from beyond the screen door.

At the sound of it, Kira's whole body went rigid. And then tears spilled down her cheeks.

I heard little footsteps pounding onto the screened porch. And then a small set of hands became visible against the door just behind Kira. Quick as a flash, Kira leapt to her feet and spun around, darting through the door. It closed with a bang behind her.

"Whoa," a man's voice said. "Deep breaths, Kiki. What did he say?"

The hair stood up on my neck. I dropped the bicycle and covered the distance to the stoop in three paces. Leaping up, I opened the screen door. A little girl stood there, with fair, curly hair and blue-green eyes. I was no good with kids' ages. She wasn't an infant, but she wasn't school-aged either. There was a babyish fullness to her face. She was three? Four? Five? I looked up at Kira.

"I'm so sorry," she squeaked.

That's when I finally understood. And I almost couldn't draw breath to speak again. "I... She... What the *fuck*, Kira?"

"That's a *very* bad word," the little girl said, accusation in her voice.

"Sorry," I said automatically. I raised my eyes to Kira's. "You... She..."

I couldn't think. There was pressure in my ears, and my pulse was ragged. *Dizzy*, I thought, absently, putting one hand on the door jamb for support.

"*Breathe*, man," the guy behind Kira said. He wore a bright pink polo shirt and an expression of concern. "Sit down. Seriously, before you crash."

I bent over and grabbed my knees. "Oh my God." The only thing I could hear was my own ragged breathing and Kira's choked sobs.

"Mama!" a little voice said, full of alarm. "Don't cry!"

The scary moment stretched on, until I heard yet another bicycle approaching outside. A moment later, another male voice called out, "Knock-knock!"

The pink-polo-shirt guy answered him, his voice full of false cheer. "Hi, Luke!" Under his breath he added, "Wow. It's raining men." Then he scooped the little girl up in his arms, stepped around me, and walked out the screen door. It closed behind him with a bang.

I just stood there, staring at my shoes, trying to catch my breath. Kira's shoes moved into my visual field, but I wasn't ready to talk to her yet. Not until my head could clear. Which would probably be sometime next week.

We stood here, awkward and quiet for a couple of long minutes. There was some low-key chatter outside, and then I heard the sound of the bicycle departing.

The guy in the polo shirt came back inside, alone.

"You're her brother." I coughed, trying to reconstruct the world into a rational place.

"Yup," the guy said. "Uncle Adam."

"Where is Vivi?" Kira asked, her voice raw.

"Luke is taking her for a little bike ride. There may be ice cream involved."

"Really, Adam?" Kira moved quickly to peer through the screen. "But that's awkward."

"Oh, honey. We have first class tickets on the HMS Awkward today. And the ship has sailed. Luke even had a pink helmet for her, Kiki. Just go with it, okay? I told him you were having a moment."

I straightened up. "She's having a *moment*," I spat out. "Is that what this is?" My pulse was still pounding in my ears, but now from anger instead of shock.

Kira was as pale as a sheet. "I was going to tell you today." She pulled a photo out of her pocket. "Here. I was trying to find a way."

I snatched the picture from her hand. "She's, what, four?" The photo shook as I tried to look at it. The little girl smiled up at the camera, a stuffed animal in her hands. It was purple. Somehow this detail made it all the more real. The little girl in the photo was clutching the purple cat I'd won at the fair all those years ago.

"She's four next month."

I forced myself to meet Kira's gaze. "And what if I hadn't run into you? Were you *never* going to tell me?"

She wasn't. I could see it in her face, where tears were drying on her cheeks.

"I was..." she stammered. "I just didn't know how. And I didn't think..."

"What, that I would *care*?" Fuck, that hurt. She was the only person alive that I expected to know better.

"You made yourself unapproachable," she said quietly. "You gave me a fake name."

"It wasn't fake!" My voice shook. "John is the name my parents gave me. After they died, my aunt changed it because... she's a bitch." I still wasn't getting enough oxygen. I took another deep breath, and it didn't help.

Kira wiped her tears. "Well, I didn't know that. But if you were trying to blow off someone, and you wanted to be sure she wouldn't ever be able to find you, what name would you choose? How does *John Smith* sound to you?"

"Kira, that's crap. You eventually knew who I was—you told me so yesterday. Any lawyer with use of a telephone could have gotten the message through. You never tried."

She dropped her eyes.

"I thought we were..." *Close.* I couldn't even finish the sentence, it was so pathetic. God, was there *nobody* on earth I'd ever been important to?

"She was just afraid," her brother said, his voice soft.

"*Afraid?*" The word made my heart lurch again. "*Fuck* no. She wasn't afraid of me. *Not of me.*"

"But you didn't see how it all went down here in the boonies," Adam argued. "The whole town slut-shamed her. Our father shamed her." Adam pointed outside. "Her ex-boyfriend called her a slut to her face. Seriously—it used to be me they sneered at, but for a couple years there they gave Kira their worst. First for getting raped, and then for getting knocked up."

And that was all I could take. My hand formed a fist, because I needed to shut Adam up.

"Whoa!" Her brother took a step back. "Hands are not for hitting."

Kira grabbed my fist in both of her hands. "Please. I need you to calm down."

I dropped my eyes to Kira's hands. I took another big breath through my nose, and I let it out. "I want to see her at least. You owe me that."

"You have every right to see her," Adam said. "Except you're losing your shit right now. And since we don't want to freak out *in front of the child*—" He looked pointedly at me. "—everybody has to go back to his own corner and cool off."

"Later, then. Today," I said.

Kira still looked terrified. "I don't think that's a good idea."

"Why?" I spat. "What did I ever do to you? Except exactly what you asked me to."

"That might be TMI," Adam whispered.

I turned around and opened the screen door. I walked down the three steps, but my knees felt like rubber. So I sat heavily on the bottom step, resting my head in my hands.

Before this moment I'd thought that my life—while lonely and a little aimless—was under some semblance of control. But that was a lie. Because there was a little person in the world who might have filled in some of the crushing emptiness in my chest. And she'd never even seen my face.

The door opened and shut behind me, but I didn't move. Kira settled on the step next to me, wiping her face with the heels of her hands. "I feel terrible," she whispered.

"You should."

She pressed her hands to her mouth, and I realized that if I kept saying things like that, she'd quit talking to me.

"Kira, was I good to you? Was I a good friend to you *every day* that summer?"

"Yes," she said, her voice shaky.

"Then why would you keep this from me?"

"It took me a year and a half to figure out who you were. I was already a mother to a little girl when I saw you on an album cover. And then there's the fact that you blew off my letter. I thought if I wrote another one, the same thing might happen again."

Bitterness settled into my stomach. Because she made a good point. I was too stupid to return her love when I'd had the chance. I'd pushed her away. "I'd never turn my back on my obligations, though. You had to know that."

"But I didn't want us to be an *obligation*," she said quietly.

Shit.

Nobody said anything for a while. Minutes ticked by. I focused on my breathing, the way I might before a concert. Until finally I felt calm. Kira slapped at a black fly beside me, and it brought me back into the present. It was still a sunny afternoon in Maine. Even if my whole world was reshaping.

"What a waste," I whispered suddenly. A waste of time. And of a beautiful friendship that could have been so much more.

"She's going to be back soon," Kira said. "We have to figure out what we're going to say to her."

"What did you tell her before? Did she ask where her father was?"

Kira gulped. "I told her that her daddy lived far away. That he was too busy making music to be someone's daddy."

My eyes burned. "Would have been nice if you'd checked to see if it was true."

"John..." She cleared her throat. "*Jonas*. I'm sorry, okay? I did wrong. I can't argue the point. But we need a game plan, and we need it now. I don't think we should tell her you're her father until she's comfortable with you."

"Why not?" How could more lying be a good idea?

She looked into my eyes, and my heart practically stopped.

Her face was so serious, and so beautiful. Sitting next to her was like living in a time warp. "I just want meeting you to be less of a shock for her. If you tell her right off, she won't know what to do with that information, and she won't know what to expect from you." Her silver eyes bored into mine. "Honestly, I'm just making this up as I go along. Parenting, I've learned, is all guesswork."

I took a deep breath and felt a little bit of the fury drain out of me. "I bet you're pretty good at it." And that was another reason Kira probably hadn't told me about our little girl. I'd never been the sort of person who looked like I should be someone's father.

Her wide eyes still took me in. "I do all right. She's easy, though. A little cocky sometimes, but sweet, too. She's a good girl."

My heart gave an unfamiliar squeeze. I heard the telltale click of a coasting bicycle approaching.

Kira leapt off the stoop and stood waiting as the bike slowed to a stop. "Hi," she said, sounding breathless.

"Hi, yourself," the guy said, setting one foot on the ground. "You okay?"

"Yes. Fine."

But I wasn't even paying attention to them, because my eyes had landed on the little sandaled foot that was visible from behind the guy's body. "You sure?" he asked Kira.

"Of course," she said quickly, ducking behind him to unclip her daughter from the kiddie bike seat.

She stretched her short arms toward Kira, leaning out of the seat, confident that she would be caught before hitting the ground. The look on her face was so happy and accepting, it nearly made me lose my shit right there.

Kira set her down and removed her bike helmet. Once I could see her properly, the rest of the world seemed to dim. She was wearing a green dress that had chocolate ice cream down the front of it. While her mother spoke in low tones to the man on the bike, she wandered towards me, and I held my breath.

"Hi," she said, an appraising look on her face. "I'm Vivi. What's your name?"

It came out as a rasp. "Jonas."

"Jonas," she repeated, trying it out. "Your shoe is untied. You're gonna trip."

I cleared my throat. "I should fix it, then."

"I'll do it." She knelt in front of me on the gravel and tugged on my laces. Her short fingers had dimples at the knuckle, the last vestiges of baby fat. As she worked on my shoe, her head tipped forward, revealing a porcelain neck. I'd never really studied a child before. Her skin looked brand new, like a little doll just out of the package. She tipped her face towards mine suddenly, her tongue caught in the corner of her mouth. "Do you like double knots?"

I nodded, speechless.

She returned to her work. A minute later, she stood back. "All done!"

I looked down to see possibly the worst excuse for a knot in the history of mankind. "Thank you." I took a deep breath in through my nose, trying to hold it together. The man on the bike had disappeared. Kira was standing back, arms folded across her chest, biting her lip.

The only person who looked completely at ease was Vivi. "I want to go in the lake now, Mama." She stomped over and put her hands on Kira's hips. "Please. You said that after you got back from lunch I could go swimming."

I stood up. "Then let's go to the lake."

Kira glanced at me, and there was a long moment where she said nothing. I stared right back, with a look that insisted I couldn't walk away right now, even if she wanted me to. Finally, she looked down at her daughter. "You need a towel."

Vivi shot up the steps and stretched for the door handle. She pulled the screen door into her nose before maneuvering around it and then onto the porch. Seconds later, she was back, a pink beach towel in her hands.

Kira was still rooted in place, an uneasy expression on her

face. But Vivi took off toward the beach, so Kira had no choice but to follow. I fell into step with her and, wordlessly, the three of us set off down the street.

As we passed Mrs. Wetzle's house, I wondered if the old lady was still alive, and still serving bad food and passing judgment on musicians.

Kira gave me a sideways glance. "Are you okay? Holding it together?" she asked, her voice low.

I nodded. *Barely.* "You?" This was difficult for her, too. She looked nervous as hell. But the day's stresses were of her own making, and I wasn't about to disappear just to let her off the hook. Ahead of us, Vivi had begun to sing as she walked. I couldn't make out what. "What's that song?" I asked.

Kira shrugged. "Maybe something from preschool. Usually, she just makes up her own."

My heart almost failed for the tenth time that hour. How could Kira think that a songwriting child would not be of any interest to me? Maybe all four-year-olds invent their own tunes. I had no fucking clue. But I sure as hell wanted the chance to find out.

The path turned toward the beach, and the shimmering expanse of Nest Lake helped distract me from my turmoil. It was so beautiful here. *My child has a nice life.*

That was something, right? That was what mattered most?

Vivi went over to the roped-off kiddie area. She dropped her towel on the strip of sand, then yanked her dress over her head, revealing a purple ruffled bathing suit. She chucked the dress down onto the sand without a backward glance, and then marched her little rectangular body into the shallow water.

I checked Kira's face. "Does she swim?"

She nodded. "Adam says her stroke should be called the Drowning Dog, but she swims. You'll see."

Sure enough, Vivi immersed herself up to the chest, then dropped down into the water up to her neck. With an indescribable wiggle, she began to swim around. Cutest thing I ever saw.

"Kira, my heart is breaking." It was a cliché, but it was true.

My child, I thought, testing the words in my head. *My little girl.* And, most surprisingly, *my family*. Those were words that I'd been sure would never apply to me, but they already did, and I'd been clueless about it.

"She breaks mine, too," Kira whispered. "Every darned day."

Ten yards away, in deeper water, a couple of teenagers took turns splashing each other, oblivious to the awkward drama playing out on shore. Vivi swam to the edge of the kiddie area to watch them. She gazed past the rope, the way a prisoner looks through the bars of his cell. "Mama!" she called. "I want to jump off the dock."

"Sweetie, I don't have my suit on," Kira replied.

Well. Here's where it comes in handy to be a party boy. I pulled off my T-shirt and dropped it on the ground. Then I took my phone and my money clip out of my pockets and dropped those, too. "Vivi, I'll go with you," I volunteered.

"Really?" Vivi began splashing her way out of the water.

"Sure." I undid Vivi's knot in my shoelace and kicked off my shoes.

Kira was frowning up a storm, but I turned my back on her and picked my way through the gravel toward the dock. As I walked out onto the dock boards, I heard Vivi pounding along behind me.

I reached the end and turned around. "I should jump in first, right?"

"Okay. You have to catch me," she said. "I don't like to put my face in."

"You mean, like this?" I asked. I turned casually around, and without breaking my movement, dove straight in. The icy temperature shocked me back to the surface. "Oh shit, that's cold!" I said, wiping the water from my eyes.

"You said a bad word." Vivi peered down at me from the end of the dock.

Damn! The cursing was going to be a problem. "You're right. Sorry." I swam out a few feet, then held out my arms. "Your turn."

"Closer." She frowned.

"Okay." I laughed, coming nearer.

"Closer," she said again.

There wasn't any more room. "Jump, little sweetness. I'll catch you."

She pinched her nose between two fingers and jumped so quickly that it took me by surprise. But I reached for her automatically, catching her squat torso as she plunged into the lake. And then I was holding my little girl in my arms.

"Shit, that's cold," she said.

"Vivi!" Kira shrieked.

I laughed, but my throat felt hot, and my eyes burned. I shifted Vivi onto one of my hips, because that felt right. I swam an awkward sidestroke into shallower water, until my feet touched the sludgy bottom.

"I wanna do it again," she said.

"Just one more," Kira said. "Your lips are purple."

"I like purple," Vivi argued.

"You're going to freeze, and so is your fa—" Kira caught herself, a look of horror crossing her sweet face.

I couldn't help but give her a smirk as I hoisted Vivi onto the side of the dock. I received one of her heels in my eye socket for my trouble. "You were saying?" I asked Kira.

She ignored me. I dove under, swimming towards the end of the dock again to catch Vivi. Again, the cold water was a shock. But there were good shocks and bad ones. Sometimes they were impossible to tell apart.

* * *

ON THE SHORT WALK BACK, I caught Vivi's hand. "What else do you like besides swimming?"

"I like school. I like Blumes. Do you like Blumes?"

"Sorry, what?"

"You add water to the pot. The dolly grows out of it."

"That sounds..." *Terrifying*. "Fascinating. I've never heard of that."

Kira snorted.

"Well, what do you play with?" Vivi asked.

"My guitar, mostly."

"Guitars are neat. My daddy played a guitar," Vivi said. Then she dropped my hand and scampered to the side of the road to pluck a dandelion that grew there.

I turned a raised eyebrow in Kira's direction.

She looked away.

* * *

WHEN WE REACHED THE HOUSE, I followed Kira and Vivi through the screen door and onto the porch, where Adam was reading the *New York Times* with a beer in his hand. I wasn't leaving until Kira threw me out. I pulled my T-shirt over my mostly dry torso and wondered what would happen next.

"You know, Vivi, it's nap time," Kira said.

"No! I'm not tired."

"Come on, sweetie."

Kira picked her up, but there was some thrashing. "Uncle Adam didn't kiss me yet."

With a sigh, Kira let Vivi slide down her body. She climbed up onto Adam, crunching his newspaper. He held his beer out of the way and let her scale him. "If you have a good nap, I'll take you out in the rowboat before dinner," he promised, planting a kiss on her forehead.

"Can I row?" she asked.

"Certainly. Now scoot." He gave her a mock spanking, and then Kira scooped her up again, heading for the dark interior of the house.

I watched every second of it. In their own way, Adam, Kira, and Vivi were the perfect little family. A much warmer one than I'd grown up in.

"Dude, I think you need one of these." Adam offered me a bottle of Dos Equis and a church key.

"I think you're right. Thanks." I threw Vivi's towel onto the seat of the rocker beside Kira's brother, and lowered myself onto it. I popped the top off the beer and took a swig, hoping Adam wouldn't think I was a lush. But the beer was cold and bracing, and I was happy to have it. "She takes naps?" I asked. I didn't know a thing about little kids. There was no point in pretending otherwise.

"Most days," he said, abandoning his newspaper. "She's a good sleeper, actually. The first year, Kira and I thought we would *die* of exhaustion." He chuckled into his bottle. "But now she's a champ."

"They've lived with you the whole time?" I had a million questions. At least.

But Adam looked suddenly guarded. "Yeah," he said quietly.

I watched his face carefully. "That makes me feel a little better, knowing she had somebody helping her."

Adam's expression did something confusing then, morphing from surprise, to warmth, and then back to cautious again. "Maybe it's weird, but it works for us."

"I can see that." The conversation lapsed into a minute or two of silence. Glancing through the screen, I spotted a familiar figure walking down the road, swinging a picnic basket. I stood up and went to the door, swinging it open. "Ethan! Are you looking for me?"

The big man turned his big head. "Jojo! What's the deal with you today? You didn't eat your lunch." He strode up and entered the porch, taking in me and Adam and our bottles of Mexican beer.

I plopped myself back into the chair. "Yeah. About that... Adam, this is Ethan. He's my tour manager. But he thinks he's my mother."

Ethan put down the basket. "And you're an ingrate."

"Beer?" Adam asked.

Ethan tilted his head to the side, considering Adam. "Love one," he said, after a beat.

Adam handed Ethan a beer, and Ethan sat down, fitting his big frame carefully onto another wooden rocker, the one opposite me. Then he kicked the picnic basket toward me. "Have a deviled egg and tell Mama why you're such a train wreck."

I dug into the basket for the dish of deviled eggs and popped one into my mouth so I wouldn't have to speak. I passed the dish to Adam, who helped himself. "I'm sorry about the radio thing," I said eventually.

Ethan shook his head. "It's okay. It was early enough in the day that Nixon was still coherent. I passed the phone to him. He made up some shit about the two of you writing the song. It was fine."

"All right." And now I was going to have to tell Ethan the very thing I was trying to process. "There's a couple of things I need your help with. People are going to give you a hard time because it's a holiday weekend, but this can't wait."

Ethan frowned. "Okay. Hit me."

I propped my feet up on his giant knee. "Call Ben and tell him not to book anything in Europe or Asia until he talks to me personally."

"All right." Ethan's frown deepened at the mention of his boss—our business manager. "But Ben already nailed down a few dates. He said something about that festival in Munich."

"He needs to hold off on any more. Tell him that I'll talk to him, and we'll go over everything on Tuesday or Wednesday."

"What else?"

"I need to get Peters on the phone. Tonight." Peters was my lawyer.

Ethan pulled a face. "On the Saturday night of a holiday weekend. Are you insane? He's probably on a golf course in Maui."

"I never ask him for anything. Tell him it's important."

"Should I assume you're talking about your lawyer?" Adam asked, his voice wary.

I raked a hand through my hair. "Yeah, but... It's not... I don't want to panic Kira," I said. "I'm not going to be an asshole about this. But I don't even have a will. And of course I want to pay child support."

Ethan choked on his beer. "What...?" He coughed violently into the crook of his arm, knocking my feet to the floor. With watering eyes, Ethan stared at me.

"I have a four-year-old daughter," I said. The words sounded entirely foreign on my tongue. "Kira is her mother, and Adam is her uncle. This is not a drill."

Beside him, Adam took a long pull of his beer. "You don't have to yank your lawyer off the golf course. There's nothing you can do or file until you get a paternity test. And that takes a week to come back, at least."

"I don't need a paternity test," I said. "Kira could never be wrong about this."

Adam's eyes got huge.

"What?"

Adam shook his head. "I'm just surprised you understand that. Kira said it was only a one night thing between you two."

"She did?" I'd been starting to feel calmer, but hearing that I'd been dismissed as a one-night-stand made my gut ache again. I couldn't sit still anymore. I stood and strode out the front door.

"Jonas," I heard Ethan say, his voice gentle.

I needed a minute to collect myself. No, I needed more than a minute. I stood under a big old elm in the yard. A squirrel snickered at me from overhead.

I'd come to Maine for a two-day break, to soak up a quick dose of happy memories. Instead, I was reeling.

I stood there a long time, staring at the dirt road and an oblique slice of Mrs. Wetzle's house. From Kira's yard, only a narrow strip of clapboards and white trim was visible. I had sat inside that back room at the foot of the bed, my guitar in my arms. I'd been patient with myself and the music. I'd learned a lot. And when it was over, I'd thought I'd come away a better man.

But now the script had been rewritten. I'd gotten a twenty-year-old girl pregnant, and then I'd blown her off when she tried to show me love. It was yet another fucked-up lesson in humility.

Kira appeared beside me on the lawn. When I turned to look at her, my heart contracted. Even though I was still angry and confused, I knew I wouldn't stay mad at her. Being so close to her did a number on me. In her khaki skirt and tank top, she looked just as fresh and lovely as I'd always remembered her. While I felt about a hundred years old.

"I'm not going away, you know," I said suddenly.

"Of course you are." Her voice was soft. "You're on tour for ten weeks."

Fuck. It was true. Summer touring was our bread and butter. "How do you know that, anyway?"

"Hush Note dot-com."

I gave her a bitter chuckle. "If you were as easy to track as I am, I might have known I had a daughter about to turn four."

"I'm sorry."

"You said that already." I looked away from her, because it pained me to look into her pretty face. She'd let me down so badly today that I almost couldn't breathe. But that didn't mean I wanted to hit back.

"Jonas, I'm sorry to say that you can't be here when my father comes home from the store."

"Why? Am I starring in a Spaghetti Western? Is he going to get out the shotgun?" I could see the storm I was causing in her face, and I wasn't proud of it. I had to get a grip. "Kira, I can take whatever your dad throws at me. Hiding from him isn't something I'd do." And she should know that already. *Fuck.*

But her frown only deepened. "You need to go, okay? Not because of what he'll say to you. Because of what he'll say to *me.* I don't have it in me to go ten rounds with him tonight. This is hard enough as it is."

Oh, hell. I wish I could just scoop her up, along with Vivi, and take them somewhere quiet for as long as it took for the shock to wear off, and for the pounding in my head to stop.

But reality didn't give a fuck about what I wanted. It never had. "All right. I'll go. But only if you promise me you won't leave town before we talk again."

Her eyes widened. "I wouldn't do that."

I bit back the obvious retort. *Why should I believe you?* "Okay," I said instead. "Do you have a cell phone?"

She nodded.

"Can I have it, please?"

She pulled it out of her pocket and handed it to me, and I got to work. First, I called my phone with hers and then added a couple things to her Contacts list. "I'm adding Ethan's phone number as well as mine. He's my emergency contact, okay?" I saved her number and one more to my phone. "I'm taking Adam's number, too."

"Okay," she whispered.

When I was finished, I handed her phone back. "Call me, Kira," I said, my voice low. "Any hour of the day. We're leaving tomorrow at eleven. I need to see you before that."

She nodded solemnly. Her troubled eyes broke my heart.

I took one step forward and pressed my lips to her forehead. I kissed her gently, inhaling the citrus scent of her shampoo. Feeling an unwelcome sting behind my eyes, I backed away. "Hey. Don't worry, okay? I'm sorry I was a dick earlier."

"You weren't," she whispered. "I had it coming."

The bike I'd ridden here was still lying in the grass. I stood it up. "Call me."

"I will," she said.

There was no more left to say for the moment, and I was beat. Just utterly spent. So I mounted the bike and rode away.

The half-mile ride was a blur. In front of the lodge, I ditched the bike. I ducked inside and threw myself at my unmade bed. Five minutes later, the weight of the day was too much, and I fell into a long and dreamless sleep.

EIGHT

JONAS

Several hours passed before I felt the side of the bed compress under someone's considerable bulk.

"Wakey, wakey," Ethan's voice prodded.

I yawned, still unwilling to open my eyes. But something smelled good, and the smell was getting stronger. When I finally peeked, Ethan was waving a bowl of chili under my face. His amazing, chunky, homemade chili, with sour cream and shaved cheddar cheese melting on top. My stomach growled at the savory scent.

"Sit up."

I didn't fight him on this. I pulled myself up and leaned back against the headboard.

Ethan put a tray on my lap, then stuck a spoon in my hand. "Eat this. Every bite."

He didn't leave after making his delivery. He sat there on the bed until the food started going in at a satisfactory rate. Ethan's last act of mercy was to open the beer he'd put on the tray and press it into my free hand. Then he left the room.

I hadn't spoken a word to him, but that was okay. Several hours ago—though it felt like several weeks—I had tried to explain to Kira that everyone who cared for me was on my payroll. When I'd said it, I was feeling sorry for myself. But tonight the payroll was seriously pulling its weight.

After eating, I left the tray on the mattress and carried the beer into the lodge's shared bathroom. The shower was already occupied, so I bent over one of the sinks and splashed water on my face. Since Quinn's toiletry bag was sitting there, I helped myself to some kind of fancy soap. Then I nabbed her brush, raking it through my hair.

I tossed it back into place as Quinn stepped out of the shower wrapped in a towel. When our eyes met in the mirror, she got straight to the point. "Wow, Jonas, is it true? You really have a kid?"

"Looks that way." My voice was rough from disuse.

"You're not sure?" Her eyes got wider.

"No, I'm sure."

"Oh honey. How come you're just finding out now?" Quinn picked up the brush I'd abandoned and began teasing the tangles from her long hair. "Five years later? Who *does* that? What a bitch."

"Don't call her that," I growled.

Quinn snorted. "Okay. Sure. But that isn't normal behavior, Jonas. What the hell was she thinking? You'd have to be a stone-cold bitch to keep that from a guy. Or else..." She flinched.

"Or else what? Just say it already."

"Damaged," she said quietly. "Either way, it's not good news for you."

I bristled, even though Quinn always had my best interests at heart. Most days her bluntness didn't bother me much, because I was pretty sure she was a little damaged, too.

Maybe we all were. I was still mad at Kira, of course. But I was just as mad at myself.

"Either way," Quinn chirped, "be careful. The media is going to eat this up. And the label will love it. They'll exploit this all summer long if it means 'Sweetness' rides the Billboard charts. I'm surprised your phone isn't already ringing with an offer to put the whole fam-damily on the cover of *People*."

Jesus. I felt sick just picturing that. Without another glance at Quinn, I left the bathroom.

The idea of paparazzi photographing Vivi made my skin crawl. Not only would Kira hate it, but what four-year-old could understand strangers jumping out of the lilac hedge with a camera?

I was accustomed to that kind of bullshit and understood my millions of dollars in the bank were fed by the media machine. But I'd made that choice myself. Kira and Vivi hadn't.

Fuck.

Back in my room, I dropped to the braided rug on the floor and began banging out pushups. It always helped me think.

Quinn could have been nicer about it, but she'd made a good point. Given half a chance, the media would eat up this story. I'd seen these things unfold. Even if everyone on the tour bus kept their traps shut, all it would take would be for some paralegal at my lawyer's office to leak the story. I might be a thousand miles away singing in some stadium in Virginia while some asshole bore down on Kira and Vivi outside their Boston apartment building with a video camera.

Shit. For the first time, Kira's decision not to tell me about Vivi seemed almost reasonable.

And the new single made it all worse, right? It wasn't a huge leap to lay the inspiration for "Sweetness" at Kira's feet.

It had taken me five years to write that song, because it had taken me that long to figure out what I was trying to say. Even now the song was far from perfect, but I'd gotten impatient with myself and recorded it anyway.

If I was honest with myself, I'd hoped that Kira would hear it. I'd gone so far as to picture her in a car somewhere, listening to a Spotify playlist and tapping her thumbs on the steering wheel. In my daydream, she'd googled the song later and figured out that I was that guy from five years ago. She'd realize I'd written it just for her.

And then—in my fantasy—she'd smiled.

But that was it. That was supposed to be the end of the story.

And now it was too late to yank it back from thousands of American radio stations.

What a total fucking disaster. I should have kept my heartache to myself.

After two sets of pushups, I rooted around in my duffel bag for my toothbrush. When I went back into the bathroom, Quinn was still there, patting moisturizer beneath her eyes. I grabbed her face in my hands and gave her a chaste kiss on the cheek.

"What was that for?"

"I love you even when you're prickly," I said, turning back to the sink. "And you're pretty smart, too."

Her eyes dipped. "I don't want to see anyone steamroll you. You're *too* nice sometimes. The world is full of people who'd take advantage."

"Maybe. But Kira isn't one of them."

Quinn's expression in the mirror made it clear that she didn't believe me.

* * *

I SCROLLED through the new numbers in my phone as I walked through the living room.

"Hey," Ethan called to me. "You okay?"

I looked up to see him and Nixon watching at me. "I will be. And thanks for the excellent chili."

"That must have been some shock, man." Nixon eyed me with an expression that was more empathetic than usual. Lately, when I looked at my oldest friend all I saw was barely concealed anger. At what, I couldn't say. And until yesterday, figuring out what the fuck was wrong with Nixon had been at the top of my summer to-do list.

If only the g-forces of reality would ease up for a minute or two, I might be able to finish a thought.

"It was a shock," I admitted.

He grinned. "I can't believe there's somebody who's gonna call Jonas *Daddy*."

"That's pretty scary, right?" Although it wasn't clear that anyone would ever call me Daddy. Kira didn't seem to want that. I took a step toward the door.

"Nah," Nixon said, giving his head a shake. "Actually, it's not scary at all. Not a thing wrong with you. That kid is *lucky*."

The words stopped me in my tracks. "Thanks, man. That means a lot." We'd been friends a long time, but it wasn't like us to sit around talking about our feelings.

"I mean... if a kid called *me* Daddy, now *that* would be scary."

I paused at the door. "Look, can you guys do me a favor? This needs to stay a secret for a while. Kira is pretty freaked out, and I don't know what's going on in her head."

Ethan chuckled. "Do you know what's in your *own* head? You're going to go all broody now, aren't you? Shit. I can't take you and Nixon both moping at the same time. That'll damn near kill me."

"Good thing we pay well." I shoved my phone into my pocket.

Ethan's face closed down. "Speaking of people who are well paid, I spoke to your lawyer. Gave him all the details—the little girl's address, that stuff. He'll get to work Tuesday morning, first thing."

"Details?" I frowned. "Where'd you get the info?" I didn't even know Vivi's birth date.

"Adam," Ethan said. "Got 'em from Adam."

"Oh."

"He's Kira's lawyer."

"Oh, of course." I wondered when my head would ever stop spinning.

"Damn convenient for her, really. It won't cost Kira anything when you sue for paternity."

I froze on the doorstep. "Wait. I don't want to *sue* anybody."

Ethan waved a hand. "Petition for paternity. Same thing."

"Dude, this has to be done carefully. And *quietly*. No reporters."

"I get it. Deep breaths, dude."

"Thanks. I'm going out."

"Ring if you need anything."

I went out into the night, banging the screen door shut behind me. It was dark, but moonlight washed across the dirt road. When I tilted my chin toward the night sky, I remembered something else about Maine. The stars were fucking brilliant. With no urban light to mask them, they dazzled overhead.

In Los Angeles, the only stars were on the sidewalk. What was the use of that?

NINE

KIRA

I left my father in charge of Vivi's bedtime, because there was someone I needed to meet on Main Street.

Walking in the dark made me uncomfortable, even though Nest Lake was a safe place. The weekly crime report was full of people getting fined for fishing without a license or the occasional kegger thrown by teens in the woods.

But for me, there were no safe places. I'd always carry the knowledge that violence was real and terrible. Still, I paused for a moment at the town beach, just to prove I could—daring myself to remember that my independence was worth the risk.

This view of the lake at night had always made me feel wistful. Spots of lamplight shimmered from the lakefront homes, and occasional laughter floated over the glassy water. As a girl I'd imagined everyone else's dinner tables were happier places than my own.

And maybe they were. My mother had left when I was nine, claiming she couldn't abide another minute in this tiny town in the middle of nowhere. Eight years later, we'd gotten word that she had drowned in a boating accident on another tiny lake somewhere in Canada.

The relief I'd felt was my darkest secret. Her death meant

that I could stop wondering whether she'd ever come back for me.

After she'd left, my father held down the fort as best he could. He loved his kids, I supposed, but he'd done so in a gruff and unbending way that had cut down me and Adam. Every year seemed to bring more tension. Adam coming out of the closet had led to a year of slammed doors and brief but spectacular shouting matches. Adam escaped to college as soon as he could, and rarely came back.

I'd been eager to follow him to Boston, and at eighteen, I'd become a bright-eyed freshman at Boston U. College life had been great, but early in my sophomore year, the assault had killed my joy along with my confidence.

I'd limped through the rest of the fall semester. Adam did his best to comfort me, but he was a busy law student, and I hadn't wanted to let on how terrified and depressed I really was. So I took the spring and summer off, hiding out in Nest Lake to try to regain my footing. It had mostly worked, with a little help from a certain guitar-playing hottie.

But my return to school was cut short after discovering I was pregnant. The week before Christmas, I packed up my dorm room, this time moving across town to Adam's little apartment, where I slept on the couch until his roommate moved out in the spring. During the last months of my pregnancy, I worked at the library, saving money and trying to prepare myself for becoming a parent.

At Adam's law school graduation in May, I'd been as big as a house.

Vivi was born on a rainy night in early June. That summer, Adam studied for the bar exam during the baby's screamy newborn days. Some nights he'd read contract law standing at the kitchen counter with Vivi wrapped in a sling around his chest.

My brother was my rock. He'd basically set aside his personal life these past four years because of me and Vivi.

But now that Jonas had reappeared, I felt the sand shifting

under my feet once again. The poor man was in shock. I never meant to do that to him. After all, I'd had a taste of that shock myself. After I'd learned his real identity, I could barely make sense of it. I read his wikipedia entry, and it was like reading about an utter stranger. Song titles and famous girlfriends and European tours and music awards.

I couldn't reconcile that information with the man I thought I knew. Except maybe the part about famous girlfriends.

Then a few more months slipped by without my taking any action. Vivi turned two. And then three. At various times I'd look Jonas up. Once I wrote down the mailing address of his L.A. management company.

But every time I pictured writing that letter, I was always reminded of that *other* letter I'd written already. And the idea of confessing something so huge in a letter left me cold. It would be like sealing my heart into an envelope and sending it into the void.

So I just didn't. And every day that I waited made it harder to change my mind.

Now, I turned my back on the lake and walked the rest of the way to my father's store. It was closed now, but I climbed the steps to the porch, where I'd left a six-pack chilling in a tub of ice. I lit the old citronella candle on the table and sat down to wait.

Five minutes later, I heard footsteps approaching.

My visitor didn't whistle, and I tried not to hold it against him.

The door opened and my ex-boyfriend Luke stepped onto the porch. I plastered on a friendly smile and took him in. His brown hair was buzzed as short as it had been while he was in the service. And even though his days as a tight end for the high school football team were long over, he still filled out his clothes like a football player.

Luke was, to quote my brother, a fine looking hunk of man. In high school, we'd been inseparable. We'd gone to home-coming together, and eventually prom. That night, on a blanket in the middle of someone's back meadow, we'd had sex for the first time.

Those were such innocent days. And they felt like a million years ago.

"Hi, Kiki," he said now, as the screen door slammed shut behind him. I jumped at the sound. "Sorry," he said, sliding into the chair opposite me. He stretched a hand across the table to cover mine. "How are you?"

"Okay," I lied. Thirty-six hours ago I'd been looking forward to catching up with him. But now I was twisted in so many knots, it was hard to focus. "I'm sorry that I never got back to you about our bike ride."

"S'okay," he said with a shrug. "I coulda called before I came over today."

Yes, you could have. "Vivi loved going with you, though," I said quickly.

"Maybe we can all go tomorrow." His brown eyes studied me. They were full of questions.

"That might work," I said carefully. "Although Adam wants to go back to the city tomorrow."

Adam didn't want to stay over on Sunday night, claiming he had an appointment on Monday. But who had an appointment on Memorial Day? It was probably just an excuse to cut the visit short. I wasn't going to call him on it.

"Have a beer, Luke." I reached down for a couple of bottles, popped them open, and passed him one.

"Thank you." He touched his bottle to mine and took a sip. Then he studied me. "Are you going to tell me what that was all about today?"

And there it is. I took a sip, playing for time. I'd been expecting this question, but that didn't make it any easier to answer. "I can't, Luke. I'm sorry." I smiled as kindly as I could, knowing he wouldn't be satisfied with my answer.

His eyebrows knitted together. "Is that man Vivi's father?"

"*Luke,*" I said quickly. "Please don't press me."

He reached for my hand across the table, giving it a squeeze.

"But why, Kira? Why won't you just talk to me? Otherwise we'll never get past it. I *know* I fucked up the first time you told me. I was young and angry, and I acted like a shit. But that was a long time ago. And now I ask one question, and you say, 'Don't press me.'"

"Luke," I whispered. "That's the only question I won't answer. Because I think Vivi should know who her father is before I tell anyone else."

"That's fair." He let out a big sigh. "Except I don't want to be just 'anyone else.' What do I have to do to convince you that I'm on your side?"

"It's not about *sides*," I insisted. Although, four and a half years ago when I'd told him that I was pregnant, everyone else in town seemed to be taking sides.

And Luke had not taken mine.

But that wound wasn't fresh anymore. Years later, I found it possible to understand that he'd only said out loud what the rest of the town had been thinking. He'd spoken out of anger and shock, and we *had* been young and stupid.

Still, it had hurt. A lot.

"Look, I've said I'm sorry, honey," he said. "I've told you so many times. My reaction was hotheaded and wrong. But that was a long time ago. And it hurts that you won't forgive me, even though I'm still here, asking you to."

I took a deep breath and let it out. "I do, Luke. I forgive you."

He accepted this with a nod. "I appreciate that, Kira. You know, I'm probably moving to the Boston area after New Year's," he said quietly. "I start interviewing for jobs in the fall, and I graduate in December."

"I'm proud of you," I managed to say. "Graduating in just three years."

"But I had it easy," he said, his fingers brushing the backs of my knuckles. "I had the GI Bill and a few summer classes. It isn't a struggle for me like it is for you."

Okay, that was a nice thing to say. I stared down at his hand, wondering when it might finally feel right to get back together with him. He wanted me, in spite of everything that had happened.

And he had apologized.

But something always held me back. At first I'd told myself that I was too busy with the baby. And then I'd told myself that a Maine/Boston relationship would never work.

Now here he was, on the verge of moving to my own city.

Raising my chin, I looked him right in the eye. I saw warmth reflected back at me. Luke was comfortable and familiar. I could get used to that kind of affection, couldn't I?

"Maybe you can help me figure out where to look for an apartment," he said, his eyes crinkling at the corners. "You know the neighborhoods."

"Sure," I said easily. "I'll help you." I tried to imagine what it would be like having Luke around. We could meet for dinner or a movie.

There hadn't been any men in my life since Vivi was born. I'd gone on maybe three dates in four years. The hurdles were just too high. Dating meant time apart from Vivi, and more babysitting hours from Adam. As it was, my brother stayed home whenever I had a night class or an evening shift at the library circulation desk. Any date I went on meant yet another night chiseled from Adam's social life.

For a single mother, dating was an impossible luxury.

But with Luke, it would be easier. He and Vivi already knew each other. And with him, I didn't have to pretend to be a typical twenty-five-year-old. He knew my story already, and he kept showing up.

"I'll probably have to rent a real shithole at first," Luke said with half a laugh. "Entry-level jobs won't pay very well."

"We'll find you something." I took a sip of my beer. A second later, the first two bars of *You Are My Sunshine* floated toward the porch on a breeze.

And just like that, the hair on my arms stood and my heart lodged in my mouth.

Oblivious, Luke smiled at me over the lip of his beer, and I tried my best to return it. Even so, I withdrew my hand from Luke's as the whistling got closer.

"What's the matter?" he asked.

I didn't know what to say. And I didn't have a lot of time to figure it out. Footsteps sounded on the stairs, and the door swung opon, revealing Jonas's outrageously handsome face illuminated in the candlelight.

My heart did a back flip.

Jonas said nothing at first, taking in the candle and the beer. He frowned, and I wondered whether he was having a flashback to the nights we'd spent in this very spot. "Evening, Kira."

"Hi," I squeaked. "You were looking for me?"

He stepped all the way onto the porch and eased the door shut behind him. "Yeah, Adam said you were out. There aren't that many places to look."

"You went to my *house?*"

"Easy." Jonas gave me a sad smile. "Adam was out on the front steps, smoking. I didn't have to knock."

"He was *smoking?*" I gasped. Adam had quit ages ago. What was that about?

"Hey," Luke cut in. "Have we met before?" My glance cut over to my ex-boyfriend, who looked unhappy about the intrusion. "You look familiar."

"People say that all the time," Jonas muttered without so much as a glance in Luke's direction. "Kira? I was hoping to hear from you tonight. Can we talk?"

"This is a private party," Luke said in a curt tone of voice.

Jonas chuckled. "Sorry, man, but I've only got fourteen hours to visit with Kira and my little girl."

Luke stiffened. He jerked his thumb at Jonas, but kept his eyes on me. "Kira, if you're keeping it a secret, this asshole didn't get the memo."

"Easy, Luke." I sighed.

"Nah. You want me to be *nice* to him?" Luke turned a glare on

Jonas. "He disappears for *five years*, and now he wants your time?"

I tensed, but Jonas didn't look the least bit worried by this show of rudeness. "Yeah, that's exactly the kind of asshole I am. You've got me pegged. And, by the way, you're in my seat. Kira put that chair here for me."

"No way." Luke's jaw went dangerously tight. "How about you fuck *off* now right back to wherever you came from?"

That's when Jonas finally dropped his smile. "How about you take your own advice. Are you the one who called Kira a slut? Or do I have that wrong?"

Luke flushed with anger. "You have a lot of nerve."

"Really? Just answer the question. Did you say that to her face?"

"That's none of your business."

"I think it is."

And now my heart was in my throat for all new reasons. Was I about to witness a *fight* between my ex-boyfriend and my daughter's father?

The Nest Lake crime blotter might get a heck of a lot more interesting in a hurry.

Luke's eyes darted from me to Jonas and back to me again. Then he let out a disgusted sigh and said to me, "Look, honey, I can see that you have a lot on your plate this weekend. So I'll call you later, okay?"

"Okay," I said quickly.

He pushed back his chair, which made an awful squeak on the floorboards. Then, without a glance at Jonas, Luke turned and ducked out the door.

This time I was ready for the door slam. I didn't even flinch.

Without hesitation, Jonas slid into the empty chair across from me. He chucked Luke's empty bottle into the ice bucket, and then leaned down to take a beer for himself. "Wow," he said. "What a tool."

"Jonas!" Now I felt my own flash of anger. "I've known him

my whole life. It was rude to go all rock-star power trip and chase him away."

His eyebrows went up. "Damn, Kira. It's going to take me an hour just to unpack that sentence. First of all, what just went down there has *nothing* to do with my day job. So that's just not fair. And more importantly, I didn't chase him away at all. He just up and walked. And *that's* why he's a tool. If a guy means to stake his claim, he doesn't walk. No matter what."

Good God. I lifted my cold beer bottle to the side of my face and tried to calm down. "I just... You..." I made a little noise of frustration.

"You're not with him," Jonas said suddenly. "And he doesn't have a prayer."

"Stop!" I spat. "That is the most caveman thing I've ever heard. Why would you assume that? And what business is it of yours?"

Jonas shrugged. "I turned up the heat on him, and he just got up and left. If he's really your man, he wouldn't do that."

"He's honoring my privacy."

"He's a coward."

"Really? His army specialty was disarming explosives." Although Adam had used exactly the same word for Luke. More than once.

"Look," Jonas continued, "I get that my weird choice of careers freaks you out, and that's because you're smart. But you know what freaks me out? The thought that you put up with a bunch of judgment from people when you were pregnant and alone. I'm going to be sitting with that a long time."

I didn't know what to do with this bit of kindness. "Jonas. Why would you use up part of your precious fourteen hours discussing my high school boyfriend? Don't we have bigger things to worry about?"

He set his beer down on the table. "I'm just trying to figure out how we got here, Kira. Maybe if I can understand why you didn't tell me about Vivi, then I'll be able to fix it. I need to be involved, but I don't want to scare you. Today you looked fucking terrified."

I *was* terrified. Seeing him after all these years made me want to jump out of my skin. But I couldn't admit that, because it was much too revealing. "Sharing Vivi is scary for me."

Jonas nodded. "I'm sure that's true. And I would never —*never*—try to take her from you, okay? But that still doesn't answer the question. When you were twenty and pregnant, that wasn't the reason you didn't call."

He had me there. God, I didn't want to say it, though. And couldn't he guess the reason? I'd written to him. I'd told him my deepest feelings, and he'd said... nothing. "I don't see how rehashing the past is going to make this easier," I croaked.

"All right," he whispered, letting me off the hook, at least for now. He leaned back in his chair and sniffed the night air.

Sitting here with him felt like a time warp. I remembered how easily we used to talk. The familiar shine of his eyes in the candlelight made my heart ache. That summer I'd lived for the hours when I could sit across from him, discussing everything and nothing. For a long time after my attack, not much had felt easy. But talking to Jonas had.

But now talking to him was hard.

"I'm sorry, you know," I whispered. "I'm sorry to give you such a shock today."

He didn't meet my eyes. "I... I know you're a good person, Kira. But it's hard to understand why you did it."

"I know I should have told you as soon as I figured out who you were. But the more time that passed, the harder it got. I knew I was going to have to deal with it eventually. When you're holding a newborn baby in your arms, you feel like you should try to control every moment of her life. But every day Vivi gets a little sharper. I knew she deserved the truth, too."

"Yeah, okay." He crossed his arms in front of his chest. And I really shouldn't have been admiring the way his muscles bulged. "But I could have helped. It kills me to think that you didn't believe that."

"That wasn't why I didn't call." I put a hand over his on the table. "I never thought you wouldn't help. I didn't want to *ask* you for your help. There's a big difference."

"Yeah. Fine. But I'm here now, and even though you didn't ask me, I'm offering. Tell me what I can do. What do you need?"

"I just need..." I swallowed hard. "I don't want Vivi to feel tension between us. So the thing I need most is for you not to hate me over this."

His eyes went soft. "I could never hate you, sweetness. I really need you to know that."

"But this is all on me. Back then... I wasn't careful. I used..." In my mind, I'd explained this to him a hundred times already, but it was so hard to admit how stupid I'd been.

Jonas only waved a hand, as if dismissing a small thing. "Birth control fails sometimes."

"Has it ever... Do you have any other children?" I asked.

He coughed on the next sip of his beer. "Not that I know about."

"Oh." I laughed, hiding my eyes. "Too soon for that question?"

"Too soon." A flicker of a smile crossed his face, and I couldn't help but smile back. For a split second, the old warmth shone in his eyes, and my heart took a swoopy detour through my stomach. To break the spell, I looked out toward the Kreemy Kone, which was doing the Nest Lake version of a brisk business. The light spilling from the service window illuminated two couples, one at each picnic table.

Jonas reached over and squeezed my hand. Startled, I turned back to face him. He was the second man to do that tonight. Yet this was the first time I wished I didn't have to let go. "Tell me what you're thinking right now," I said.

"I'm thinking that I have to head to Quebec City tomorrow for a music festival. But I'm coming to Boston in nine days to play a concert at the waterfront. And I'd really like you and Vivi to come to it."

"Oh," I said slowly. "A concert?" In just nine days? I thought I'd have a little longer to get my head on straight.

Jonas frowned. "I can see that you don't love the idea. But it would be a favor to me. And if Vivi hates it, you can always bail after the first song."

"Well..." I couldn't expect Jonas to have any experience with preschoolers, and now I was going to sound like the mom that I'd become. "I don't know if you can take a four-year-old to a rock concert. How late does it start?"

"That's the lucky thing," he said. "Because it's outdoors, and the noise bleeds, everything starts earlier than usual. Seven, I think?"

"Um." Could we really do that? Maybe if Vivi took a good nap first. "I'll think about it."

"I hope you will. You were right when you said I'd be busy for the next ten weeks. I've asked Ethan to try to find me a couple other dates when I have time off. He's going to see if there are any gaps when I could fly to Boston. The tour finishes up in August, but I don't want to wait that long to see you guys unless I have to."

Whoa. That made it sound like Jonas was already set on being a part of Vivi's life. That meant he'd turn up from time to time. Maybe at the kindergarten graduation. Or the third-grade Christmas concert. I pictured Jonas flying in for the weekend to take Vivi to the zoo, or whatever it was that part-time fathers did.

That meant years and years of my stomach turning somer-saults every time he showed his face. Jonas knew—or he'd known at one time—how deeply I felt about him. We would have to brush that under the rug and behave as if I'd never thrown my heart at him. And as if he'd never stomped on it.

I was in for a good fifteen years or so of torture.

But hey—I should look on the bright side. Paying Vivi's college tuition had just gotten easier.

"A penny for your thoughts," Jonas said, fingering his beer.

"I'm just trying to picture it," I said.

"Picture what? The concert?"

"The future."

"Ah," he said. "I'm not sure that works too well. But we all try, anyway."

I took a sip of my beer. The bottle was sweating in the warm summertime air. And even if my thoughts were in turmoil, the silence between us felt more comfortable now.

"I lost my parents when I was seven," Jonas said suddenly.

"That's young." I'd read all about it on his Wikipedia entry. "It was a car wreck, right?" I'd often wondered if that was what he'd been talking about when he told me that the squeal of brakes frightened him.

"Yeah. A horrible thing. We were at a music festival, and I was standing in line for ice cream while they waited nearby. So I saw it happen." He looked away. "It was bad enough losing them. But what happened afterwards was bad, too. I went to an aunt who had three kids of her own. She didn't want another one."

"Oh." That wasn't the sort of thing that showed up on Wikipedia. "I'm so sorry."

"I just... I don't want to sound morbid. But if I have a child on this earth, I'm going to make myself available, okay? I don't know if I'll be any good at being somebody's dad. But I couldn't stand for Vivi to think her father didn't care to try."

"Okay," I whispered.

He dropped his voice. "You trusted me once before, Kira. You're going to have to trust me again."

"I know," I choked out. I was scared, and the future felt so uncertain. And it was humbling to finally face up to all my secrets. But Jonas was so beautiful in the candlelight, and I didn't want to look away.

"What's the matter?" He covered my hand again and squeezed.

I shook my head to try to clear it. "I just don't know what happens next."

"Of course you do, sweetness. That's easy. We drink a couple of beers, and then I walk you home." He leaned back in his chair and smiled at me.

Wow. That smile. I'd missed it so much.

He made it sound so simple. But it wasn't simple at all. My heart was fit to burst. "It's weird to be here with you again."

"It's not weird, Kira," he said, quietly. "It's fucking awesome."

And my poor little pounding heart agreed with him.

TEN

KIRA

On the trip back to Boston the next morning, I let Adam drive. After twenty minutes, I turned around to peek at Vivi. My daughter had fallen asleep, Purple Kitty tucked onto her shoulder and under her resting chin.

Purple Kitty used to be all we had of Jonas. But now he was on his purple bus somewhere, headed to Canada, with my number in his phone. As if that weren't weird enough, he was coming to Boston in just over a week.

I felt a nervous rush just imagining it.

"Adam," I whispered to my brother. "We have to talk."

"Yup." He sighed. "You first."

"Hush Note is playing at the waterfront in a week, and Jonas invited all of us to go. Can you come too?"

"Hmm. I hope so."

"Do you have a better offer?"

He shook his head. And that's when I noticed how grim he looked.

"Hey, is something wrong?"

"Is Vivi asleep?"

I took another peek. "Yes."

"Okay." He cleared his throat. "Kiki, do you remember when

you told me that you were pregnant? You said, 'I need to tell you something, and I need you not to freak out.'"

"I remember."

There was a brief silence, and then Adam took a breath. "I need to tell you something, and I need you not to freak out. And what's more, there's no reason to freak out, okay?"

My heart lurched. "You're scaring me."

"I'm sorry, but I can't put off telling you any longer. Last week a doctor told me that I have testicular cancer. He also said that it's going to be okay."

"No!" I gasped, and then took care to lower my voice. "That's impossible."

"Unfortunately, it isn't. However, the survival rate is between ninety-six and ninety-nine percent. Basically, if you ever get the big C, you want to have it in one of your nuts."

Ninety-six to ninety-nine percent. It was hard to deny it sounded survivable, but my eyes filled with tears anyway. "Are you sure? You're too young to have cancer."

"I'm sure. And it's guys fifteen to thirty-four who typically get it," he said. "I'm right on schedule."

Ugh. "Do you *promise* those are the odds? You didn't just say that so I wouldn't get hysterical?"

Without taking his eyes off the road, Adam reached over and gave my elbow a squeeze. "I promise, Kiki. It's going to suck. But then I'll be okay again. I have to have surgery."

"Are you in any pain?"

He shook his head. "Nope. There are no symptoms, except for a lump where there shouldn't be a lump. And I have a doctor's appointment this afternoon to get pre-surgical blood-work done. The surgery is really pretty simple, too. It's not supposed to be any worse than a bad root canal."

I let out a nervous laugh. "The dentist never asks me to drop my pants, Adam."

He chuckled, too. And after a couple of seconds, both of us were trying not to completely bust a gut. Just two full-grown adults, trying to drive down a country road while cracking up over a cancer joke.

Adam let out an ill-timed hiccup, which only set off another round of giggling.

"Oh my God," I gasped. "We've gone off the deep end."

"Yup," Adam said, flicking a mirthful tear from his face. "This shall be known as The Weekend Of Overabundant Drama."

"That spells WOOD."

Adam snorted. "There are so many jokes in there just waiting for their chance to shine."

I blew out a breath. "Adam, how can I help you? Can I come to your doctor's appointment?"

"Today's appointment is just a needle stick. But I have others this week, because I'm getting a second opinion. You can tag along and hear what they have to say."

"How soon will you have the surgery?"

He shrugged. "Within the next two weeks, I think."

"Okay," I said. "Maybe I won't go to this concert. Whatever. Let's just focus on getting you through this. Let me know as soon as you schedule the procedure. I can cancel some shifts at work."

"Thank you," my brother said quietly. "I knew I could count on you."

"Always."

We both settled into our private thoughts as the miles went by. No wonder Adam had been acting strangely. According to Jonas, he'd been smoking. That had to mean that he was more worried than he let on. "I'm sorry," I blurted into the silence.

"What for?"

"Being such a drama queen this weekend."

Adam gave a low chuckle. "It's not your fault. We'll handle it, okay? All of it. We always do."

* * *

UNFORTUNATELY, the next few days were sobering.

I went to Adam's second round of doctor's appointments. I heard many words of encouragement. "Chance of five-year survival above ninety percent," and "probably caught it early enough," and "no long-term health consequences."

But the second team of doctors suggested a different treatment protocol, which left us googling "testicular cancer surgery" six ways till Sunday, and drowning in medical jargon.

With Vivi in her last week of preschool for the year, I called in sick to work and went with my brother to yet another consultation. Sitting there in the sterile waiting room while he had more scans done, I felt numb with fear.

It just wasn't fair. I didn't want Adam to have to go through this. He was already the oldest twenty-nine-year-old I knew. He supported a family of three, and cared for a child he had not created. And all without complaint.

Meanwhile, Jonas had tried to call me twice. The first time, I'd been watching Vivi in the bathtub, so I couldn't take the call. The voicemail he'd left was really sweet, though. "I'm thinking of you two, and I'd love to hear your voices," he'd said. "Call me."

But Vivi had a bedtime meltdown, and after she'd gone to sleep, I couldn't quite find the nerve to call him solo. Obviously, it was Vivi he wanted to speak to.

He'd called again today, when Adam and I were waiting for the results of one of his tests. Since Adam wanted to keep his illness private, I didn't take the call.

An hour later, he'd followed up with a text. ***Can you tell me when is a good time to talk? J.S.***

For years I'd dreamed of getting that text. Sometimes I'd even fantasized about him turning up on my doorstep with my love letter in his hand. "There was a mistake, and I didn't get this until now," he'd always said in those dreams. "I'm sorry, my love. But I'm here now."

Right. My brother's sci-fi TV shows had more realistic plots.

Later in the evening, Adam came home from work looking so

grim I assumed he'd gotten some terrible news. "What is it?" I asked, panicked. "A test?"

He shook his head. "I'm fine, Kiki."

But he did not look fine. I'd made one of his favorite foods for dinner, and he wasn't eating it.

"Adam," I whispered when Vivi darted into my bedroom in search of a doll. "If you're refusing my white lasagna with spinach, I'm going to call the paramedics."

He pushed his plate away. "I got a pile of legal documents from Jonas Smith's lawyer today."

My water glass froze on the way to my mouth. "Really? What do they say?"

"They weren't what I'd hoped." He folded his hands on the table. "Although it could just be posturing. Some lawyers are just dicks by default. If they want you to take two steps, they'll first ask for twenty."

"Adam! Just tell me what they said."

"Most of it is standard." He chewed his lip. "They're requesting a paternity test, after which, they'll file a complaint to establish paternity."

I made a noise of dismay, but Adam held up a hand. "No lawyer would negotiate child support without those things, Kira. That's just standard procedure. But I don't like their cover letter. It hints that they're going to push for joint legal custody."

"Legal custody," I whispered. "That means he could make decisions for her?"

Adam nodded. "But, like I said, the guy might be posturing. I expected him to ask for what's called 'reasonable visitation.'" He made quote marks with his fingers.

I felt as though the floor were dropping out from under me. "He said he'd never try to take her away from me. That was three days ago."

"Mama?" I whipped my head around to see Vivi standing in the doorway. "Where is Purple Kitty?"

I took a deep breath and steadied myself. Then I got up to help Vivi find a tattered stuffed cat.

* * *

LATER, when Vivi was asleep, Adam and I sat together on the couch, plotting together in low voices.

"I'll call his lawyer tomorrow," Adam promised. "I'll try to figure out what he's really trying to accomplish. The problem is that after you swab for a paternity test, it takes a week or ten days to come back. And he has no incentive to level with me until he has the results."

I fingered my phone. "Jonas has been calling me, but we haven't connected. What am I supposed to say to him?"

Adam's gray eyes were full of concern. "You could tell him that you can only speak through your lawyers for now. If he's going to play hardball, then so can you."

"God, I'm no good at hardball."

He smiled. "You are when it comes to me."

"Are you suggesting that I hide the plaintiff's clean underwear until he does what I asked?"

He shook his head. "That judge may construe that as harassment. However, as your lawyer, I'd advise you not to hide his *salami* until this is settled."

"Adam! I would *never*."

He raised an eyebrow. "Um, *never?*"

"That was a long time ago."

"He's still hot, though."

"No kidding." But that didn't help my case. "Adam, what's the worst thing that could happen here?"

"The worst thing? A meteor hits Boston."

I gave his knee a little shove. "I'm not kidding. Don't mock."

"I'm not." He leaned back against the couch, making himself comfortable against the cushions. "A lawyer's job is to prepare for the unlikeliest scenarios. It's your job to worry about the likelier ones."

"Fine. What's the worst *likely* outcome, then. Hit me."

"Well, if he's a vindictive asshole, he'll pursue this joint-custody thing for real. The judge isn't likely to grant it, though, because the state cares about Vivi's welfare. And a child who lives in a good home shouldn't be yanked out of it. That's common sense."

I sensed a "but" coming. "Then why are you worried?"

He toyed with the piping on the edge of the couch. "Because they might have a shot at convincing the judge that your deception is grounds for an unusual decision. The other side could argue that if he'd *known* about Vivi, he wouldn't be a stranger in the first place."

I groaned.

He reached over and pulled on my ponytail. "You asked me for the ugly version. I still think it's just posturing."

"I hate this."

"I know. But this too shall pass."

I made another irritated sound and picked up my phone. Tapping the message app, I stared at Jonas's message. *When is a good time to talk?*

I wanted to reply: *Does never work for you?*

But I didn't do it. I didn't reply at all.

ELEVEN

JONAS

I lay in my bunk on the tour bus, staring at the ceiling, feeling tense. A movie blared from the big screen in the forward lounge. Since I heard frequent gunfire, I supposed Nixon had chosen the film.

It got quiet, and for a moment I could almost hear my own thoughts. Just when I was beginning to relax, the blast of a Hollywood explosion tore through me.

I sat up fast, nearly bumping my head. Pushing the curtains aside, I slipped to the floor and stomped up the aisle. "Could you turn that fucking thing down?"

Two faces turned in my direction, each one reflecting mild surprise.

Yes, I'm about to lose my shit, here. Thank you for noticing.

They turned back to the screen, but Nixon reached for the remote, and a few seconds later the sounds of faux brutality dimmed somewhat.

I went back to my bunk and put on a pair of noise-canceling headphones. But now I'd have to hold my phone in my hand, in case Kira finally called me back. If I couldn't hear the ring, at least I'd feel the vibration.

And where was she? The silence was killing me.

It had been six days since my life blew up bigger than the blasts on my friends' movie screen. And every hour that Kira avoided me left me feeling lower than the hour before.

One thing was clear. If I'd had the balls to answer Kira's letter five years ago, this could have been avoided. I'd have a daughter who knew my name. And possibly a wife.

I'd had a chance at something real, and I'd blown it. Spectacularly. I'd let Kira think that I didn't care. And all because I was afraid to put my heart on the line.

All I'd had to do was pick up the phone. And everything would have been different.

There would still have been difficult conversations, I reminded myself. When she'd discovered she was pregnant, I would have panicked for sure. And maybe wrecked everything.

But maybe not. And now I'd never know.

My phone vibrated.

Ripping off the headphones, I craned my neck to read the screen.

FLASH SALE! Up to 40% off brand name amps and pedals!

Fucking email. I dropped my head back onto the pillow. Then, because I couldn't help myself, I tapped Kira's phone number, dialing her. *Again.*

It went straight to voicemail. *Do not pass Go, do not collect proof of her existence.*

This was getting a little ridiculous, right? I'd been trying to give her a few days to get over the shock of seeing me. But my bus would arrive in Boston in forty-eight hours. And if she wouldn't take my calls, how was I going to arrange to see her?

It was time for the nuclear option.

I pulled up her brother's phone number and tapped it. Adam's phone rang, at least. "Hello?" he answered tentatively.

"Adam, this is Jonas Smith," I said. "How are you doing?"

"Fine, thank you." His voice was cool. "But I think it's best if you communicate through your lawyer for the time being."

"My lawyer? What the hell for?"

There was a pause before Adam spoke again. "Jonas, you

need to talk to your lawyer. Because he's asking Kira for things that make it difficult for her to take your call right now. You can't have it both ways."

"What? I'm not asking for *anything*."

"If that's true, then you need to have your lawyer call me," Adam said.

Then he hung up.

I stared at my phone for a second, wondering what the hell had just happened. Then I slid off my bunk and ran to the rear of the bus, past the stainless-steel kitchen with its shiny glass tiles. Past the tiny marble bathroom. Past each ridiculous show of opulence that some clown had decided belonged on a bus.

Instead of knocking on the door to the rear lounge, I slid it open and burst inside. "Ethan?"

The big man looked up at me over the rims of his reading glasses. He had itineraries spread out in front of him on the built-in table. "Yeah?"

"What did Peters do?"

Ethan removed his glasses with a frown. "I have no idea. But from the look on your face, I'm guessing it wasn't good."

I slid the door to the lounge shut. After sitting down across from Ethan, I repeated what Adam had said, word for word. "If Peters went in with guns blazing, then we need to hire somebody else to handle this."

Ethan pushed his itineraries out of the way and took out his phone. "Let's take a deep breath first. You don't haul off and fire the firm that's negotiating your next contract with the record label."

"Fuck the contract. This is more important. Times a hundred."

The bald man looked up from his phone and smiled at me. "Okay, Jojo. I'm with you. Let's divvy this up. You call Peters and try to figure out how big an asshole he's been. I'll work on scoping out a new lawyer."

"How are you going to do that?" I asked, scrolling for Peters's number.

Ethan didn't answer, because he'd already placed a call. "Hi Adam, this is Ethan, do you remember me? I sure remember you." A private smile crept across his face. "Aw, I like your grumpy lawyer voice. It's hot. But this is a business call, after all. It seems we might need a new lawyer. Preferably in Massachusetts. And preferably one who listens when we talk. I was hoping you could save us some time and recommend someone." He grinned to himself again. "Sure, I'll hold."

"You're *flirting* with Kira's pissed-off brother?" I hissed. "How is that a good idea?"

"It's a *fine* idea," Ethan said, picking up a pen. A moment later he jotted a name and a number onto the corner of one of his file folders. "And this is a good guy? You trust him? Okay. Awesome. We'll be in touch, once we figure out what the fuck is going on. Thank you." Ethan hung up.

I reached across the table for Ethan's glass of ice water and drained it. "God, how did we end up here?"

"Oh, honey. Did they not teach sex ed at your school?"

I gave him an irritated groan and put my forehead down on the table. I'd been so angry at Kira for not telling me about Vivi. And now that I was getting used to the idea of having a daughter, my lawyer was fucking everything up.

I'd been an idiot to walk away from Kira. And I hoped I'd get the chance to say so.

TWELVE

KIRA

I was cleaning up from lunch on Monday when I got a text from Adam. ***New paperwork from Jonas's new lawyer. Reasonable visitation! *fist bump****

I dialed Adam immediately. "This is good, right?"

"Hey!" he said, sounding happy. "I'm just running into a meeting. But yeah, this version is *much* better. You can relax. But now I have to go. I'm trying to cram as many billable hours into this week as I can. I have a client dinner tonight, too."

"I know. Sorry." Instead of trying to relax and think positive thoughts, poor Adam was working overtime to prepare for his medical leave. "You can show me the papers tonight. I'll wait up."

"Tell you what. I'll messenger them over. You'll feel better if you read it yourself. Gotta hop."

I let him go. Since Vivi was singing her way through nap time instead of sleeping, I went into her room and sat on the bed. "I don't have to work today. So we can go to the park later."

Vivi sat up so fast that her curls bounced against her face. "How 'bout now?"

I should have seen that coming. Adam sometimes referred to her as the Little Negotiator. He'd suggested that we should be setting aside money for Vivi's inevitable law school tuition. "Not yet, sweetie. I'm waiting for a package."

Her eyes got wide. "For my birthday?"

"Not this time," I said quickly. "It's just some boring papers. But after it comes, we'll go out to the swings."

"Can I push my doll stroller?"

"Sure."

"Can we get ice cream?"

It was like living with *two* lawyers. "Maybe."

Vivi clapped her hands, as if it were a done deal. Then she wiggled off the bed and went to choose which dolls would have the honor of riding to the park.

* * *

TWENTY MINUTES LATER, the intercom buzzed.

That was fast. I went to the door and pressed the button allowing the messenger access to the elevator.

Vivi came skidding out of her bedroom. "Your boring papers are here?"

"I think so. Unless you ordered a pizza."

Her forehead crinkled. "We already *had* lunch."

I laughed. "I'm kidding. Go find your shoes."

Vivi tore out of the room again. The messenger tapped on the door, so I pulled it open.

And came face to face with Jonas.

For a long moment, I just stood there like an idiot, staring into his indecently attractive turquoise eyes.

"Hi," Jonas said quietly, his lips twitching.

"Why are you... here now?" I sputtered.

He frowned. "I told you I was coming to Boston for a show."

"Tomorrow night," I protested. I'd assumed I'd have a good twenty-four hours before we shared a city. *I'm not ready.*

There had been other times when his band played Boston venues, I'd wondered where he was, and if he'd even remember me.

If a girl could get a degree in self-torture, I'd already have the diploma. With honors.

Jonas put a hand to the back of his neck, still peering at me. "The show is tomorrow night, that's true. But we drove all night so that I could sign papers for my new lawyer."

"Oh," I said stupidly.

Vivi clattered into the room behind me. "I'm ready!" she yelled.

I turned to see her pushing her toy double stroller, a doll strapped into each side. When she saw Jonas at the door, she stopped. "Oh, it's you again."

Jonas burst out laughing. "What a greeting. From both of you."

Vivi had her hands on her hips. "Did you bring the boring papers? I can't go to the park unless they come."

He held his hands out to the sides, empty. "Sorry."

"You want to see my dolls?"

"Sure!" Before I could argue, Jonas had slipped past me into the living room. He went right over to the rug and sat, criss-cross applesauce, as if it were a perfectly ordinary part of his rock-and-roll day to plop down for a tea party. "Introduce me."

Vivi began an elaborate description of the merits of each doll. I stood by my open door like a zombie, trying to figure out just how this had happened. The door buzzer went off again, and because I was standing right beside it, I jumped.

The messenger had finally arrived. I buzzed him up and signed for the package.

"Yes!" Vivi leaped to her feet. "We can go to the park now."

Jonas caught her by the hand. "Give your mom a minute to read her boring papers, okay?"

I didn't know whether to be grateful that he was trying to distract Vivi, or annoyed that he'd show up in the first place. I walked past the two of them, slitting the big envelope with my thumb as I went.

"Do you know it's my birthday soon?" Vivi asked.

"I'd heard that," Jonas said gently. "What do you want for your birthday?"

"A pony," Vivi said immediately. "Or a rowboat. But I can't have those because we live in the city."

"Ah," he sympathized. "Ponies don't like elevators."

My daughter continued to babble to Jonas, and I tuned them out so I could skim the contents of the envelope. The first sheet was a short letter.

DEAR KIRA,

Please accept my apology for the documents you received from my previous law firm. I would never try to take your daughter away from you.

(My new lawyer did not want me to put that in writing. Lawyers are trained to think of all the outlandish possibilities. But since you're not the kind of girl who is likely to start a meth lab in your kitchen, I'm just going to go out on a limb here and assume that my intervention for Vivi's welfare will never be necessary.)

Enclosed please find a standard "complaint to establish paternity." (I don't like the word "complaint," but that's what they call these things.) After a judge helps me establish that I am Vivi's father, I will request "reasonable visitation." But not before discussing it with you.

Again, I apologize for any anxiety my crack legal team has caused. That was never my intention.

Sincerely,

John Jonas Smith

The complaint to establish paternity was the only other document in the envelope. It was not quite two pages long and entirely straightforward.

I let out my breath for what felt like the first time all week.

THIRTEEN

JONAS

Kira's shoulders visibly relaxed. Thank fuck. If there was any justice, I'd make it through the next forty-eight hours without finding brand-new ways to alienate her.

It was pretty trippy to be sitting in her apartment. I wanted to wander through the rooms and get a better picture of her life. Or—even better—to sit beside her and ask questions. I wanted to take a seat at one of those barstools separating the kitchen from the living area and listen to her talk about her day.

Years ago, I'd loved sitting at the general store's counter in Maine, letting her musical voice wash over me and watching the flutter of her pulse at her neck as she worked.

But that wasn't in the cards today. Because every time I managed to get close to Kira, I found a way to ruin it. It was tempting to blame this latest disaster on my ham-fisted West Coast lawyer, but as usual, I'd been asleep at the wheel when it counted.

Beside me, Vivi was describing the life cycle of a butterfly. My baby was a talker, that was for sure. A lucky thing. It gave me an excuse to observe her, taking in the sound of her high little voice, and the way her eyes were quick and warm, like Kira's.

"...And then the larva eats and eats. And then it finds a leaf to stick on."

"It has to make a cocoon, right?" I put in.

"Nope," Vivi corrected me mercilessly. "You call it a chrysalis. Cocoons are for moths. That's different. A butterfly has a chrysalis. Chrysalis, chrysalis, chrysalis!"

"Got it."

From the kitchen, where she was watching us, I heard Kira snort.

"And then the next part is boring, because it takes ten days. But when the chrysalis starts to wiggle, you know the butterfly is going to come out. That's good to watch. Except when the chrysalis breaks open, some stuff that looks like blood drips out, only it's not called blood, it's called something else."

"What's it called?"

"The teacher said, but I forgot. The butterfly is sort of wet for a while after it comes out, and it has to just sit there getting dry before it can fly."

"You know," I told her, "babies are wet when they're born. But I think a nurse just dries them off with a towel."

Even as the words came out of my mouth, I knew I was saying a stupid thing. If I got Vivi going on the topic of babies, then she was bound to ask me where babies come from, and I did not have any fucking clue what people told four-year-olds about *that*.

Kira would murder me, probably.

Vivi opened her little mouth to ask a question, and I braced myself. "Do you like grapes?"

"What?" I reeled from this abrupt change of topic. "Yeah. Yeah, I like grapes! Especially after someone has made them into wine. Or a nicely aged cognac." I was blathering like an idiot, and another snort erupted from the other end of the room. But as long as we weren't talking about babies and vaginas, it was probably okay.

"Do you want to eat your grapes, Vivi?" Kira called.

"Yep."

Kira set a bowl of grapes at the dining table, and Vivi scampered over there to eat them.

I got up off the rug, relocating to the sofa. "Kira?" I asked softly. "Can I speak with you for a moment?"

Her expression was wary, but she made her way over to sit beside me. "What's up?"

"Tomorrow night," I whispered. "I want you and Vivi to come to the concert. And Adam, too."

She pursed her lips, causing me to notice how pink and full they were. "Maybe we should wait until..."

"Until what? Don't say court, because that's only a formality. I just want to see you guys." Since she still looked as if she was searching her brain for a good reason to decline, I kept talking. "I'm staying at the Waterfront, because that's where the venue is. Why don't you come at five? That way I can see you before the show. We go on at seven thirty. There wouldn't be any waiting around—you'd get to your seats right before we play, and afterwards, Ethan would whisk you into a car."

"Okay." She was still frowning. "We'll give it a shot. But if Vivi asks for beer or a blunt afterward, it's going to be your fault."

I barked out a laugh before I could think better of it, which brought Vivi running. "What?" she wanted to know.

"Your mama is funny," I said, rising to my feet. "That's all."

"It's okay to say someone is funny," Vivi mused, "but not that they're funny-*looking*. Because the teacher will give you a time-out."

I held in my laughter this time. But just barely. "I have to go now. Have fun at the park."

"You're not coming to the swings?"

I shook my head. "I can't. I have a meeting for work."

"Like Uncle Adam."

"Yeah, like that." I took a step closer to Vivi. She reminded me of a little bird, hopping from idea to idea, alighting only briefly here and there. I knelt down again. "I'll see you soon, Vivi. Maybe tomorrow."

My daughter reached out and put her hands on my face, one on each cheek. "Okay." Her fingertips tickled me.

Vivi was just so... disarming. Little kids didn't know all the grownup rules about who you could touch. She didn't know that you weren't supposed to say exactly what you wanted, and instead bury your desires under ten layers of self-doubt. Vivi let it all hang out.

When exactly had I stopped doing that? And why?

I gave her one more smile, then got up to go.

Kira followed me to the door, her expression unreadable. "Thank you," she said, and then her face softened. "I guess we'll see you tomorrow night."

Without thinking, I leaned in and kissed her temple. The moment we connected, I inhaled the citrus scent of her shampoo. It was so familiar that I wanted to weep.

Kira went absolutely still at my touch. So I lingered a half beat longer than was friendly. But goddamn it, I wanted to pull her into my arms and kiss her for real. And maybe I would have, but Vivi was right there on the rug, adjusting her dollies.

"Please come at five," I said, making myself pull away.

Kira nodded swiftly, her eyes on her shoes.

"Goodbye for now, sweetness." It was an effort to open the door and leave.

FOURTEEN

KIRA

The next text I'd received from Jonas instructed me to go to the check-in desk at the hotel and give them my name. *They'll be expecting you*, he'd written.

Gotcha, I'd replied.

I got a room for you and Vivi, he'd added.

No need, I'd quickly tapped out. *We're 20 minutes away*.

I want us to have breakfast together in the morning, he'd argued. *The bus leaves at 9. Please stay?*

I had not replied to this message, but I'd packed an overnight bag, anyway. If I changed my mind, I could always grab a taxi and take Vivi home after the show.

At the hotel, I gave my name to the desk agent. The suite that Jonas had booked was on the club-level floor. "You'll need to insert your key card into the elevator slot, or the doors will not open on the club level," the woman at the desk explained in hushed tones.

"Gotcha," I said, thinking that it sounded silly. Making something exclusive just for the sake of exclusivity. Vivi yanked on my hand. "Just one more minute, sweetie."

"There is a complimentary buffet of snacks and beverages on

the club level," the woman added. "It's quite useful with kids, actually."

Hmm... Maybe I would need to revise my opinion of the club level, after all. "Thank you."

The moment we stepped off the elevator, Vivi made a beeline for the snack table. "Cookies!"

"Don't touch," I said automatically. "Let's get into Jonas's room, and then we can come back out here and get a snack."

When I found the right door, the plaque above it read *The Harbor Suite*. There was a creamy envelope taped to it, addressed to "K."

I removed a note from the envelope. *Kira—if we're not back from sound check, make yourself at home. The double room is for you.*

Instead of swiping the door open, I knocked, then waited nervously. I wished I didn't feel this way. *Hey*, I tried to tell myself. *It's no big deal to walk into your rock-star hookup's hotel penthouse.*

Right.

Nobody came to the door, and I heard no voices. So I tapped my card against the lock mechanism, and the lock gave way. I opened the door onto a decadent living room.

"Wow," Vivi said, marching past me as if she owned the place. "I want this apartment."

Hotel room, I nearly corrected her. But really, was there a difference? At one end of the room, in front of a floor-to-ceiling view of Boston Harbor, was a gleaming dining table set for six people. Behind that, a kitchen stood ready. It was as big as the one in our apartment.

Through one doorway I spotted a king-sized bed with a duffel bag resting on it. The other open doorway led to a room with two queen-sized beds.

Wow, I thought, echoing Vivi. Somebody liked to throw his money around.

"Can I have a cookie now?" Vivi asked.

I set my overnight bag down beside a sleek leather sofa. "Sure. But just one, because it's almost dinner time."

* * *

AFTER A COOKIE (and a five-minute unsuccessful plead-a-thon for more), I pulled out the book that I'd been reading to Vivi for the past week. I gave myself a mental high-five for packing a distraction good enough to interrupt her survey of the suite, where she'd opened nearly every drawer and cabinet.

I'd read only one chapter when I heard a tap on the door. Then it opened, and Jonas stuck his head around the door frame. I saw him take us in, curled up on the sofa. When he smiled, my stomach swooped and dived.

This was why I hadn't wanted to stay here tonight. We'd spent exactly one night under the same roof together, and it had set quite a precedent.

But that was all your doing, I reminded myself. So as long as I didn't throw myself at the guy this time, all would be well.

"Hi, ladies," Jonas said, closing the door after entering the room. "I'm sorry I was late."

"S'okay," Vivi said. "There are cookies. But Mama only lets you have one."

Jonas grinned. "It's almost dinner time, though. The food will be here in a few minutes."

"Food?" Vivi asked, climbing off the couch. "What kind?"

"Hmm," Jonas said, pretending to think. "Ethan said the food had to be stirred up. Like this." He grabbed Vivi under the arms, then quickly spun her around in a circle.

Vivi let out a shriek at a pitch that only a little girl can achieve.

I caught myself smiling, the back of my throat strangely hot. I'd always wondered what the two of them would look like together.

Happy. That's how they looked.

Someone knocked on the door. "Room service!"

I jumped up to open it, and a bellman rolled a cart into the room.

Vivi was dizzy. She took a swaying step and crashed into

Jonas's leg. The hand he dropped to her back to steady her was so natural that I couldn't help but stare.

"But we already have a table," Vivi said. "It's right there."

The bellman winked. "Now you have two." He began placing dishes onto the dining table, arranging the linen napkins and heavy flatware.

Jonas signed the check. "Enjoy your meal," the bellman said before bowing out.

"Hungry?" Jonas asked. "Ethan sent us a few choices."

I was not, in fact, hungry. A small fleet of Vivi's nursery school butterflies were doing a dance in my stomach. But Vivi climbed right up into one of the heavy dining chairs and surveyed the plates. "I like mashed potatoes."

"I'll fix you a plate." I cut up a piece of chicken for her, adding a good dollop of creamy potatoes.

I took a second plate and put a tiny amount of food onto it for myself. Jonas sat down on the opposite side of the table, taking nothing but a soda. "Aren't you eating?" I asked him.

He shook his head. "Can't eat before a show. But I'll make myself a plate, and stick it in that fridge." He tipped his head toward the kitchen. "Because the later you call room service, the longer it takes."

"Ah. If I'd finished that hospitality degree, maybe I could tell you why."

His eyebrows lifted. "You switched majors?"

"Yes. To education. I wanted teachers' hours." This conversation did nothing for my nerves. Could it be any more obvious that we didn't know each other anymore?

Jonas looked like he wanted to ask another question, but Vivi began talking about sprouting potatoes at school. "You have to use organic ones, because the grocery store ones have chemicals."

Vivi to the rescue. And this was how "reasonable visitation" might be survivable. Whenever the conversation got too personal, or when I slipped into the memory of Jonas's hands on my skin, I would just let Vivi take over the conversation.

I took a small bite of chicken and reminded myself that tomorrow Jonas would leave town again. He'd come and go from my life, and I would just have to deal with it.

* * *

AFTER DINNER, Vivi hopped down from her chair and began to tear around. "What's in here?" she asked, darting into the room with two beds.

"Well..." Jonas glanced my way. "That's your room for tonight."

A little head came peeping out again. "Really? Yay!" Vivi yelled.

"Thanks for the subtle invitation," I scolded. Of course Vivi had already scrambled up onto one of the beds. She was lining up to leap over the four-foot chasm between them.

"Sorry," Jonas said lightly. "But you did bring a bag. So I assumed it was settled."

I had brought a bag, damn it, but I couldn't argue with him, because I had to rescue Vivi from making her jump. "Whoa," I said, rounding the bed to stop her. "This is not a playground, sweetie."

Vivi gave a whoop and began to jump up and down. And, yay. Now I looked like the worst mom ever, since Vivi didn't listen.

"I wish I could get that excited about hotel rooms," Jonas said from the doorway. "By July, I'm so tired of little soaps and trying to remember my room number that I just want to cry."

Vivi slid off the bed and ran through the living room and into the other bedroom. "What's in here?"

I followed in hot pursuit. Vivi was already jumping on Jonas's king-sized bed. "Vivi, I mean it. Knock it off." With my luck, we'd end the night in the ER.

She dropped to her bottom on the bed. "Can I watch TV?"

"Sure," Jonas said, at the exact same moment that I said, "No."

I shot him another look as he leaned against the door frame. "Actually, she doesn't watch any TV."

"Not ever?" he asked, his eyes wide.

I shook my head. "We're just trying to avoid screens until she's older." I could've cited the scientific research, but it would've made me sound like a weirdo.

"Jonas said I could!" Vivi yelped, grabbing the remote off the bedside table. "We don't have one at home."

"You little trickster," Jonas said, stepping forward to scoop her up by the hips. "Are you going to listen to your mom?" Slowly, he tilted her little body sideways, until she began to laugh.

"No." She giggled. The remote slipped out of her hand and onto the rug.

Jonas tilted her further, stepping over to the bed. She reached for the surface, squealing. The reversal of gravity made her T-shirt ride up, and he planted a loud raspberry on her belly.

Vivi howled with laughter, trying to escape his grasp. "I'll... listen!" she gasped. He released her suddenly, and she fell into a heap on the bedspread.

He swept the remote off the floor and handed it to me. "Do with this what you will."

"This bed is biiiiig!" Vivi hollered, performing a forward somersault on its surface. "I like it. It's fun to play on."

At that, Jonas winked at me, a grin spreading across his mouth. My face flamed.

"Mama?" Vivi stopped flopping around and sat up.

"Yes, sweetie?"

"Harper went to a hotel at Disney World with her mama and her daddy."

"Did she?" I braced myself, certain that Vivi was about to ask when it would be her turn to meet Mickey Mouse.

"Mama? Is Jonas my daddy?"

My brain short-circuited.

Across the room, Jonas swiveled around in surprise, his wide eyes asking a question. *Well? What now?*

Confused, I just stood there for a moment. So this was happening now? I wasn't ready! And yet, I didn't want to lie to Vivi's face...

I glanced again at Jonas, giving him a tiny nod.

That was all the permission he needed. He closed the distance to Vivi, plucking her off the bed and kissing her on the forehead. "You are very, *very* smart," he said, his voice husky. "And you are, in fact, my baby girl."

"*You're* my daddy?" she asked, her little voice reedy. She turned to me for confirmation.

I didn't trust my voice. I could only nod and swallow hard.

"Wow," Vivi said. "Are you going to live at our house? That would be neat."

"Well..." Jonas chuffed out a laugh and held Vivi close to his chest. His back rose and fell as he tried to control his emotions. "I'm going to see you as much as I can. Your mama and I are trying to figure that out. I live far away."

"You could stay in my room," Vivi offered. "Once, Grandpa slept on my floor. The bed isn't big. Not like this one." She wiggled out of his embrace, and Jonas set her gently on the bed, his eyes bright and shiny.

There were two knocks on the outer door. "Hey, Jojo?" a voice called. It sounded like Ethan. Jonas met my gaze again, uncertain if he should walk away.

"Go," I mouthed. I knew that Vivi wasn't finished with this topic. She'd come at me later with more questions. She'd circle back, always catching me off guard.

I plucked her off the bed and carried her through the living room and into the other bedroom. Behind me, I heard Jonas take in a deep, steadying breath. Then he went to answer Ethan's knock.

I sat down heavily on one of the beds, feeling shaky. Vivi climbed onto my lap. "Love you, Mama."

"Love you too, sweetie," I whispered.

"Can I watch TV now?"

"Nope."

"Bummer."

* * *

AFTER THAT, the suite began to fill with people. Band members arrived one by one. They were polite to me and Vivi, but clearly had no idea what to say.

I was starting to feel like we were in the way when Adam texted me. *Where are you? I'm in the lobby.*

Let me figure out how to get you upstairs, I tapped out, relieved that he'd decided to join us. *There's a secret handshake and everything.*

Will this make me cool? Adam returned. *I've always wanted to be cool.*

We are about as cool as we're ever going to get. Sad but true, I replied. "Hey, Ethan?" I stopped the big man as he walked by.

He turned around with a smile. "What do you need?" I got the same greeting he gave everyone tonight. As far as I could tell, his job was to put out everyone's fires.

"My brother is in the hotel lobby..."

"There's a key card for him at the front desk," he said immediately. "Under his name." With a wink, he strode off to answer someone else's question.

A few minutes later, Adam knocked on the door, and I was right there to let him in. "Hi," I said, grabbing him into a hug. "Guess what Vivi figured out? The truth."

"Seriously?" Adam gave a low whistle. "You can't get anything past that kid. She's probably going to be president one day. Or head of the CIA."

"She still believes in Santa," I reminded him.

"Maybe she's just humoring us."

Ethan skidded to a stop in front of us. "Hey! Good to see you again," he said, grabbing Adam into a hug that was tighter than the one I'd just given him. Huh. "Thanks for helping me with the lawyer thing."

"No problem," my brother said. And if I wasn't mistaken, Adam's cheeks got a little pinker than normal.

"Glad you could make it tonight."

Adam's lips twitched. "It's pretty hard to drag me to a free concert when I could be at my desk right about now."

Ethan clapped him on the back with a hand the size of a dinner plate. "Thanks for making the time." Then he hurried off to help someone find his security pass.

The last person to arrive in Jonas's suite was Quinn. She wore skin-tight black jeans and a shimmering, form-fitting tank top. Her eyes were smoldering in expertly applied makeup, and her lips were painted man-killer red. It was the kind of look I'd never pulled off in my life.

Quinn greeted her bandmates first and then paused in front of me, Vivi, and Adam. "Hello there." She smiled at me. "I like your blouse."

"Thank you," I said, surprised by the compliment.

I was just opening my mouth again to pay her a compliment, when she added: "My mother has one just like it."

And I felt like I'd been slapped.

I was trying to formulate a response when Vivi piped up. "Mama tried on LOTS of shirts. Like all of them. They're still all over her bed."

Adam clamped a hand over his mouth, while Quinn let out a snort.

Speechless now, I wondered why this fancy suite did not come equipped with a trapdoor for quick escapes. It really needed one.

Club level my ass.

"What did I miss?" Jonas asked, coming up behind me, putting a warm hand in the center of my back.

Quinn's eyes got squinty. She turned and headed for the other end of the room.

"Nothing at all," I said a beat too late.

"Ethan says the cars are two minutes away," Jonas said.

"Cars? The concert is... a hundred yards from here, no?"

He made a face. "We can't walk it. Too many people between here and there. Sorry."

Ethan clapped his hands and asked everyone to proceed to the elevators.

It was show time.

* * *

AS PROMISED, Vivi, Adam, and I were ushered into front-row seats just a minute before the PA system announced, to shrieking fans, that Hush Note was about to take the stage. The overhead lights went out, and Vivi scrambled immediately into my lap.

There was a charged silence while fifteen thousand people waited to see what would happen next. My heart thumped harder as bodies moved around on the stage in the darkness.

The sound of a fast guitar riff gave me goosebumps. And then a yellow beam of light illuminated Nixon, and the audience screamed its approval.

After a few bars, the bass and drums came in together, and more lights came up as my heart rate increased to match the drumbeat. Around us, the audience got to its feet, and I let Vivi stand up on the seat, holding her body so she wouldn't fall.

Finally, a spotlight came up on Jonas. As the audience lost its mind, I experienced a moment of cognitive dissonance. He was standing up there in the same jeans and T-shirt I'd seen on him a few minutes ago, but now he looked like a stranger with the stage lighting washing over him and a microphone in his hand.

"I turn up on Saturday nights and always find you in this spot," Jonas sang. *"Used to think it was a coincidence, but now I think it's not."*

His voice sent shivers down my spine and across my shoulders.

The song was "Start Something With Me." I knew it well. I hadn't set out to become a Hush Note fan, but after I'd discovered who Jonas was, I'd become unwillingly tuned into him, like a radio signal that suddenly sharpens from static to clarity. I'd heard him everywhere—on the radios of cars passing by on the street, at the drugstore, and even in an ad for dog food.

"Start Something With Me" was like a family member. I hadn't chosen to memorize the lyrics or hear the tune in my head, but it was there just the same.

God, I could never let Jonas get ahold of the playlists on my phone. I didn't want him to know that I owned his music, and listened to it sometimes, especially in summer, when I was most susceptible to him. He'd written most of *Summer Nights* during that summer in Maine.

Until a few short days ago, the music was all I had left of his voice.

"Wow," Vivi yelled. "My daddy is loud."

I couldn't disagree. At least Vivi was sporting a pair of hot-pink headphones that fit snugly over her ears. They were special ones, for noise protection. Just before we'd stepped into the car, Ethan had torn them out of a plastic package, and Jonas had fitted them carefully over Vivi's ears. "You have to wear these for the whole concert, okay? Otherwise the music will hurt your ears. Promise me you'll wear them?"

Vivi's face had become solemn. "Okay, Daddy. I promise."

I'd had to blink away tears, and Adam had, too.

After clearing his throat, Ethan had given a tiny plastic packet to both me and Adam. "And you two should wear these. Jonas and I always do." We'd tried on the ball-shaped earplugs, with little tubes sticking out of them. I'd thought they made us look like aliens.

"God, I have enough trouble looking cool without the science fiction headgear," Adam had grumbled.

For some reason, Ethan had found this hilarious. And then he'd shut our car door and rapped on the window as a signal to the driver to go. Just like in the movies.

* * *

THE CONCERT WAS AMAZING on so many levels. Seeing Jonas work the stage was surreal and overwhelming. There were two of him up there—both the guy I knew and the famous stranger, all wrapped up together. He prowled the stage under the multicolored lights, eyes on the audience, his brow glistening with effort.

My eyes were fixed on the way his hands danced over his bass guitar. It was impossible to believe that those hands had once played my body. An entire lifetime had passed for me since that night.

And after each song, a deafening wave of applause rolled over me. I hadn't been to a big concert like this since my teen years. I'd forgotten the sheer power of live music—the way the crowd's energy seemed to rise up from their waving hands into the sky, and the way the bass echoed inside my chest.

It was big and wild, and one thing seemed absolutely certain. Jonas was never mine, and he never would be. I'd bet a dozen homemade whoopie pies that every person in this stadium felt an equal sense of ownership.

They played one of my favorite songs near the end. After another loud crash of applause, Nixon began picking out the beginning of a slow tune called "Heavenly." His strumming shimmered through the amplifiers, breaking over me like goosebumps.

Jonas began to sing about the pain of indecision. I'd heard the song before, of course, but watching him perform it was a different experience. His voice was supple and easy, though there was sweat coursing down his face. His body seemed to bend with emotion, squeezing the high notes from some place deep inside.

The crowd ate it up. As I watched, a scrap of something red sailed through the air and landed on the lip of the stage. I was close enough to see it was a lacy red thong.

And here I thought thrown panties were just a myth. And how was it done, exactly? Had the panty-tosser wiggled out of them? Or had she brought a spare pair in her pocketbook?

Adam cupped his hand over my ear. "Are you going to toss yours?"

I gave him a sharp look. "I did that five years ago."

He shrugged, grinning like he knew a secret.

I'd better learn how to tamp down my reaction to Jonas. And I'd better learn to do it soon.

Vivi shocked me by staying awake for the entire concert. Even so, she leaned more heavily on me after each song, her little body sagging with the lateness of the hour.

Finally, on the heels of thunderous applause, Jonas unhooked the microphone and announced their last song of the evening. "We're going to play you our new single, just released last week. I thought I'd tell you a little something about it. It's called 'Sweetness.'"

"Hey!" Adam poked me in the arm. "Isn't that what he calls you?"

"About five years ago I met somebody wonderful. And then I spent five years trying to write a song about her. But I couldn't do it. Every version was worse than the one before. But then last year I finally figured out where I went wrong with the lyrics. And everything fell into place. This is a song about meeting the right person at the wrong time. It's a song about regrets. And I hope the girl in the song knows that I mean every word. Because I'm really hoping the story isn't over yet."

The audience hooted its approval, and Quinn clicked her sticks together four times, bringing the rest of the band into the groove. By the time Jonas sang the first lyric, I was holding my breath.

IT WAS many years ago now
  That summer was my saving grace
  We were so much younger then
  But I will not forget her face

SO I MIGHT NEVER BE the same
  Since that night that meant so much

I will never mind the pain
But I'll always miss her touch

I WANT *her to be happy*
Hell, I pray for it sometimes
I never found what I was after
At least I know the reason why

SWEETNESS...
I let the good one get away
Sweetness...
If you found love I'll be okay.

"WOW." Adam nudged my shoulder. "Fire up the panty cannons. That is so romantic."

"It's...something," I stammered. Confusing was the first word that sprang to mind.

After the last chord died away, Nixon yelled, "Thank you very much!" and walked off the stage.

"All done?" Vivi asked with a yawn.

"There might be one more," Adam cautioned.

Indeed, after the audience stomped and whistled for five solid minutes, a solitary stagehand appeared with a chair. He set it in the middle of the stage, then placed a microphone in front of it. A moment later, Jonas walked onto the stage alone, carrying only an acoustic guitar, and sat down.

The crowd got quiet to see what he'd do.

"I hope you'll indulge me in an encore, unplugged," he said, his voice whiskey-rough from a night of singing. The crowd applauded, and he went on. "I don't remember much about my parents. They died when I was young. But one of my memories is having my hair washed by my mom. And she used to sing to me while she did it. One day I started to cry, and she thought it was because she got soap in my eyes. But really, it was just the song. It's one of those that's both sad and happy."

He strummed the guitar absently while he spoke.

"Five years ago almost to this day I started whistling it to a friend of mine. I don't even know why it popped into my head. Just one of those things, I guess. But it's the perfect song, and I'm going to sing it to you now."

Oh hell, I thought. And then the stage got blurry as Jonas sang the first words to "You Are My Sunshine." By the time he sang "please don't take my sunshine away," I had to wipe tears from my face.

"Huh. Shot scored," Adam said.

"I know this song," Vivi said from Adam's arms. Then she gave a big yawn, and put her head on Adam's shoulder.

"Your daddy said that he was singing this one just for your mama," Adam said. Vivi's response was to fall asleep.

* * *

AFTER THE CONCERT ENDED, we waited by our seats, avoiding the crush of the crowd. But as the audience drained away, I saw Ethan waiting for us at the end of the row.

"Follow me," he said, fullbacking through the stragglers towards a stage door. A beefy guy in a SECURITY T-shirt stepped aside when Ethan showed him a pass.

After a quick walk through the back of the outdoor venue and into a cordoned-off area, Ethan opened the door to a shiny sedan. There was a car seat set up for Vivi, and Adam poured her into it and clipped the harness.

"Jonas wanted me to tell you he'll be a half hour or so behind you," Ethan said as I slipped into the back beside my daughter. "He has a few hands to shake before he can get away."

"I'm sure he has plenty to do," I said. In fact, I should probably just head home. Except I'd left my overnight bag in Jonas's hotel room. *Nice job, subconscious.* "Are you getting in?" I asked my brother.

Adam raked a hand through his hair. "Well... I think I'm going to stop by the afterparty for a little while."

I could only blink up at him in surprise. "Oh! Sure. You should totally do that." Who knew my nerdy lawyer brother would want to drink with a bunch of rock stars?

He blew me a kiss. "Goodnight." The door closed, and a few seconds later, the car headed for the hotel.

FIFTEEN

JONAS

After the show, I was cornered by a beefy Boston radio DJ who wanted to talk about "Sweetness." We were standing outdoors under the awning at the rear of the band shell.

"It's like poetry, but with a poppy backbeat," the DJ gushed, swigging a beer. "And the bridge is just seminal."

"Thanks, man!" I kept my smile pasted on, but my eyes drifted to where Ethan stood. That man needed to get the hell over here and rescue me from this fuckwad.

"This one's gonna go big," the DJ said, sweating through his Hawaiian shirt.

"I sure hope so," I returned, trying to sound modest. Trying to sound even half civil.

I wondered if Kira had made it back to the hotel suite yet. And—more importantly—what the hell she was thinking. I'd just spent the last two hours seeing my life with fresh eyes. Now I was dying to know how put off Kira was by the onstage strutting and the screaming hordes.

The music didn't embarrass me. The music was good. At least, it was as good as I could make it. The songs I wrote always sounded better in my head than they did in the recording studio.

But I could live with that. Creative frustration came with the territory.

The circus of a concert, though, that was something else. I'd forgotten about the underwear throwing, for starters. It's not like I had a collection at home.

What *did* happen to all those flying thongs, anyway? The stadium must have a dumpster out back just for women's panties.

And then there was the line of hardcore fans outside the ropes. Security men were planted in a row, like shrubberies, one man every three or four feet, just to make sure the fans didn't storm the place. Some of them would be teenage boys who'd spent all their free hours learning guitar riffs in their bedrooms. I'd been one of those, once, too. I could almost understand waiting like penned cattle for a glimpse of a favorite player and for the slim chance of a hand-shake or an autograph.

But quite a few of those fans were drawn to fame for fame's sake. Some people wanted a taste of us just because other people wanted a taste of us. We were desired simply because we were desired.

God, it made my head spin. And when I imagined explaining it to Kira, I didn't even know where to start.

What sane woman would want a guy that dealt with all this craziness? She'd probably rather be with a guy who came home every night at six, and whose coworkers weren't drunk or stoned half the time. And who didn't have to make a lot of small talk with radio DJs. The guy in front of me was *still* talking.

"Jonas," Ethan's voice rumbled over my shoulder. *Finally*. "You have that conference call with your Chinese record label in three minutes," he said.

"Dude, you're right," I said, reaching out to shake the DJ's hand one more time. Ethan and I used this same fake excuse at least three nights a week. "Duty calls," I lied, begging off.

"Great show, man. Great show," the DJ said before walking off.

I felt suddenly weary. I let Ethan lead me over to a bank of lockers, where the big man extracted my wallet and phone from one of them, handing them over. "Here you go, Jojo. The car is ready to take you to the hotel."

And to Kira. "Can I get a beer?" I heard myself ask.

Ethan had a Sam Adams in his hand. He offered it to me.

"What, I don't get my own? Just a sip from Mom's bottle?"

"I thought you were leaving. There's plenty of beer in your hotel room. I checked."

"Maybe I should stay," I wondered aloud. "I could keep an eye on Nixon."

Ethan shook his giant head. "No. No, Jojo. Don't do this."

"Do what?"

"You're stalling."

"No, I'm not," I lied.

"Maybe I'm your paid slave, but I am not an idiot," he said, his tone as grumpy as I'd ever heard it. "Man up, would you? Go back to the hotel and tell your girl that you meant every word."

"She's not my girl," I muttered. I'd been an idiot to say all those things on stage. In Maine, Kira had accused me of going all "rock-star power trip" in front of that ex-boyfriend of hers. And I'd vigorously denied it.

She'd been *right*, too. The sight of another man sitting across the table from Kira had made me crazy. The pull I felt whenever I looked at her was undeniable, but that didn't make me worthy of her. I couldn't make myself into a better man just by wishing for it. And I couldn't make her trust me just by telling a large audience how much I loved her.

She was probably back at the hotel right this minute, thinking of all the different ways she might tell me to take a hike.

"Look," Ethan said. "Someone has to watch Nixon, but that someone is me. If you stay at this party, then I have to look out for *both* of you fools. I'll have to keep him from self-destructing, and save you from your broody self. Do me a favor and get the fuck out of here. I might get laid tonight if it doesn't all go sideways."

"Wait." I laughed. "You want me to go home, so you can hook up?"

Ethan gave me a little shove toward the venue gates. "There are a hundred good reasons for you to go back to the hotel right now. I'm just sharing the highlights. Can I tell this driver that you're on your way? Pretty please?"

"Fine."

Ethan took out his phone and tapped the screen.

I scanned the party, trying to see it through Kira's eyes. Nixon had already locked onto a couple of fans. The three of them stood, beers in hand, getting to know each other a little better before they all got stoned and naked, probably in that order.

Then there were the roadies carrying equipment to the trucks. They had no hope of getting either beers or girls until all the work of breaking down the show was done. Against one wall, Kira's brother Adam stood listening as one of the guitar techs told a story, gesturing madly with his hands while Adam grinned.

"Let's roll," Ethan said, pocketing his phone.

He pointed to a car, and the two of us jogged toward freedom. Security staff began moving the fans aside, making way for us. "Jonas! Jonas!" the women screamed. "Over here, baby!"

When I was younger, I used to shake hands and sign autographs with the fans on the other side of those ropes. But I'd learned interacting only fed the beast. The types who rushed the security ropes after a show could be pretty fucking scary, thrusting things at me to sign, grabbing my T-shirt, trying to yank me over the rope.

The moment the car door opened, I launched through the parted clot of outstretched arms and dove into the sedan. Ethan slammed the door behind me, and the driver hit the locks. Then the car began inching forward, nudging through the crowd that formed around the darkened windows.

This was why we'd sent Kira ahead, alone. If she got a look at this, she'd take her daughter and run like hell.

It took ten minutes to thread through the crowd, and then

only two minutes to drive to the hotel. The driver brought me to the service entrance, and I slipped into a maintenance elevator without incident. I put my key card into the slot granting me access to the club level, and seconds later I was standing outside my door, letting myself in.

I tiptoed inside, wondering if Kira was still here. The lights were low, and the door to the double bedroom was still open, so I crept around, slipping my gym bag to the floor before poking my head into Kira's room. She lay on the bed fully dressed, next to Vivi's short little form. Even as I sneaked across the room toward them, Kira put a finger to her lips.

I stopped beside the bed. Vivi's satin eyelids were shut tight. In one arm she clutched a purple kitty—the same stuffed animal I'd won at the fair all those years ago. It was smaller than I remembered, and it had not aged well. Some of the fur had been rubbed off its head.

I couldn't have looked away to save my life. And it was impossible to say which of the two girls on the bed was responsible for the lump in my throat—the beautiful child asleep on her pillow, or the gentle eyes of her young mother looking up at me.

How many times had I returned to a hotel room after a show? Three hundred times? Five hundred? Never had anyone of any importance ever been waiting for me. Not once. I had never allowed myself to imagine how this would feel—finishing up a grueling performance (they were all grueling) and finding a family waiting.

I pushed that thought aside. "Kira," I whispered, bending down next to her ear. "I'm going to shower, because I am disgusting. But I was hoping you'd have a drink with me." I pointed towards the living room.

She nodded, and my heart gave an optimistic tug. I made myself turn around and walk back to my room, closing the door as quietly as humanly possible.

Alone in the marble shower stall, I tried not to think how

badly I wanted to remove all of Kira's clothing and spread her out on the king-sized bed.

But I knew better than to expect her to feel the same. Just because I'd basically told fifteen thousand people that I still loved Kira didn't mean she wanted a demonstration of how much.

I rinsed the soap off my body, turned the shower off, and dried with a big, fluffy towel. Then I pulled on some jeans, but no shirt. After a summer concert under thousands of watts of lighting, it always took hours to stop perspiring.

There was no sign of Kira in the darkened living room. So I grabbed my dinner plate out of the refrigerator and put it in the spotless microwave oven. I was leaning against the counter, drinking a quart of water and wolfing down reheated chicken and potatoes when she emerged from the bedroom, closing the door softly behind her.

"Hi," she said quietly.

"Hi, yourself." I set down my empty plate as Kira made her way over to me. "So. What did you think of the whole circus?"

She shoved her hands in her pockets. "Where to start?"

"That bad, huh?" I opened the fridge and pulled out two beers.

"No, it was amazing. But—Jonas—it's weird to be you. All those women screaming your name."

"Some of the men, too," I joked. "But that's just another day at the office for me."

She gave me an assessing stare as she accepted the beer. "That's what you're going with?"

"Yes? No? You're right. It's super weird. But when I sat down to write my first song at age fourteen, I wasn't gunning for that. I just wanted to write something pretty. It's not really my fault that people yell my name. I'm sure it's skewed my world view, but I can't tell you how much because I'm trapped here in my own weird existence, where people follow me into the bathroom and it seems normal to spend two grand on a hotel room."

"Two *grand*." Kira glanced around, looking more horrified than impressed.

"Hotels force us onto pricey floors for security purposes."

"Eesh." She took a sip of beer. "So tell me—what am I doing here?"

"Obviously you're here to validate my fucked-up world view."

She rolled her eyes.

"Kidding! You're just here having a beer with me. Like we always did."

"Jonas, there was no *always*. There was just one weird summer, when neither of us was living in the real world." She took another sip of her beer and regarded me in a way that was almost cool. Now that the shock of seeing me again had worn off, she looked more calm and collected than I'd ever seen her.

I wasn't, though. I would never be able to play it cool when she was around. She was *the one*. And suddenly I felt desperate to let her know that. "Come sit down with me."

I flipped off the kitchen lights and crossed the big living space with only the city lights illuminating my path. The darkness was a nice change from the stage. I sat down on the sofa.

Kira sat down too—about five feet away from me. It was not the encouraging sign I was looking for.

"Are you hungry?" I asked her. "There's still food in the fridge. Or we could order something for you."

Kira shook her head. "Thanks, I'm fine."

I tipped my head toward the door where Vivi lay sleeping. "She *sleeps* with that purple cat?"

"She loves Purple Kitty. I don't know why." Kira paused a beat. "Actually, I once told her that her daddy gave it to me."

Oh, man. That had to mean something. Didn't it? "You know, that cat has seen better days. Seems like her daddy should spring for a nicer stuffy."

At that, Kira finally flashed me a smile. "That's the funny thing. She has dozens of stuffies. Every one of them is newer and fancier than that one. She says she loves them all, but she keeps coming back to Purple Kitty. I have to trick her into washing it every once in a while."

"Purple Kitty has been through the washer?"

"Sure. Purple Kitty leads a dangerous life on the front lines. When the tummy bugs happen, Purple Kitty is right there."

"Unlucky kitty!" I laughed. "You know, I have a friend who swears that rock and roll is good training for being a parent. Because you already know how to stay up all night, and you're not afraid of a little puke."

"Interesting theory," Kira murmured, watching me from the other end of the couch. She'd tucked her legs up, putting up even more barriers between us.

"I'm not saying I know anything about raising kids. But I'm ready to learn. You must have had a hard time, Kira. I can't imagine how you've done everything—taking care of Vivi and going to school, too."

She shrugged. "I seem to be on the ten-year plan at school. But every mom of little kids does some juggling. I've learned that it's never easy. I'm just one of the ranks."

"But I know it's held you back. You can't tell me that you didn't sacrifice a lot to have her."

"Sure. But I get back a lot, too. It sounds counterintuitive, but being a single mom proved to me that I was tougher than I thought. Taking college courses with peanut butter on my T-shirt... It's not the end of the world. Even without a child, I wasn't destined to be much of a party girl."

"Money must be tight." It was a topic that needed to be discussed eventually.

"We get by okay," she said quickly. "There are single moms at Vivi's daycare who don't have enough money to buy their kids an ice cream cone. Honestly, Adam has sacrificed more than I have. Both time and money."

Interesting. "He seems really involved."

"You have no idea. He's supported us for four years, although he doesn't like to hear me put it like that. We live with him, and I pay no rent. Whenever I talk about maybe working full time instead of chipping my way toward graduation, he talks me out of it. He says, 'We're doing fine. We don't need the money, and you need the degree.' Adam has a good job at a great law firm, so he's not lying about the money. But he doesn't have much of a life."

"Why?"

She was quiet for a moment before answering. "I take classes at night, or work as a teaching assistant at the university. So he's home babysitting. He hasn't had a boyfriend since Vivi was born, because he won't bring guys into the house."

"How come?"

"Well... he's funny that way. He's totally out of the closet, of course. But my father has always told him that it's unnatural and has said some things about how wrong it is to raise a child in a gay household. He said, 'At least Kira didn't have a little *boy*.' I get mad just thinking about it. But it's as if a little part of Adam believes him."

I whistled. "This is your father who calls his son unnatural and his daughter a slut? And Adam listens?"

"I know it doesn't make sense. But he's our dad. He's gruff and ornery even when he's trying to be nice. We try not to hear the worst of it, but it's hard."

"You know what, Kira? I just spent the last week asking myself if I'm fit to be somebody's dad. But I can sure as hell do better than that." I plucked Kira's ankles off the sofa, pulling her feet into my lap. "Are you okay? You look tired."

"I am tired," she agreed. "I didn't sleep all that well this week."

"And then I dragged you out to a mediocre concert."

She sipped her beer, her big eyes studying me. "The concert was amazing, Jonas. But I don't know why you're fishing for compliments. You already have the world's approval."

"Maybe yours matters the most."

She stared at me like I wasn't making sense. "I loved the concert. Do you need a sticker for your sticker chart?"

A bark of laughter escaped me. "Maybe I do." She smiled at

me, then, and it made me foolishly happy. I put my hands on the arches of her bare feet and squeezed. God, I wanted to touch her. Hold her. I wanted all the things.

And I only had a few more hours in her presence.

I put a hand on her bare leg, skimming two fingers from her ankle to her calf. Kira's eyes snapped downward, watching me. "Look," I whispered. "It's only fair to tell you that I want to spend time with you. Not just for Vivi's sake." I gave her knee a light caress.

Kira's eyes were still locked on my hand where it touched her. "Why?"

"What do you mean, *why?* Because I miss you like crazy. And I always have."

Kira let out a shaky breath and shook her head. "You can't say things like that to me."

"Why not? It's true." I gently shifted her feet to the floor and slid across the sofa until we were hip to hip. I wrapped an arm around her, pulling her close to me. *Finally.* "That's better. I've been wanting to hold you for, oh, about a million years."

Kira shivered, so I did what came naturally. I turned my head, brushing a kiss across her temple. It was barely a kiss, more like a warm breeze on a summer night. Still, I felt her shiver again. I threw caution to the wind and went for it, turning to find her mouth with mine.

And it was just like that day on the dock. Our mouths came together like this was meant to happen. Like we had no other choice. Warm, soft lips parted for mine.

The kiss was as soft as I could manage. But I needed her so badly that I was lucky to keep it on the right side of civilized. It didn't help that her soft hair caressed my shoulders, making me too aware of my bare skin. Making me feel crazy. On a groan, I slanted my mouth across hers, deepening the kiss. And when she let me taste her, it was glorious.

She was *meant* to be mine. Nothing would ever convince me otherwise. Pulling her body flush against my own, I kissed her long and hard. The next few minutes were the sweetest victory I'd ever tasted.

"Wait," she gasped suddenly, pushing on my shoulders.

Five years later, the word still penetrated my lusty haze. I pulled back, breathing like a sprinter after the hundred-meter dash.

"You don't get to toy with me like this," she said, leaning away from me. "'Poor little lonely Kira. We had a hot night once. And she wanted more, but I blew her off. But, hey! We're in the same zip code for a night, so let's get it on.'"

My head swam as I tried to follow this sudden transition. "It's not like that."

"I think it is."

"Never," I breathed. "You mean more to me than anyone else ever will."

"How can you say that?" she yelped. "You didn't sing that tune when you had the chance!" She slid off the couch, scrambling to her feet. I saw a sheen of tears in her eyes as she turned away.

"Kira," I ground out.

But it was too late. She slipped into the darkened double bedroom and closed the door with a firm click.

I sat there for a minute, trying to calm my pounding heart. I'd fucked up *again*. Kissing her had been so very stupid. *Way to be trustworthy, asshole.* It's just that I wanted Kira to know how I really felt. And even though I'd won a Grammy for writing songs about heartbreak, this time I hadn't used my words.

Yup. I blew it.

I blew out a frustrated breath, stood up, and adjusted my jeans. Heading into my room, I went into the marble bath to brush my teeth.

Steady, I told my reflection. This wasn't over. In fact, it was just beginning. Tomorrow, before my tour bus left, I would figure out my next chance to see Kira and Vivi. And I wouldn't fuck it up again.

Kira deserved patience. It had been patience that had given me our magical night together. And it had given me Vivi.

I'd been waiting five years. I could wait five more if I had to.

Back in my bedroom, I stripped off my jeans, tossing them onto a chair. I got into bed in the nude. Sliding across the expanse of the king-sized bed, my erection brushed against the cool, high-thread-count hotel sheets.

Heated kisses—and memories—had me all fired up and ready to go. There were, of course, dozens of women at that show tonight who would have happily solved this problem for me. But I didn't want any of those women. I wanted Kira. Alone in the giant bed, I flexed my hips a single time to acknowledge the yearning. Wanting her felt right and necessary.

I jammed the pillow into the hollow of my neck and made myself as comfortable as I could. Patience would be me new mantra. It would have to be.

SIXTEEN

KIRA

In the silent, darkened room, I perched on the edge of the empty bed, trying to figure out what had just happened. Not that it was tricky.

I panicked. And then I blamed it on Jonas.

So I made everything awkward. Yay.

There were plenty of good reasons not to make out with Jonas on the sofa. He and I were in the midst of legally negotiating his relationship with Vivi. That was no simple matter. I needed to keep a clear head.

But who was I kidding? There was no keeping a clear head when he was around. Every encounter with him since the first one had left me quivering with desire and uncertainty. Why would tonight be any different?

I liked to think that I'd changed since that summer when we met. I was more confident now. I'd come a long way from that tentative girl who needed a man to walk her home every night. I was close to finishing my college degree. I held down a job. I was a terrific cook and a single mom.

There was one big gap in my confidence, however, and that gap was sex. Physical intimacy was still mysterious to me.

When Jonas kissed me, my response had been so swift and

thrilling that I freaked right out. Not like before—I wasn't afraid for my safety tonight. But boy, had I been overwhelmed.

And now I was just embarrassed.

I pulled out my phone to check the time. It was ten thirty. I was too wired to go to sleep yet, so I texted my brother. *Was it a good party?*

I soon got an answer. *Yeah. Still ongoing.*

Now *that* was a surprise. It was so unlike Adam to go out drinking with strangers. I tapped out a hasty reply. *Who is this and what have you done with Adam?*

Very funny. Are you OK?

Ugh. Not the question I wanted to answer. *Fine*, I lied. *I didn't throw my panties.*

Smart, he replied quickly. *I don't trust him.*

I flinched. It was all well and good for me to hold Jonas at arms' length, because I knew that Jonas made me stupid. But if Adam didn't like him, then maybe I should pay attention.

My brother sent one last message. *Got to go. Guy I've been flirting with has brought me another beer.*

Have fun, I replied.

He replied only with a smiley face.

I pocketed my phone and let my eyes adjust to the darkness. In the other bed, Vivi was sacked out on her tummy, dreaming of ponies and cupcakes, probably.

And what would I be dreaming of, exactly? I'd just shouted down the hottest musician in North America. I'd pushed away the only man with whom I'd ever had a transcendent sexual experience. Now I was supposed to go to sleep, even though my nerves were still jangling.

Standing beside the bed, I peeled off my clothes in silence. I picked up my bag and carried it into the bathroom for a better view of its contents. After closing the door and flipping on the light, I was confronted by my naked reflection in the mirror. Appraising my body was something I rarely did, but the mirror took up most of the wall, and there was no escaping it.

Really not bad, was my first reaction.

I was twenty-five years old, inhabiting a body which had given birth to a nearly eight-pound baby girl, but my waist was still slim, flaring to feminine hips. After nursing Vivi for a year, my breasts weren't precisely the same shape as before. But my skin was smooth, and my curves stood out. I was still young, damn it. But for how much longer?

The girl in the mirror was frowning now.

With another sigh, I found my nightgown in my bag. It was new, actually. I usually slept in oversized T-shirts that I stole from my brother. But this morning, on the way back from the playground, I had dragged Vivi into a shop to purchase this nightgown.

Now I held the traitorous object up to the light. Black jersey, with flowers printed on it, the V-necked nightie wasn't silky or particularly low cut. But it had black satin trim and spaghetti straps. And more to the point, I'd bought it because I'd thought there was some chance, however small, that Jonas would see it.

You hypocrite, Kira. Nicely done.

I had just given Jonas an earful for daring to kiss me. And yet I'd spent forty-two dollars to look sexy for him.

I yanked the fabric over my head then took one more look at the girl in the mirror, at the expanse of skin that never got touched by hands other than my own. The gown made a nice line of cleavage across breasts that had tightened in anticipation when Jonas had kissed me.

Guess what? Regret runs in two directions, genius. I could tell myself that Jonas didn't really mean all the loving things he'd said to me tonight, and I might even be right about it. But there was no prize for being right, except for loneliness. I could hold Jonas off, and try to make him prove that he meant what he said. But how long was long enough? A month? Six?

And what if we *were* a good match? When would he grow tired of trying to prove himself to me? On one of those future visits, when Jonas swung by to take Vivi to the zoo, he might someday say, "I've met someone." How would that feel?

Horrible. That's how.

I turned off the bathroom light and padded back through the bedroom. Then, before I could change my mind, I opened the door and tiptoed across the living room. I put my hand on the knob. For a millisecond, I worried that Jonas had been so fed up that he'd locked the door. But no. It clicked open, and I slipped inside, closing the door behind me.

The room was lit only by the clock on the bedside table, but I could see him lying on his side, facing the windows. "Jonas?" I whispered, trying not to startle him. "I'm sorry I yelled at you. I just panicked a little."

He rolled onto his back. "I fucked up, Kira."

"It's okay," I said quickly.

Jonas shook his head. "No, I mean five years ago." He sat, propping himself against the cushioned headboard. I got an excellent view of his bare chest and tried not to stare. "Hey, come here, will you? Let me explain."

I hesitated for a beat. But Jonas patted the vast expanse of empty bed beside him, so I climbed on top of the bedspread. As soon as I got near him, he tugged me closer, looping an arm around me, until we were sitting side by side. He kissed my temple just once, and quickly. "Thank you," he whispered. "It's easier for me to tell you all the stupid shit I've done if I don't have to shout."

"Like what?" I asked, squeezing my eyes shut to keep from staring at the lush geography of his abs. But there were other distracting sensations that came from being tucked against Jonas. He smelled like clean linens and man, and his skin gave off a delicious heat.

"I didn't answer your letter," he whispered.

My heart spasmed. "Did you even read it?"

Jonas used his hand to tip my head onto his shoulder. "Here's where it gets weird," he said in a low voice. "I read it every day for two years. I carried it in my pocket wherever I went. That letter has been to Australia and Japan. And a bunch of other places, too."

"What? Why?" I breathed.

Jonas let out a sigh. "Because that's how much I liked it. Reading that you cared about me felt like winning the lottery. I wanted to see you again so bad. But I was afraid of fucking things up. I didn't trust myself enough to follow through."

"That makes no sense," I argued.

He turned to kiss the top of my head. "It doesn't make sense to *you*," he said, "because you're not an immature twenty-five-year-old guy."

"I am too twenty-five."

He chuckled, and I was so close to him that I felt the vibration in my own chest. "Kira, the fact that I'm five years older than you is not even *enough*. You already have more sense than I ever will. And that's why I didn't tell you all of this right away. I want you to believe in me, even though I've been such an idiot. It's not an easy sell."

"Well... I'm not sure what you want me to say."

"I want you to say that we have a chance. Or at least that you'll consider it. Not just for Vivi's sake. I'd want you whether we made a baby or not."

There were goosebumps on my bare shoulders. It wasn't easy to keep my wits about me when I was cuddled up against the hottest man I'd ever met. And he'd just said something about making babies.

Focus, Kira. There were still lots of reasons why this was a bad idea. "It's not that I think you're trying to... trick me or something. But you haven't thought this through. You and I lead very different lives. You're traipsing the world, but our life in Boston is quiet. A big event at our house is like... taco night."

Jonas gave a sexy little grunt of disagreement. "I think you're overestimating this so-called big life of mine." He palmed my lower back and gave it a squeeze that I felt *everywhere*. "What looks like a big life to you can feel pretty damned small. When I got in the car tonight after the show, there were a dozen girls yelling my name. But they don't know me at all, Kira. I'm too old to think that's cool anymore. I just want..." He seemed to be reaching for the right words. "I just want two girls who look up at me when I come in the door at night. I want to hear, 'Hey, we *missed* you today. And by the way, it's taco night.'"

I tried to picture it—a future in which *People's* Sexiest Man Alive came home after work to eat tacos in my kitchen. Even Vivi's yearnings for a pony sounded more realistic. And if it didn't work out? Disaster. "If things went badly between us, it would hurt Vivi."

He rubbed my back. "Is that your objection? Because if things are great between us, that's good for her, right? I want us all to be together."

I tipped my head to look him in the eye. "You say that," I whispered, "because you feel guilty." He opened his mouth to object, but I raised a hand. "I know you're going to love Vivi, because she is irresistible. But you shouldn't assume that there really is more between us."

His turquoise eyes got wide. "There was *always* more, Kira. That's what I've been trying to tell you."

"Five years was a long time ago, Jonas."

Slowly, he shook his head. "When I look at you, it feels like five minutes."

"We weren't even together then."

"We should have been. I loved you so much more than the ex-girlfriend I'd just left. Every time I'd come to Boston, I'd think about you the whole time. I just wish I'd done something about it."

I turned away, because it was too hard to keep the shock off my face. "When you're in Boston, I look for you in the crowds," I admitted.

"*Jesus,* Kira," he breathed. "What a waste, right?" He held me a little more tightly. Tipping his head back against the pillows, he closed his eyes. "I won't rush you, sweetness. But I have to say that just having you next to me right now makes me so happy. I've loved you a long time."

My eyes got hot, and my throat felt tight, which was all very inconvenient. What I needed was a few hours alone to try to process all the things that Jonas had said. I could just say so, and toddle off to the empty bed in the other room. Except his fingers were tracing a soft circle on my back. It wasn't an overtly sexual touch, but it might as well have been. There was no place that Jonas Smith could touch my body that wouldn't make me instantly and urgently aware of him.

"Jonas," I said, my voice roughened by both emotion and desire. "It's hard for me to put aside the fact that you could have anyone."

"But so could you." He pulled me even closer. "There isn't anyone else I want, sweetness. You *disarm* me, the way nobody else can. I don't know any way to prove it to you. But it's true." His thumb brushed my lip with such tenderness that I almost couldn't bear it. "Be with me, Kira. In my heart, I really just want you."

The world went a little blurry then, and I felt Jonas's thumb sweep a tear off my cheek. "I worry that it's not that simple," I said, my voice cracking.

"It's *just* that simple," he whispered. In the darkness, the color of his eyes was lost, but not their intensity. For a moment, we only stared at one another. But then we were kissing again. I wasn't even sure how it happened. I probably started it.

But I wasn't sorry. His lips were firm and hungry against my own. When he kissed me like this, it was possible to believe that he needed me as badly as he'd said.

On a sigh, I opened for him. He swept inside, his mouth hot and needy. When his tongue slid between my teeth, I heard a guttural groan, and realized that I'd made it myself.

The sound brought me back to reality. I broke our kiss, burying my face in Jonas's neck.

His arms softened around me. "I won't rush you," he whispered. "I want you to get used to the idea. Used to me."

"Mmm," I said, listening to my heart galloping like one of Vivi's storybook ponies.

"I can be a patient man," he said.

"Okay," I whispered. The trouble with that idea was that his rock-star body was still pressed against my own. My skin felt feverish everywhere we touched.

"Here," he said, scooting down to lie on his back. "Put your head right here. Just let me hold you."

That sounded nice. I flipped the comforter down and slid in beside him, so I could cuddle closer. I put my head on his shoulder and a hand on his chest.

"See?" He sifted a lock of my hair onto his chest. "This is perfect. Never thought I'd hold you again." He kissed the top of my head.

It was perfect. Except that the most lickable chest I'd ever seen was currently in use as my pillow, and the desire circulating through my veins with every pump of my heart was difficult to ignore.

I let my hand wander on his torso, exploring all that beautiful skin practically begging to be touched. Jonas sighed, closing his eyes.

When my hand dipped beneath the bedclothes, I discovered that no clothing impeded me at all. My hand slid freely past his waist, my fingers trailing through the soft hairs on his belly. His muscles contracted, and I grazed his erection as I quickly withdrew.

I whimpered at the discovery that Jonas Smith was naked in this bed.

Jonas caught my hand, bringing it up to his mouth. He kissed my palm. "Sweetness, you're making it hard for a guy to be patient."

"It's your fault," I whispered.

"How's that?"

"You're so *hot*." I jerked my hand free of his grasp and put it under his chin, where I could feel him chuckling. With my thumb, I skimmed his lower lip, measuring his smile, until he opened his mouth, sucking my thumb inside. He moaned, his tongue warm and wet against my skin.

"Oh my God." I felt myself flood with desire.

He released me with a groan. "Okay. I tried. I really did."

One second later, Jonas rolled on top of me, and the spark that was always between us ignited into flames. His kiss was hot and demanding, his hard body a satisfying weight on mine.

"Damn," I gasped, stunned at how unbearably good he felt, and how badly I wanted him. Jonas was both passionate and beautiful. And when he inevitably withdrew the hot blaze of his attention, the chill he'd leave behind would be devastating.

But this was no time to worry about that. With each kiss, we were more lost in each other. Arms grasping, legs tangled, I never wanted it to stop.

"Kira," he finally rasped between kisses. "Am I allowed to take this off?" He skimmed a big hand down my nightgown, pausing to gently squeeze my breast, before plunging down to my hips and thighs. "Or are we waiting?"

I tried to take in enough oxygen to understand the question. "For what?" I gasped.

"I don't know." He chuckled into my neck. "I want to make love to you. But only if you're ready for that. I feel like I talked you into it."

"I got into your bed, Jonas. I talked myself into it."

Still breathing hard, he grinned at me. "Every guy wants to hear that a girl has *convinced* herself to climb into bed with him." He lifted off my nightgown nonetheless.

"I didn't mean..."

"I *know* that. Just a little joke, okay? Because I need a minute to calm down." He tucked me into his side, rubbing my back. "It's been a long time since there was anyone special in my life. The last person I was out-of-my-mind excited to hold was you."

That idea made my stomach flutter. "Well. The last person who did hold me was you."

The hand on my back went still. "Really?" His voice was rough.

I probably shouldn't have said that. It would only make me feel more self-conscious. "I've been a little busy. It's not all that strange, for someone with a toddler."

"That's..." He blew out a breath. "I'm sorry, Kira. You deserve better than that. I never wanted you to be alone."

"I'm not alone right now," I said.

"I guess not," he said in a low voice.

Somehow, a little twinge of sadness had stolen under the door and drifted into bed with us. I wanted to chase it away. I ran an admiring hand down his chest. "You're so beautiful."

"Isn't that my line?" He sat up, tugging on my hand until I sat up, too. Then he wrapped his arms around me in a hug. "It feels so good to touch you, Kira. I never thought I'd have another chance."

"It's crazy," I whispered.

"No..." He kissed the sweet spot just beneath my ear. "It's *right*." He spent a long moment exploring all the sensitive little places down my neck. "I wonder how much attention I can give you before the sun rises," he asked, his voice gruff. "I'm going to spoil you."

"Mmm?" I was barely listening now. He was sliding both his hands onto my breasts.

"I'm going to spoil you so good," he whispered.

And I believed him. Because everything about the night we'd once shared had been *so good*. I drank in more of Jonas's kisses. He smiled against my lips, any sadness being chased away by his warm hands.

"Come with me, sweetness. I need to find a condom." He patted my thigh, and I slid out of bed so that Jonas could get up.

He went into the bathroom, which was dimly lit. I followed him, drawn like a moth to the flame. I kissed him between the shoulder blades while he opened a bag and fished a packet out. He tore the wrapper open. "Now, sweetness. Tell me how you want me. Just like you did the last time."

"Last time I was in charge."

"That's fine," Jonas said quickly.

"No, it isn't. These days I'm always in charge, twenty-four seven." I held up a hand. "I know that's my choice. But not tonight."

Jonas's expression grew serious as he cupped my face. "Funny. Every damned thing I do is for me alone, and I'm done with that, too. You need someone else to be in charge, for once?"

I tipped forward, wanting to feel his skin against mine. "If only for an hour."

He wrapped his arms around me. "Two would be even better." His hands skimmed the bare skin of my back, my waist... my ass. When he spoke again, it was in a husky voice. "Last time was all about you doing something you needed."

"Yes," I said into his shoulder.

"This time, there's something I need."

"Mmm?" It was hard to think when we were both naked, and he was touching me.

"I need to prove it to you." He dipped his head to kiss me.

"Prove what?" I asked against his lips.

"That you're mine," he rasped, kissing me again. "For keeps."

My belly quivered. Jonas slid a hand down my torso until his fingers grazed the outer fringe of my sex, and my quiver gave way to trembling.

"This." He teased me with the barest tips of his fingers. "I'm keeping this."

I swallowed a moan. I wasn't sure how I felt about his possessive tone. My body, on the other hand, didn't have any issues with it.

Jonas grabbed my hips and turned my body toward the bathroom mirror. "See this?" he asked. "Mine. These..." He rubbed his palms over my hips. "Mine. And this right here..." He bent to nibble at the place where my neck met my shoulder, working it with his lips and then his tongue. I bit the inside of my cheek to keep from gasping. "Mine," he said.

Feeling unsteady, I leaned back against Jonas, but more contact made things worse. His firm, hot body radiated heat and desire, and his ambitious erection stabbed me in the back.

I swayed, but he caught me, wrapping me in his arms. "Mmm," he groaned into my ear. "These," he cupped my breasts.

"Definitely keeping these." He made that point very convincingly, too, by teasing my nipples.

I gasped, forgetting to hold it in.

Jonas let go of me to grab a folded towel off a stack nearby. After placing it on the counter in front of me, he took my elbows in hand and gently leaned me forward. And I did as I was asked.

With a groan, Jonas pulled my hips back. As he curled his body around mine, I watched us in the mirror. Jonas hovered over my shoulder, his expression serious, eyes closing as his lips traced my shoulder. With one hand he cupped the side of my flushed face, and with the other, he stroked my quivering body. Then he opened his eyes, his gaze locking onto mine. I shivered with pleasure. He was impossibly sexy, the muscles in his arms flexing as he ran his hands over my ribcage. His eyes flashed in the low light, and then his forehead creased with longing. Just the desire on his face made me feel crazy.

Without breaking eye contact, Jonas lowered our bodies slightly, pressing his hard chest against my back. Between my legs, the head of his cock massaged my opening. The slick pressure made me shiver with happiness.

Jonas moaned. Without warning, he bent his knees and entered me in one quick slide. "Oh, fuck yes," he gasped. I agreed, but couldn't spare the words to say so. Because he was just so overwhelming.

He took a steadying breath and then dropped his head to the crook of my neck, kissing me tenderly. I raised a hand to his head and held him there, my heart quivering with excitement.

"Okay?" he asked.

I nodded, still unable to answer.

He curved his body around me, his forearms bracketing mine. He held my hands, his thumbs stroking toward my wrists. I watched his face in the mirror as he began to move against me in short, exquisite thrusts. His eyes fell briefly closed with pleasure, before snapping open again to meet my gaze. "I love you," he mouthed in the mirror, that sexy mouth puckering on the last vowel.

I groaned, pushing my bottom back against him. He flexed his hips, and I felt him so deeply that my breath caught. His tongue worshiped the nape of my neck. I turned my chin, trying to catch his mouth with my own. I wanted everything he could give me, and I wanted it right now. A frustrated huff escaped my lips.

He chuckled, nudging my chin until I faced the mirror again. "Who is in charge here?" he asked. "Tell me."

"You are," I gasped.

"That's right. Touch your breasts for me."

"What?" I asked, lost in a sex haze.

"You heard me." He grasped my wrists and crossed them, filling my hands with my bouncing breasts.

"Yessss," Jonas hissed, thrusting harder. "Good girl. You're so beautiful."

Something was beautiful, that was for sure. I had never seen anything as erotic as the two bodies in the mirror. His face was flushed, his eyes heavy with arousal.

He palmed my shoulders and pulled out. "Turn around," he demanded, and I did. Immediately. He grasped my hips, lifting me onto the counter. "I need you to hold me while I fuck you, Sweetness."

His words made me groan again. I had never in my life found the f-word sexy, until I heard Jonas rasp it into my ear. With shaking hands, I found his shoulders. He pushed my knees apart, making room for himself. The newer, braver Kira could do this— she could *fuck* on the counter of a hotel bathroom.

I could do it because the man who now tucked his hips tight against my body had such love in his eyes.

With one smooth thrust, he was inside me again. I drew him closer, until my breasts rubbed against his chest with each grind of his hips.

"Yes," I gasped into his neck.

"You like that?" He slipped a hand between our bodies,

forking his fingers over our connection. "Come for me," he demanded. "I want to hear you." His lips dipped down to catch mine, and then we were kissing again.

The multisensory assault was too much for me. "Oh..." I moaned into his mouth. I jerked my hips against his body and absolutely *shook* with pleasure.

In that exquisite moment, it was hard to believe that I'd seriously considered turning my back on him tonight.

SEVENTEEN

JONAS

I swallowed each of Kira's moans, the sound nearly finishing me off before I was ready. Holding her tightly, I took a slow, calming breath. "Beautiful," I rasped against her lips.

Her answer was a deep kiss, which I greedily accepted. I scooped her off the counter. Still inside her, I carried her to the bed, losing the connection only when I set her down. Kira scrambled backward, yanking down the covers. I prowled over her, admiring the sweep of her hair against the bedspread in the dim light.

I dropped my head to take her nipple in my mouth, swirling my tongue over her perfect breast. This gorgeous body had brought my child into the world. I wished I could have been there. But there was some amount of consolation in touching her beautiful body everywhere she'd allow it. "Mine," I whispered, moving over to show her other breast the same attention.

Kira made a noise of argument even as she arched her back, pushing more of her breast into my mouth.

Chuckling, I kissed my way back up her body, pausing to worship her neck and the sensitive spot below her ear.

Then, taking my time, I nudged her legs apart. "Mine," I whispered, teasing her entrance again.

"Doesn't it cut both ways?" she gasped.

"Does it?" I teased. "Do you want what's yours?"

She hummed, lifting her hips. I couldn't resist any longer. "Fine," I whispered, sinking slowly into her.

Kira spread herself even wider for me, making me groan. "Fuck, Kira." I rocked into her. "So good." My mouth dipped down to kiss a trail across her collarbone, finding the delicate pulse point at the base of her throat. The rhythm I set with my hips was like a slow, steady heartbeat. I never wanted it to end.

She reached for me, pulling me down until I was basking in sweetness and curves. This *was* mine. Mine and hers. The moment belonged to both of us, and we'd waited a long time for it. Nobody had ever held me quite like this—as if she needed me to anchor her to the earth.

"Tell me," I demanded. "Who loves you best?"

"Jonas..." she breathed.

I kissed her fiercely. "That's right, sweetness. That's what I needed to hear."

"I missed you..." She sighed against my mouth. "Missed you so much."

The sound of those words unhooked whatever control I'd had left. "Now you've done it. Fuck, I have to come." I let out a growl. Then, shaking, I planted myself deeply, and the sudden friction made Kira quiver beneath me.

"Jonas," she gasped, as if surprised. She arched her back, clutching my cock with her body.

"Jesus Christ." With a shameless moan, I clung to her as she rode it out. "So fucking beautiful."

Completely spent and not wanting to crush her, I rolled onto my side, taking her with me. We were both breathing hard, and I gave her slow, unfocused kisses. "I just need you, Kira," I panted.

She buried her face in my neck.

I wasn't sure how long we lay there together. I was too blissed out, and too exhausted to care.

"I should check on Vivi," Kira whispered eventually.

I roused myself a little, stroking her shoulder. "Can you just open the bedroom doors? I'll put on my shorts."

"Okay," she agreed. She stayed in my embrace for another minute and then slid off the bed. After putting on her nightgown, she opened the door and slipped out.

I staggered to my feet and made a brief visit to the bathroom. I put on a pair of boxers, then met Kira back in bed.

She turned, curling into me, and I took a deep, happy breath. There was no place on earth better than where I was right now —pressed against the only woman I'd ever loved. She smelled of sunshine and fresh air, and her smooth arms encircled me, holding on tight.

I caught Kira watching me, her eyes glinting in the dark.

"What is it, sweetness?"

"The condom was a smart move," she whispered. "You don't need more surprises from me."

I settled her head into the crook of my shoulder and held her tightly. "So far, your surprises are some of the best things that ever happened to me." I felt her body go absolutely still after I spoke. I knew she'd heard me, but she didn't reply.

I had the wildly romantic impulse to add that maybe we should skip the condom next time. If we had another baby, I could experience all the things I missed the first time around. But I didn't say it, because my gut told me that Kira had already put her heart as far over the line tonight as she could.

So that could wait. I stroked her silky hair, my eyelids pleasantly heavy. I dozed off for a while. When I opened my eyes, the clock read three thirty. Kira was asleep beside me, her hair tickling my bare chest.

During my tours, I'd often wake up in the night, my subconscious poking me to make sure I was in a safe place, and alone. But there would be no more wildness in my life. No more drunken exploits after a show. Lying here next to Kira, I knew that I wouldn't even be tempted.

She stirred in her sleep, and I couldn't resist pulling her a little closer. After a moment, her fingers splayed gently on my belly, tickling the fine hairs growing there. I lay awake just listening to her breathe. I could sleep tomorrow on the bus, when I'd be all alone again.

It wouldn't seem so lonely, though. Not anymore.

* * *

THE NEXT TIME I WOKE, I knew all was well before opening my eyes. I was lying on my side, my ankles tangled with Kira's, my hand resting on her hair.

It was the sound of soft little footsteps that roused me. They passed by Kira's side of the bed, then turned at my feet. There was a scramble for purchase, and then the sensation of someone crawling over my legs, trampling down the bedclothes between me and Kira.

A warm little body filled the valley there. "Me too," was all she said.

I held my breath as a little hand found my forearm, resting on my skin. I lay still, afraid to move a muscle. Maybe this perfect moment might last.

Vivi teased the hair on my arm with her fingertips, and Kira continued to breathe with a soft, sleepy rhythm.

Kira and I would never have childless years together. We'd skipped some things that normal couples enjoyed. We'd never duck out for a late dinner on a whim, or jet off for a carelessly romantic weekend.

But I'd squandered those years, hadn't I? I'd done every whimsical thing that there was, and come up empty. I'd played concerts on four continents. I'd gotten drunk in every four and five star hotel you could name.

Kira hadn't sewn any wild oats, though. And I began to imagine all the ways I might be able to make it up to her.

EIGHTEEN

ADAM

I hadn't done the walk of shame in years. But now I stood in the hotel lobby feeling hungover and a little embarrassed.

Last night, after warning my sister against throwing her panties at a hot musician, I'd thrown mine at the band's sexy tour manager. Hypocritical, much?

Technically, Kira never had to know. I could've snuck out of the hotel and gone home alone. But that meant making Kira and Vivi ride the T home just so I could save face.

That would have been a chickenshit move. So instead, I used the key card I'd been given yesterday to take the elevator up to the club level. Then I tapped on the door to Jonas's suite.

Silence. The only thing I could hear was the pounding in my own achy head.

I waved the card in front of the sensor and opened the door. "Knock-knock," I said, the sound of my voice muted by plush carpeting. I ventured further into the living room, peeking through an open doorway into the master bedroom.

What I saw there made my eyes prickle, because the three people lying quietly on the king-sized bed looked a lot like a real family. One of Vivi's hands was on Kira's belly, the other absently fingering her father's wrist. It was just about the sweetest damned thing I'd ever seen.

But it frightened me. If Mr. Hottie swept Kira off her feet and moved her to Seattle, I'd be devastated. Especially now, at this odd and stressful juncture in my life.

Kira opened her eyes and looked right at me. Quickly, her expression turned sheepish. *Sorry big brother. I went to bed with him after all.*

I gave her a wink and walked all the way into the room. I traveled around the giant bed and flopped down next to her. "So this is where the party is," I said, followed by an involuntary groan. "Oh, my head. Kiki, do you have any aspirin in your bag?"

"Sorry, Uncle Adam," she said. "I didn't plan ahead for you to party like a rock star."

On the far side of the bed, Jonas chuckled into his pillow. "I've got you covered. I travel with a quart bottle of Advil. We also need breakfast and a vat of coffee."

"I'm going to take a quick shower," Kira said. "Move, Adam."

"Make me," I said, my eyes closed against the dull ache at my temples. But a few seconds later, I yelped "Ow!" as my sister rolled right over me to get out of the bed. "Meanie." I gave her a little kick as she walked away.

And then I noticed something. "Hey, new nightie?"

"Mama bought it yesterday!" Vivi piped up.

At that, Jonas lifted his head. "Reeeeeeally?"

"I hate you all," Kira mumbled, heading out of the room. "Except Vivi."

With Kira gone, that left me next to Vivi. "This bed is big," she said in her muppet voice. My niece crawled over to me and flopped her head onto my chest. "Which bed did you sleep in, Uncle Adam?"

"Uh," I stalled, trying to think through my headache. This was one of those moments when the truth was not a good option. "Hey, Vivi? Do you want to watch TV in your room?"

"Yeah!"

"I bet you can't turn it on by yourself!"

"Can too!" Vivi scrambled off the end of the bed and was out of the room in a nanosecond. A minute later I heard the television power up in the other bedroom.

"Nice save." Jonas chuckled from his side of the bed.

"Yeah. Kira won't like it."

"It's better than the alternative." Jonas dropped his voice to a whisper. "Vivi, can you say *walk of shame?*"

My face got hot. Vivi's departure had left me alone in bed with Jonas. I checked the other man's expression, and to my relief, his eyes were twinkling. "Your day is going downhill already," I muttered. "Now it's just you in bed with some strange guy."

"Oh, well..." the rock star yawned, stretching his arms overhead. "I've seen worse. Let's find you that Advil."

He really *was* gorgeous, all lean muscle and golden hair. No wonder my sister couldn't turn Jonas down. You'd have to be legally blind, and probably deaf as well. Seriously, though. The dude had better have a heart made of twenty-four karat gold if he planned to stick around Vivi and Kira. I'd be watching.

Jonas grabbed his phone off the bedside table and wandered into the bathroom, returning a minute later with a pill bottle. "Heads up." He tossed it onto the bed.

"Thanks, man."

"*De nada*. Hey—is Ethan awake yet? He gets pissy when I wake him up with business."

I couldn't quite meet his eyes when I answered the question. "Uh, yup."

"Awesome." Jonas hit a button on his phone, and turned back into the bathroom. "Morning, Ethan," I heard him say before the door closed. "Party time is over. There's a couple of things I need before we leave..."

The bathroom door clicked shut, and I was alone. I lay there a moment, gathering my thoughts. More had happened to Kira, Vivi, and me in the last ten days then I could even process. And last night I'd broken my own dry spell in a big way, with enough alcohol and sex to make up for months of lost time.

However.

Reality was about to sink its ugly teeth into my (pleasantly sore) ass. In the next week, my surgery would be scheduled and then performed. As if that wasn't miserable enough, I'd begin the process of adjusting to life as a one-nut wonder.

With another groan, I rolled off the bed and went into the other bedroom. I sat on the bed next to Vivi, turned the TV down to a reasonable volume, and prayed for the pain reliever to kick in soon.

* * *

A little while later, the bathroom door opened. Kira had showered and changed, and was drying her hair. When the hair dryer stopped, I pulled my hungover self off the bed and went to stand in the doorway.

Kira leaned toward the mirror, applying lip gloss with a tiny brush.

"You never wear makeup," I said automatically.

She gave me a withering look in the mirror. "You never get wasted and stay out all night. But I wasn't going to point that out."

Well, ouch. "I'm sorry. Can we have a truce?"

Kira didn't answer, either because she was upset, or because she didn't want to ruin her top lip.

"Last night... I shouldn't have said that I didn't trust him."

"But you don't," she said, meeting my eyes in the mirror.

"I don't *know*, Kira. It's not my place to judge." I rubbed my aching head. I should have known better than to have this conversation right now. Anything I said was going to come out all wrong.

"Are you going to be okay?" Kira asked. "You smell like a distillery."

"Switching to scotch was probably a bad call." I cleared my throat. "Look, I did a few things last night that are out of character, too. The difference is... I'm never expecting to see him again."

She capped her lip gloss and turned around. "I thought you

were going to say that the difference was Vivi. That's my only real hesitation—it's not just me who could get hurt."

"Just be careful."

She sighed. "What does that even mean? You and I are the most careful people we know. We also spend a lot of time watching movies on our couch. Coincidence?"

"I'm sorry," I said again, hoping to bail out of this conversation before I put any more feet in my mouth. "It's really none of my business."

Kira's eyes got wide. "Adam, that's just code for, 'I would like to disagree in a humble-sounding way.'"

"No," I argued, "I'm just doing everything in a *hungover* way. God, don't even listen to me today, okay? I retract everything I said. Can you just do me one small favor?"

Kira crossed her arms. "Does it involve keeping a closer grip on my panties?"

"No. Don't tell anyone about my surgery."

"Okay," she whispered, her expression softening.

"It's embarrassing to me."

"Fine."

I took a step forward and hugged her carefully, mindful of that pink stuff on her lips. "Kiki? Let's not fight. I'm sorry."

"Okay. Me too. It will be all right."

I sure hoped that was true. And I hoped that "all right" did not mean that Jonas Smith would steal my family away to some mansion on the West Coast. I could only imagine how he lived. Would Vivi go to preschool in a limo? How repulsive.

My head gave a stab of pain.

* * *

In the elevator, I noticed that Jonas had donned sunglasses and a baseball cap. And when we reached the hotel restaurant in the lobby, he asked the hostess for a table in the corner, and then sat himself on the side of the booth that faced away from the other tables. Only then did he remove his shades, tucking them into his shirt pocket.

It almost worked. But when the young waitress came over to

our table, her jaw dropped comically. "Oh my God!" she squealed, putting her hands up to her cheeks. "Will you sign my order pad?"

Jonas gave her a tight smile. "Only if you can do me a little favor," he said. He put a finger to his lips.

The waitress looked to her left and then to her right, like a badly trained secret agent. "Sure." She thrust her pad and pen into his hands, and he signed. Then she ran off to get the coffee pot.

"Does that always happen?" Kira asked, her voice wary.

"Nope," Jonas said, opening the menu. "But there's a forty-five-foot purple bus with my face on it right outside. That raises the odds considerably."

Good save, I thought, and my estimation of Jonas notched one millimeter higher. At least the guy knew my sister well enough to understand that his fame was a strike against him.

Vivi opened her menu. She didn't read yet, but this menu was the kind with pictures in it. "Can I have pancakes?" she asked, hope in her voice. "And strawberries. And bacon."

"Let's see," Kira said, scanning the offerings. "Those things don't come all together. It says *no substitutions*."

"Oh, sure they do," Jonas said as the waitress came back. He raised his coffee mug toward her. "The little skeeter would like pancakes, bacon, and strawberries," he said. "Can you make that happen?"

"Sure!" the waitress practically yelled, pouring coffee into our mugs. "Let me get rid of this pot before I take the rest of your order."

"Take your time."

When she went away, Kira gave him a smile. "I guess you can get whatever you want from Miss Perky."

Jonas only shrugged. "The recognition thing is mostly a pain in the backside. So I have to take the good with the bad."

The waitress came back with crayons for Vivi. She took our order and scampered off. I had no doubt that all her other tables would suffer while we received excellent service.

A big shadow fell over our table, and I tried to keep my face impassive when I saw who it was.

"Morning, all," Ethan said. "Everybody doing well?"

"Yes, Mom," Jonas said.

"Don't sass me, boy. I've done a lot of work for you already today." He set two envelopes down on the table along with an itinerary that was marked up in green pen. "I found three dates when you can get away for two days or more. The first one is this Sunday night."

Jonas picked up the sheet. "Awesome."

"But you have to charter the return trips. Because I will not pace around a venue praying for your flight delays to resolve themselves."

"Fine."

"Ben has his panties in a wad about the European tour dates. You need to call him from the bus. We have to make our load-in time, because the New York guys are always cranky, and they'll fine you if we're late. The bus leaves in..." He looked at his watch. "An hour and fifteen."

Jonas flinched. "Okay. Got it."

Ethan swept his eyes over the entire table, noting Vivi hard at work with her crayons. Then he ducked his big body down quickly and kissed me on the neck, before turning around and walking away.

As I watched, Kira's eyes bugged out of her head. But Jonas only snickered into his coffee cup.

"Interesting," my sister squeaked.

I just shrugged, my face burning.

"So..." Jonas cleared his throat. "Can we talk about money for a second? I know it's not your favorite topic."

"Now is not a great time," Kira said quietly, tipping her chin to indicate that they shouldn't talk money in front of Vivi, even if she was busy with her crayons.

"I can help with that," I offered. Kira wouldn't like this maneuver, but I didn't want her to duck the money discussion forever. "Hey, Vivster?" My niece looked up. "Want to see Elmo on my phone?" Vivi gave a squeal of happiness as I pulled up the video I had squirreled away for just such emergencies. I dug my earphones out of my pocket and handed them to Vivi.

"Really, Adam?" Kira asked.

"Emergencies only," I said, handing the phone to Vivi, who inserted the ear buds with more familiarity than was optimal. "Okay." I nodded at Jonas. "You have six minutes."

"That will do." Jonas picked up one envelope and passed it to Kira.

"What's this?" she asked.

"Four years of back child support."

With a wary glance at him, she opened the envelope. Her eyes grew large when she looked inside. "Jeez! That's almost a hundred thousand dollars! I can't—"

"Take the money, Kira," Jonas pressed. "It's yours. In fact, your lawyer here will probably explain to you that this is just the state's figure. A judge might give you a lot more."

"Dude," I objected. "Your new lawyer would piss himself to hear you say that. In fact, what lawyer would let you write that check without a paternity test? I can't believe he'd do that."

Jonas laughed. "He hated the idea. He might even regret that you referred me to him. But I don't need a paternity test. I don't mean to brag, but look at her."

"The eyes," I admitted. "It's uncanny."

"She has my hands," Jonas whispered, his voice raw. "Guitar fingers. It's the craziest thing I ever saw."

"Here," Kira said, thrusting the envelope toward me. "This money really belongs to you."

"Wait," Jonas said. "I thought you might do that. So I did this." He picked up the second envelope and handed it to *me*.

The hair stood up on the back of my neck. "What?"

"I asked Ethan to write the check twice."

"Damn." I just stared at the envelope in my hand. "You didn't have to do that."

"I know, but I wanted to. Adam, thank you for raising my kid for four years."

I didn't know what to say. And what's worse, I didn't like how suspicious it made me feel. On the one hand, it was an incredibly generous offering. Jonas was saying, not in so many words, that my care was valuable.

But I also felt as if Jonas might be trying to buy me off. And I was not for sale.

"I don't think I can cash this," I admitted even as I privately recalculated my law school loans down to zero.

"Just consider it," Jonas said, with a nudge to the hand that held my check. "If it really makes you that uncomfortable, put it in a college fund for Vivi."

The perky waitress chose that moment to arrive with our plates. Vivi was still staring at the video on my phone, and ignoring her breakfast plate. So I cut a bite of Vivi's pancakes with her fork, then held it up to her mouth, which opened like a little bird's.

"Thank you," Kira said quietly after the waitress had left. "I should use this money to finish my degree next semester. If I don't have to work for minimum wage in that library, it won't take me so long to graduate and get a better paying job."

At that, Jonas raised her hand to his lips and kissed her knuckles. "You use it however makes sense to you," he said. "That's just what I owe you for past years. We can work out the details going forward whenever you're ready."

I took a bite of my omelet and tried to squash my uncharitable thoughts. It had been a while since I'd experienced this kind of big-brother angst. And I didn't know how to make it go away.

Taking a strawberry from Vivi's plate, I put it in her hand. Then I watched as Vivi slowly raised her hand to her mouth, eating the berry while staring at the tiny screen.

"She's really anesthetized by that thing," Jonas said.

"Yeah. Elmo is more effective than morphine." I watched Jonas watching Vivi. And the man's eyes were soft, his expression full of wonder and quiet joy. One of his arms was looped around

Kira, holding her in a casual, comfortable way. The way that Kira deserved to be held.

Well, fuck. Either the guy was exactly what Kira and Vivi needed, or he was a slick devil who would break both their hearts.

I fed Vivi another bite of pancakes, and tried to keep an open mind. Not that it was easy for a guy with cancer in one of his nuts and a once-a-year hangover.

I picked up my mug and took another hit of that life-giving force known as coffee. Maybe that would help. It would have to.

NINETEEN

KIRA

Back in the hotel room, I had only a couple of minutes to throw our things into the duffel bag. "Where is Purple Kitty?"

"Here!" Vivi yelled, running over to me.

I tucked the stuffy into my bag and then looked around to make sure that we hadn't left anything else behind. Purple cat? Check. Toothbrushes? Check. Envelope with a hundred grand inside? Check.

"I'm taking Vivi down with me to get the car," Adam said, snapping off the TV. "Can we meet you out front?"

My brother seemed to be trying to give me a moment alone with Jonas. That was nice of him. "All right. Thank you."

"No problem. Come on, princess. Say goodbye to your..." He stopped short of finishing that sentence. I wasn't the only one who found the transition strange.

"Bye, Daddy!" Vivi said, as if it was the simplest thing in the world.

Jonas jogged across the stupidly large suite and scooped her up. "Bye, Vivi. I'll see you soon."

"When?" she asked.

"Well, your mom and I have to figure that out." He set her down, pulling the itinerary out of his back pocket. "Looks like the first opportunity is in just five days. What are you all doing on Monday?"

I glanced at Adam, who was standing by the door. His surgery wasn't scheduled yet, and wouldn't be until later today or tomorrow. "Can we talk tomorrow?" I asked Jonas.

"Sure." He put a hand on Vivi's head and sifted through her curls one more time. Then he bent over and kissed her head. "Bye, baby girl," he said, his voice thick.

"Bye, my daddy."

Vivi followed Adam out of the room, leaving Jonas in a crouch on the floor. When the door clicked shut, Jonas hung his head. "Shit."

"What's the matter?"

"How do people do this?"

"Do what?" I zipped my duffel closed.

"*Leave.*" He got to his feet and disappeared into the other room.

He seemed to need a moment to himself, so I just let him go. A minute later, I heard him arguing with someone on the phone. "Ben, I said we'd talk about this *later*. I'm going to call you from the bus in an hour, okay?" He paused. "No. No more dates in Europe *at all*, and nothing in Asia. I'm taking time off after the North American tour. I've got a family crisis, okay? We'll talk later." Then Jonas laughed. "That's where you're *wrong*, Ben. I actually *do* have a family. Got to go! Ethan's waiting for me downstairs."

Jonas stuck his head around the door frame. "This is it, Kira. Can you walk me out?"

"Of course." I grabbed my bag and tried to look calmer than I felt. Because it *was* weird. I didn't know where I stood with this man, and I didn't know when that might become more clear.

Jonas took my hand in his as the elevator descended, but neither of us seemed to know what to say. The elevator doors parted at the lobby, and I stepped out, but in the ten minutes since we'd gone upstairs, the lobby had transformed into a madhouse.

"Fuck," Jonas whispered under his breath, his hand tightening on mine. Instead of stepping forward, he pulled me back into the elevator. He slapped at a button on the control panel, and the doors began to ease closed again, even as people began to run in our direction.

It took me a second to figure out that the surging crowd was aimed at Jonas.

A shriek rose up, and I had a moment of true fear that I couldn't really explain. Mercifully, the doors closed before any of the people charging our elevator reached it.

"Fuck!" he repeated. "I'm so sorry."

The car descended again. "Where are we going?"

"There's always a way out to the back from the basement of a hotel. Always." The doors opened again into a cement hallway lit by fluorescent lighting. We stepped out, and he looked left and right. "This way."

"How do you know?" The only signs read *Laundry* and *Maintenance*.

"The loading dock has to be near the laundry." He squeezed my hand once. "Stick with me, babe. I know things." His smile was sad.

Sure enough, after we walked twenty yards or so, the laundry appeared, and beyond it yawned the open doors of a loading dock. Jonas stopped, pulling me into his arms. "Kira," he whispered. "I hate leaving you right now."

I pulled back far enough to look him in the eye. "You have no choice."

He kissed me quickly. "I know. But it feels too much like the last time. One night together and..." He broke off, pinching the skin at the top of his nose. "I need to know when I'm going to see you again. Both of you."

"Soon," I whispered. I reached up to run my fingers along his jaw. "We'll figure out a date." He felt so good under my hand. But I understood his emotions. No matter how beautiful our night together had been, walking away made everything feel strange.

Jonas's phone began to vibrate in his pocket. He yanked it

out and answered it. "Yeah. I'm in the basement, just inside the loading dock. Can you swing by for me? When I see the bus, I'll come out there."

He pocketed his phone and put his hands on my shoulders. "I wish I weren't touring right now. It's not always like this."

"Isn't it?" I asked, my heart contracting.

"No, sweetness."

But even as he said it, the bus's hydraulic brakes shrieked nearby and voices yelled, "It stopped!"

Beyond the loading dock, the bus doors opened. Ethan appeared, beckoning to Jonas. "Right now, dude. We need to get out of here before..." He pointed toward the alley, where there was the sound of pounding feet.

Jonas gave me the world's fastest kiss then ran for the bus. A bunch of fans got there at the same time, and Ethan jumped down to put his big frame between their outstretched hands and Jonas. A second later, Jonas disappeared inside. Ethan hopped back in, and the doors swung shut.

Disappointed, the fans dissipated, not sparing me a glance.

The bus pulled away, leaving nothing but a slice of June morning visible through the doors. It was as if Jonas had never been there at all.

* * *

THE NEXT WEEK wasn't easy.

Connecting with Jonas on the phone proved difficult. When I tried to call, he was usually sleeping, because he kept such late hours on the road. The texts we exchanged were of the sorry-I-missed-you variety.

And then Adam's surgery was scheduled, and that became my primary focus. We had only a few days to wait, but they were long ones. My usually upbeat brother became quiet and withdrawn.

I didn't know what to do for him, except to keep my unconvincing smile pasted on. Helpless in all the important ways, I did the only thing I could think of. I baked several dozen cookies.

"These are amazing," Adam said after eating his fourth one. "But I need you to hide them from me now. I don't want to get a gut."

It was supposed to be a joke, I think, because Adam was thin as a rail. Running half marathons was his only hobby.

I put the cookies away and tiptoed through the darkened apartment toward my room. Climbing into bed, the words wouldn't stop rolling around in my brain. *Adam has cancer*.

Checking my phone, I saw that Jonas had tried to call me earlier. I listened to the voicemail. "Sweetness—please call me when you can. I should be available after ten. It's been too many days, and I want to hear your voice."

I redialed his number and listened to his phone ring. And ring.

I was about to give up when he finally answered. "Kira!" In the background, many voices were talking at once. "Wait—let me find a quiet corner." A moment later, the roar in the background dulled. "There. How are you?"

"Okay," I hedged. "It's been a busy week."

"Has it?" he asked, his voice concerned.

"Yeah," I said, although I couldn't say why. Adam had made me promise.

"Is everything okay with Vivi?"

"Yes—totally fine. She's all hyped up, actually, because it's the last week of preschool. They had a birthday party at school for her today. I made strawberry cupcakes with pink frosting."

Jonas groaned. "Did you save me one?"

"No." I laughed. "They were *pink*, Jonas. If Barbie made cupcakes, they would look like these."

"You're right," he joked. "I need manly cupcakes. My birthday is in November. Be ready."

I stopped smiling. It was awfully depressing that we didn't even know each other's birthdays.

He must have felt the change in my mood. "You know I'm joking, right? That sounded bad. Like I was putting in an order."

"Uh-huh. So you don't *want* the cupcakes?" I knew I should try to lighten up. Not that it was easy this week.

"Sweetness, I want anything you make for me. Maybe I'm a caveman, but the fact that you used to cook for me made me so fucking happy. I could not wait to walk into the store every night just to see what you'd come up with."

"It wasn't much, Jonas. The kitchen at the store isn't all that great."

"That is not how I remember it," Jonas insisted, dropping his voice to a whisper. "I ate so many of your little savory pies that you started making other things for me. It was thoughtful. And I liked knowing that you were thinking about me."

There was a lump in my throat now. "It was just food," I said. But that was a lie. I *had* enjoyed feeding him. So much.

"To me, it was more than that. Do you still think about opening a cafe?"

"Sometimes," I admitted. "But I switched tracks because teachers have a more stable work life."

"Can you switch again?" he asked. "If you have a little more of a cushion now, you could do what you wanted."

"It's not just money, though. I don't want to leave for work at four thirty in the morning, or four thirty at night. Those are hours that I would miss out on seeing Vivi."

"Ah," he said, sounding defeated. We were both quiet for a moment, and then Jonas said, "I'm coming to Boston in forty-eight hours to see you both."

"Wait. You are?"

"Yeah. Unless you tell me not to. I can get a ten thirty flight out of Philly after my concert Sunday night. I'll go to a hotel if you want me to, because I'll land pretty late. But then I'm all yours on Monday. I can bring Vivi her birthday present. And I'll fly back to rejoin the tour on Tuesday morning, with plenty of time to reach Nashville so Ethan doesn't have an aneurysm."

I felt a tingle in my chest at the idea of seeing him again so soon. But the timing wasn't great, because Adam's surgery was supposed to happen immediately after that. "Wow. The timing sucks, though."

"Does it?" he asked, sounding sad.

"Yeah, Adam..." I broke off.

"Adam doesn't like me," Jonas said bluntly.

"Adam is having a hard time, Jonas. We're just a little... busy."

There was a silence. "Okay." I could hear him trying to figure out why I would be so vague. But I'd promised Adam to keep his secret. "Should I not come?"

I thought about it for a second. "You should," I decided. Vivi didn't know about Adam's illness, and it's not like we'd planned to sit around all weekend discussing it.

"All right," he said, still sounding hesitant. "I want to."

My heart fluttered again. I was going to see him again in just a few days? "Vivi is going to be so excited to see you." *And so will I.*

"I hope so. Oh, Christ. Ethan keeps calling my phone because he can't find me."

"Why can't he find you?"

"Because I'm in a closet."

I laughed. "If you're going to come out of the closet, I think we need to have another chat."

"You crack yourself up, sweetness. Can I call you tomorrow?"

"Of course."

"Good night, my love."

More flutters! "Good night," I said, sounding a little dreamy.

I hung up the phone feeling lighter. And I couldn't wait to tell Vivi that her daddy was coming to town.

I shut off the light and made myself comfortable under the covers. Monday night, Jonas might actually be lying here beside me. How crazy was that?

I rolled my smiling face into the pillow, wishing he were here already.

TWENTY

JONAS

Everything about Sunday night's show was a little off.

Although the crowd probably didn't notice, Nixon and I weren't communicating very well. "Sweetness" was supposed to be the third song in the set. At least, that's what I thought we'd agreed upon. But Nixon played the intro to "Start Something With Me" instead.

So I followed along, even though I was holding my Gibson and always played that song on my Fender. I glared into the wings where my guitar tech stood. As if this was all his fault. But the man just shrugged, as if to say, *I gave you the instrument you called for, dummy.*

And maybe it was my fault. I was awfully distracted tonight. My overnight bag was packed. The moment the final encore ended, I'd sprint to the bus, take the fastest shower of my life, and jump into the waiting car. The airport was only a twenty-minute drive from the venue.

It would be a little tight if we hit traffic, but I knew it could work.

Thinking all of this through, I accidentally sang the third verse of "Start Something with Me" twice. A glance at Nixon earned me a cocked eyebrow.

Whoops. I really needed to concentrate a little more. But it wasn't easy when I was *this* close to seeing my girls.

The crowd was huge, but I couldn't make out many faces, because of the footlights. I was blinded by stage lighting and deafened by the music coming through the wedge speakers.

The first time I'd played big venues, I'd been scared shitless. The crowd was like a big, hungry beast vibrating in front of me.

But now? Just another day at the office. Between songs, I took a swig from my water bottle, smiled at the masses, swapped guitars with the instrument tech, and listened for Nixon's next intro. I could do this. I was good at this. And then I'd get to see my girls.

* * *

WHEN THE SHOW FINALLY ENDED, I ran for the exit with two security guards. Avoiding the aggressive fans waiting by the green-room doors, I slipped out a side door into the darkened parking lot. I tapped the access code into the bus's keypad lock (the code was Ethan's birthday.) The doors swung open for me. I thanked the security guards and locked myself in, alone.

I trotted to the back of the bus, threw the duffel down and stripped off my sweaty concert clothes. In the quirky little bathroom, I hopped beneath the shower spray before it was even warm. Shampoo. Soap. Rinse. If there were records for this, I broke them. Snatching a towel out of their protected cabinet, I covered myself before opening the door again. You never knew who you'd find on a tour bus. And sure enough, the sound of Nixon's laugh was already coming from the forward lounge.

If, on my way out, I had to walk by Nixon fucking some girl on the sofa, it wouldn't be the first time. At least they'd left me the rear lounge, and a quiet place to dress. I swiped the towel over my body and got to work. Not two minutes later I was lacing up my shoes. A text confirmed that my driver was already waiting just outside the bus.

Nixon and his girl still had their clothes on when I hurried past them with my duffel bag. He palmed something on the table, hiding it from view as I went by. "Have fun with your girls," he called, his voice a little sloppy. That had to be a record, actually. He was drunk within twenty minutes of finishing a show.

"Thanks," I said without a backward glance. I didn't have the bandwidth to worry about Nixon tonight. I unlocked the front doors and jumped down the steps and into the waiting sedan.

"The airport?" the driver asked.

"That's right," I confirmed as the car began to accelerate.

In the backseat, I tried to relax. There were bottles of water in the cupholders, in case I was thirsty. And a spread of magazines and newspapers was fanned out in the pocket on the back of the driver's seat. But I was too jumpy to read anything. I tucked my hands behind my head and thought about Kira and Vivi, both of whom were probably asleep in their apartment already.

I'd dropped by their building unannounced last week for two reasons. Kira had been ducking my calls, but I also wanted to be able to picture their place. And it was as homey as I'd imagined, with Kira's dogeared cookbooks on the countertop, and Vivi's toys on the rug.

I was glad they lived on a nice leafy street close to the park, too. I didn't know much about Boston beyond good lobster and Paul Revere. Tonight I'd booked myself into a boutique hotel in Back Bay. But tomorrow I'd get up early and take them out for breakfast. Kira could give me a tour of the neighborhood. And I could give Vivi her birthday present...

Shit!

I leaned forward to speak to the driver. "Dude, I'm really sorry, but I forgot something important."

The driver braked and switched into the right lane. "You want me to go back?" he asked in disbelief. "You might miss your flight."

I checked the time on my phone. "There's no traffic, so I think we can make it, and it's something I need. There's an extra fifty bucks in it for you if we get to the airport by ten forty-five."

The car made a sharp turn, and my heart accelerated, too. I hoped that turning around wasn't a stupid decision. But we'd been driving for only five or ten minutes...

Four aggressively driven minutes later, the sedan pulled up beside the bus. I leapt out, pounding the code into the keypad once again. I skated up the steps into the darkened bus, but then tripped over something heavy.

What the...?

I leaned down to put a hand on the obstacle at my feet. The thing I'd tripped over was Nixon.

* * *

NINETY MINUTES LATER, Ethan's voice boomed through the ER waiting room. "The last name is Winters, and I'm his emergency contact."

Finally.

The big man was out there, but I couldn't exactly flag him down, because I was hiding on a bench beside a dispensary closet, a seat I'd won through sheer stubbornness. "I will *not* sit in that waiting room," I'd said fifty times already. "If you send me out there, this will be all over the tabloids, and he'll sue you."

That last bit was probably an empty threat. But if I was spotted in an ER after a concert, there would be a lot of speculation over why, all of it bad for the band's reputation. It wouldn't take the vultures too long to hone in on the story.

I'm in the hallway behind the desk, I texted Ethan.

A minute later, he came trotting down the hall. He skidded to a stop in front of me. "How is he?"

"If only I knew. Good luck figuring out who's in charge. I'm not supposed to be sitting here, so I've been blacklisted. They're all, like, 'Make sure you don't give any information to the jerk on the bench.'"

Ethan sat down beside me with an irritated sigh. "Who gave the bad drugs to our man?"

"I've never seen this girl before. And I don't even know what it was. Pills, I think. Because there was no evidence of smoking or—" I stopped short of the word *injecting*. I didn't know what the hell Nixon was into these days. And I felt horrible for not anticipating this crisis.

"Shit." Ethan shook his head. "I meant to check in with him earlier."

"You're not responsible for every stupid thing he does, right? I should have paid more attention. I mean... I *saw* them hiding something from me, and I didn't even stop." Tonight I'd let so many people down. And most of them didn't even know it yet. "I shouldn't have told Vivi that I was coming to Boston tonight. Fuck."

"Is your girl going to be pissed?"

"I have no idea." It was too late to call Kira. I'd have to reach her in the morning and beg forgiveness. I should have known that I couldn't even go ten days without fucking things up with her. My record already spoke for itself, didn't it?

"I'm sorry, man. You want me to call a car and see if I can pay somebody to drive your ass up to Boston?"

"No," I said, putting my head in my hands. "I have to wait around for Nixon to wake up. So I can fucking kill him myself." It was tough talk. But I was terrified for Nixon. *Come on, buddy*, I privately begged. *It doesn't end like this.*

We waited. As one does at hospitals. At some point a doctor finally deigned to tell us that Nixon was stable, and that they were admitting him to a room upstairs.

"Can we keep his face covered when you take him up?" Ethan asked.

"Sure. Whatever. You can do it yourself." He gave Ethan a look of pure disgust.

I didn't even blame the guy. We were playing the part of fucked-up musicians flawlessly tonight. If I'd met myself for the first time tonight, I'd write myself off as an asshole, too.

* * *

I SPENT the night sitting in a chair beside Nixon's bed, feeling sorry for both of us. And it wasn't until gray light had begun to seep into the hospital room's window that Nixon finally woke up.

"Shit," he said, his voice like sandpaper. "Shit."

I rose from the chair slowly because my ass had fallen asleep. "I don't know whether to kiss you or kill you."

"You're not my type," Nixon tried to joke. But he sounded so sick that it wasn't funny at all. "So thirsty," he complained.

I couldn't give him a drink if he was flat on his back. I found the button to raise the bed and pressed it.

"Stop!" he said as the bed began to rise, his body clenching under the sheets

I grabbed a plastic pan off of a table and handed it to Nixon, who began dry-heaving.

Ugh. I collapsed into the chair again. "We're really living the dream now."

A nurse walked through the open room door, took one look at Nixon and steadied the bed pan.

"I didn't make a mess," Nixon said when his stomach's ugly dance had stopped.

"Congratulations." The nurse sighed. "Did you get dizzy when the bed was raised?"

"Sorry," I mumbled. "Rookie move."

"I'll get him some ice chips," the nurse said, leaving again.

"Aurrgh," Nixon moaned. "Just kill me already."

"I'm tempted."

"I'm sure that's true. I fucking hate summer."

I studied my friend. There was a hollowness to his face that shouldn't be there. "Are you ever going to tell me why you hate summertime?"

"Doubt it."

"Then tell me why you swallowed *fentanyl*, for fuck's sake. I'm supposed to be in Boston right now. And you'd be dead if I didn't screw up and come back to the bus."

Nixon closed his eyes, and I thought he might have gone back to sleep. But he answered the question eventually. "She called them her party pills. And I know better. I just didn't care last night. I was drunk and nothing seemed to matter."

"Well it does," I snapped. "You can't take that kind of risk again. Not ever."

"I know."

"Is it the tour? Do you hate touring?" I almost wanted him to say yes. If there were some way I could snap my fingers and finish the tour, I would. Even with a new hit single—"Sweetness" entered the chart at number twenty-six last week—I didn't give two shits about the tour.

"It's not the tour. Hell. I think I'd be in worse shape if I didn't have to be sober for three hours every other night. And we can't quit the tour, Jojo. That's a dick move."

He wasn't wrong. The tour could not be wished away, and neither could Nixon's issues. "I've got to call Kira," I said. It was seven thirty, so she and Vivi would be awake. They got up early and went to bed early—the exact opposite of my schedule.

Kira had warned me that there were a hundred obstacles to being together, and right this minute every one of them felt insurmountable.

I went out into the hall and rang them. "Is this Daddy?" a little voice answered on the second ring.

The ache in my chest doubled. "Hi, Vivi," I said, my voice thick. "Happy Birthday."

"It's over," she said. "We had cupcakes."

"I know. I heard they were pink."

"With sprinkles. Are you coming over?"

No, and I am an asshole. "Vivi, I couldn't get on the plane to Boston. I'm going to have to try again soon."

"Why?"

Because my friend is a world-class dumbass? "My friend needed me. I had to stay with him. He was sick, and it was an emergency."

"Oh."

"I'm sorry," I said uselessly. I would have given anything not to be making excuses to my little girl.

"Mommy wants the phone."

"Vivi, I'm really sorry. I wanted to see you today..."

"Hello?" Kira's voice cut in.

"Hi," I said. "I'm still in Philly. I'm so sorry."

"Oh," she whispered. "You're not coming?"

"I would be there right now if I could," I said quickly. "Nixon had an emergency, and I brought him to the hospital."

"Jeez. What happened?"

I did *not* want to tell Kira that my best friend overdosed. She'd think... *Shit*. "He has some issues, Kira. And I'm trying to help him."

"Yikes. That sounds serious."

"It is."

She was quiet for a second. "I wish I hadn't told Vivi that you were coming."

"I know. Lesson learned. I mean..." *Damn it all.* The "lesson learned" wasn't supposed to be that I was unreliable.

"Things happen, Jonas. I know your life can be really hectic."

Her words were understanding, but they sounded an awful lot like an indictment of our future. "It's not usually like this," I said, the excuse sounding lame even to myself.

"It's okay. We were going to take you to the aquarium today. I'll take her anyway."

"I'm sorry Kira. So sorry."

"Me too," she said. "I hope Nixon is okay."

"He will be. Thanks."

I told her I missed her, and that I hoped to call soon with better news. Then we hung up, leaving me feeling like Asshole of the Year.

I slipped back into Nixon's room, where the nurse was

fussing over him. "The attending will come in to take a look at you in a little while," she said on her way out the door.

Sitting down, I rubbed my gritty eyes. "At least we don't have a show tonight. I wonder if you'll be able to play Nashville Wednesday night."

"I'll play it," Nixon said gruffly. "I'll probably stop puking by then." He was quiet for a moment. "I'm sorry about Boston."

I groaned. "It just sucks, you know? I kept telling Kira that we could make this work. I said it a dozen times. Your timing sucks, my friend."

"It always has," he agreed.

TWENTY-ONE

KIRA

"That smells good," my brother said cheerily as he came into the kitchen.

I was sautéing his favorite chicken dish and trying not to worry. Adam was trying to cheer *me* up, which was completely backward. He was the one going under the knife tomorrow. "Thanks. It's really no trouble."

"There's something I need to discuss with you for ten seconds. And then we can never speak of this again, okay?"

My stomach dropped. "Hit me."

"There's a folder in my desk labeled 'In Case of Emergency.' It's a living will and a copy of my actual will, a list of accounts, and crap like that."

I flipped over a piece of chicken so that it could brown on the other side. "I remember." After Vivi was born, Adam made sure we both had wills, naming me as his beneficiary and giving him custody of Vivi if anything ever happened to me. It was the kind of formality that lawyers took care of.

Still, I shivered.

"That's all," Adam said, moving over to the cupboard to take out three plates. "Serious discussion over."

Lately it was all serious, all the time, though.

Vivi came into the kitchen, Purple Kitty dangling under her arm. "Mama? Is my daddy coming to see us?"

Since Jonas canceled on us, I'd been getting this question several times a day. "I hope so, sweetie. But he's very busy right now." I hated saying that. It was the very same lie I'd fed Vivi before she met Jonas. But now I found it to be one hundred percent true.

"Where is he? On the purple bus?"

"The bus went to a city called Nashville, I think. That's in Tennessee." But a four-year-old just didn't have the context to understand where that was.

"Can we go there, too?" She shifted Purple Kitty, balancing the stuffy on her shoulder.

"No, sweetie. Tomorrow you're having a play date with Ada, remember?" Our neighbor across the street had agreed to take Vivi all day so I could be at the hospital for Adam's surgery.

Vivi considered this, a furrow playing over her brow. "Can we call my daddy on the phone?"

"Not right now." Although I owed Jonas a call. There were three new messages from him already on my phone today, but I hadn't called back. Yet. I was in a dark mood, and I wasn't ready to share it with him.

Instead, I served my sesame chicken with a side of false cheer. I'd made a cold noodle salad—another of Adam's favorites —to go with it.

"This is awesome," Adam said over his first forkful.

I was sick of fake-smiling and pretending that everything was fine. "It's just chicken."

"No, Kira," he said quietly. "It's a lot more than just chicken. Thank you for all your help this week."

My eyes suddenly stung with tears. Jonas had said the same thing about the dinners I'd made him. I really should call him. But one thing at a time. I had to get through Adam's surgery first.

Sitting here with Adam and Vivi felt bittersweet tonight. As long as we were all healthy enough to sit here together again very soon, I really shouldn't ask the universe for anything more.

No matter how beautiful his eyes.

* * *

ALONE A FEW HOURS LATER, I checked my phone. There was a new text from Jonas. *Kira, where are you today? Please call tonight. Done with the show by ten*.

A peek at the clock revealed that it was half past ten. And just like that, I crumbled like one of Vivi's animal crackers on the kitchen floor. I tapped Jonas's phone number and then listened to it ring three times.

Just when I was ready to give up, someone answered. "Hello?" It was a woman's voice. That was... odd.

"Uh, hi," I said carefully. "Is Jonas around?" *Who is this*, I felt like asking. In the background, I could hear other voices.

"Oh, he's *around*. But I didn't leave him in any shape to take calls right now." Then she let out a naughty laugh.

"How's that?" I heard myself ask. Did I even want to know the answer? A prickle of unease crawled up my spine.

There was a smirk in her voice when she spoke again. "He's been a very busy boy. But if you insist, I'll let him tell you himself."

I felt as though I'd been slapped. With a quick tap of my finger, I disconnected the call.

For a full minute, I stared at the phone, wondering what had just happened. It was all too easy to picture the laughing woman with Jonas's phone in her hand, on a bed in a hotel room somewhere. And it was impossible not to remember the high-pitched sound of those women in the hotel lobby running towards the elevator.

My face grew warm, as if I'd been caught doing something embarrassing. And I guess I had. Because Jonas and I had never had a discussion about whether we'd be exclusive. I'd only assumed that if he wanted me, then he'd want *only* me.

But I never asked. And clearly I was an idiot for making assumptions.

We didn't know each other very well. That seemed obvious now.

God, I was such an idiot.

I set down my phone and shut off my lamp. I curled up in my bed, staring into the darkness. At any other point in my life, I would probably have burst into tears. But instead, I only felt numb. I shouldn't even be thinking about Jonas right now. Adam's illness was the important thing. We just had to get through his surgery.

I closed my eyes and willed myself to fall asleep.

* * *

THE NEXT MORNING was simply too busy for wallowing in my own misery. Vivi and I had to take care of the grocery shopping.

"When can I go to Ada's house?" she asked, bored by the long line at the checkout.

"Soon, sweetie. Right around lunchtime." I moved the cart forward. "Listen, Viv? Adam has to go to a doctor's office today, and they're going to fix a little thing in his tummy." This wasn't a lie, exactly. As it happened, the surgeon was going to go through an incision in Adam's pelvis. He wouldn't be lifting his niece onto his lap anytime soon.

"Why?" Vivi asked.

Why, indeed. "There's a bump there that they want to take out. And he has to stay overnight. But tomorrow he'll come back home, okay?"

"Okay."

"He'll have to sit around for a couple of days and read a lot of magazines."

"And watch videos on his phone?" Vivi asked hopefully.

"We'll see." In my pocket, my own phone vibrated. I snuck a peek at the screen, just in case it was Adam calling.

No dice. *Missed calls: 3 from Jonas.*

"It's daddy!" Vivi yelled.

"What?" I asked. Could Vivi suddenly *read?*

She clapped her hands. "The song, Mommy."

I went still. Sure enough, "Sweetness" was playing over the store's sound system. Good grief. Was there no way to escape that man? I heaved a five-pound box of rice onto the conveyor belt with a little more force than necessary.

It used to be easier to hear Jonas's songs on the radio, back when he was just a vivid memory. Now these songs were like the soundtrack to my own stupidity.

You'll always be my sweetness.

Right. And to think I'd believed that he meant it. But pop songs were meant to seduce the masses. And clearly Jonas took that seduction seriously.

I put grapes and onions, potatoes, chicken, ground turkey, cheese and crackers on the conveyor belt. And a six-pack of Adam's favorite Mexican soda. Real love wasn't set to a four-four drum beat in a recording studio. Real love was accomplished *this* way—by caring for the people who needed you.

I would try not to forget it.

TWENTY-TWO

JONAS

Three of us sat under a leaden sky on Ethan's hotel room balcony.

"I've always liked Nashville," Nixon said, his feet up on the railing. "But I liked it better when I didn't feel like road kill."

I did not reply. My opinion about why Nixon felt half alive would not be welcome. And I had no opinion on Nashville, and very little to say about anything at all today. Kira had not called or answered a text in three days, and I was about to lose my mind.

"I really can't figure out that building, though." Ethan pointed into the distance. "It looks like Batman."

"It's the AT&T building," I muttered. The logo was visible right at the top of Batman's head, between the ears.

"No kidding. But why? Did the architect *mean* to make it look like a superhero? It can't be an accident. Nobody could draw that shit on a big roll of paper and miss the connection."

Ignoring him, I hit "refresh" on the weather app on my phone for the thousandth time. "Chance of thunderstorms, seventy-eight percent."

"Fuck," Ethan groused. "A little rain would be okay. But you can't play if there's lightning. This is going to be a total shit show."

"When does the venue have to decide?" I asked.

"Soon. If there won't be a show, they have to let people know." He looked at his watch. "It's eleven now. Sound check in an hour. Doors open at four. I'd say they have to make the call by two."

"Hmm." I tapped out an impatient rhythm on the arm of my chair. If this concert was canceled, it would create a window *just* wide enough for visiting my girls. So long as I could find a flight to Boston. I'd have to leave again tomorrow, catching a flight to Atlanta to rejoin the tour.

But it would be worth it to check in on Kira. I needed to make sure she was okay, and apologize in person for my most recent fiasco.

"What's on your mind, man?"

I looked up to find Ethan staring at me. I shrugged.

"You're plotting something, aren't you? Going to try to go to Boston if we cancel?"

"Do it," Nixon encouraged.

I squinted at the sky again. "I might. But she isn't taking my calls right now."

"That's cold," Ethan said.

But was it? I'd be mad, too. "Maybe I should just leave her alone for a little while. I told her that she wouldn't regret getting involved with me. But she already does. We have a big life, you know? We have things that other people only dream about. But maybe you just can't have everything."

Nixon's snort sounded a whole lot like agreement. He got out of his chair and headed toward the room.

"Where are you going?" I asked.

Nixon stopped halfway through the sliding glass doors. "To the john. That okay with you? I don't think I'll find any contaminated pills between here and Ethan's toilet."

"Don't be a smartass," I grumbled, scrolling through my phone, hoping to see a new message from Kira.

There wasn't one.

"Hey, Jonas?" Ethan interrupted my thoughts. "There's something I need to tell you."

I looked up in alarm, because discussions that began that way never ended well. And the big man's face wore a grim expression that was already ratcheting up my anxiety. "What is it?"

"I've been offered a job with Premier."

Oh, hell. I held back a groan. "Is it a really good job? Because the timing is really rough, dude. Do they expect you to quit in the middle of my tour?"

Ethan chewed on his lip before answering. "It *is* a really good job. I already have a really good job, though."

I sure as hell didn't know what to say. I did *not* want Ethan to leave. Not ever. But making him feel guilty about it wouldn't be fair. "You have to do what's right for you," I said. "If they're offering you something you can't refuse, then I'm not going to be a dick about it."

"That's it?" Ethan tipped his head slowly backward until it collided with the wall. "That's all you're going to say?"

The prickle of discomfort that had hovered at my temples all morning now blossomed into a full-blown headache. "That's not all I *want* to say. But I just told you I don't want to be a dick."

Ethan crossed his arms across his enormous chest and frowned. "Then *say* it, man. Now is your chance."

"All right. I wish you wouldn't go. Nobody else could do the job like you."

Unless I was mistaken, Ethan seemed to relax a degree or two. "That's good to hear."

"I mean... Because you do so many things that aren't really in the job description. It isn't in your contract to give a fuck whether I ate lunch, you know? You always go the extra mile for me. I don't know. Maybe it isn't even fair to you. Maybe you should take the other job and just do the minimum. You'd still be doing more for those lucky shits than any other manager did."

Ethan's face fell. Then he banged his enormous head into the stucco behind him several times in a row. *Thunk. Thunk, thunk.* "Jojo, stop talking now."

"What did I say?"

"You..." He made a noise of irritation. "Why do you think I *do* all that extra stuff? It's not like I misread my contract. I don't think it says 'Make homemade chili when Jonas is sad.' You think I'm an idiot, or just an overachiever?"

"Neither," I insisted. "But I also don't know what you're trying to tell me."

"Sometimes you're kind of an asshole."

"You think I don't know that?"

"See, I don't think you do! The reason I work out with you every morning and listen to you bitch is because we're *friends*. I care about you. And the fact that you don't understand that does *not* make me happy. I don't want to go work for some other dudes, Jonas. But if you really don't give a shit about our friendship, I'll do it."

"I..." My neck got hot. "I'm sorry I haven't been a good friend."

"That's the thing, though. You *are* a good friend. If it was me who suddenly had a lot of family complications, what would you do?"

"I'd help," I whispered. I would, too. I'd flown down to Texas with Ethan when Ethan's brother died in a trucking accident.

"That's right. You would. But you never give yourself any credit for being a good guy. So you write off all the relationships you have, insisting that nobody actually gives a damn about you. You say that Nixon only needs you to write songs. You say that I'm only here for the paycheck. You let all your friends off the hook for everything. And it's because you're afraid to count on anyone."

"I'm not *afraid*."

Ethan just shook his head. "Call it what you will. And I'm not saying you didn't come about this shit honestly. Watching your parents die would fuck anybody up. But what if you tried admitting that you need the people in your life? There are people who would love you back if you figured out how to count on them."

"I take care of myself. I don't need to count on people."

"But you *should*," Ethan insisted. "Nobody is supposed to take care of himself all alone. It's better with help."

There was a flaw in this logic. "Who takes care of you, though?"

Ethan rubbed his head. "You guys do, in your own way. I'm part of the family, not just some employee. We jam together, and you let me muddle along on the guitar, like I'm not just your lackey."

It was true, too. Ethan was one of our crew. Not just an employee. "I really don't want someone else on my bus, E. Please don't go."

Ethan tipped his head to the side, a slow smile lighting his face. Then he leaned over and grabbed me around the shoulders, squeezing me into a tight hug.

I couldn't draw a breath for a second there until he released me.

"See that, Jojo? That right there. A gay black man does not feel welcome everywhere. But on your bus I'm good."

"Of course you are."

Ethan raised his eyebrows in a knowing look. "You see that? You got to give yourself a little more credit, if you want other people to do the same."

"Sure, okay," I said to appease him.

"Now, go tell your girl the same thing. Tell her you *need* her. Tell her it isn't okay for her to shut you out. Sometimes your job is going to get in the fucking way, but you will *not give up*."

He made it sound so simple. "I do need her. I need her so bad. But she's been alone for *years* because of me. And I don't know why she'd forgive me for that."

But Ethan wasn't even listening. He was already dialing someone on his phone. "Ben? This thunderstorm looks bad. I can't have all this equipment out in the lightning. And your boys are at risk. Call the venue and tell 'em how it's gonna be."

"Really?" I asked Ethan after he disconnected his call. "You didn't want to give it more time?"

"You. Go to Boston. Get the twelve thirty flight, bud. Before the storm shuts down the airport. I'm calling you a car."

"There's a twelve thirty flight?"

Ethan didn't answer. He was already on the phone again.

I jumped out of my chair and went to throw a few things into a carryon bag.

TWENTY-THREE

KIRA

Pacing the surgical waiting room was my new hobby. After several more laps, the clock revealed that only two minutes had passed.

I was going to make myself crazy before Adam's surgery was over, but I didn't have the first idea how to calm down.

For a change of pace, I powered up my phone and decided to worry about Vivi for a few minutes. I ducked into the linoleum hallway to make a call.

Eight missed calls, complained my phone. And every one of them was from Jonas.

Ignoring those, I pulled up my friend's number and dialed.

"Hi Kira," Kathy answered. "The girls are doing great together."

"That's good to hear. Should I say hello to her, or just let them carry on?"

"Vivi is too busy to miss you right now."

"I'm sure you're right."

"Any news on Adam?"

"Not a word yet. But thanks for asking."

"Hang in there," Kathy urged. "It's all going to be fine."

"I can't thank you enough for taking Vivi today."

"Stop saying that! It's nothing. Now go be there for Adam."

"Thanks. I will."

I disconnected the call, just as a text message popped up. *Sweetness. Please call me. I'm getting really worried.*

Oh boy. Making Jonas worry had never been the point. **We are fine**, I tapped out. *Just need some time.*

His response was immediate. **Where are you?**

I didn't really want to get into it. But maybe if I gave him a clue about what kind of a week I was having, he'd leave me alone. *I'm at Mass General*, I typed. That sounded dire, so I added: *Adam is having a small surgical procedure today. Sorry, can't talk now.*

I sent the message, then went back to pacing the waiting room. Adam's surgery wasn't supposed to last very long, but they'd taken him into the OR forty minutes ago already. I shouldn't have had that third cup of coffee. Big mistake. My stomach behaved as if it meant to climb up my esophagus and eject.

A doctor came through the double doors leading to the operating rooms, and every head swiveled in his direction. "Barnaby?" he called.

The Barnabys, lucky souls, jumped out of their chairs and went to consult with him. I walked over to the window for the fiftieth time and looked out. It was still the same view of the dumpsters, with a narrow slice of a congested roadway in the distance.

Sigh.

Twenty more minutes crept by without incident. In the best case scenario, Adam would have a successful surgery with no follow-up radiation treatments. "Although radiation isn't the end of the world," he'd told me a few dozen times.

Theoretically, this bad dream might be a distant memory by the time the trees on the Common turned orange. If Adam was lucky.

"Kira Cassidy?"

I spun around to find a doctor in the doorway, and I trotted over to her in a big hurry. "I'm Kira."

"Adam is out of surgery. Everything went fine."

"Was it contained?" I asked, breathless.

"Yes. No surprises." She gave me a quick smile. "The tumor hadn't spread any further than we could see on the scan. So we took exactly what we expected to. And the oncologist will follow up with Adam after he heals."

"Can I see him?"

"Sure." The doctor beckoned. "Come with me. He'll be very groggy, so don't ask him to make any sense. But you can see him."

I tiptoed into a recovery room, where three patients lay on gurneys. A nurse hovered, checking IV lines and taking vitals.

Adam lay under a blue sheet, his hands still at his sides, his eyes closed.

I couldn't help but touch him. "Hey," I whispered, squeezing his hand, brushing a lock of hair across his forehead. He looked so pale.

His eyes flickered open and then locked on mine. "Hey," he rasped.

"It's all done," I said, my throat closing up. He looked so vulnerable lying here.

"Already?" he squeaked. His eyes seemed to open wider, although his gaze was a little unfocused. "Something wrong?"

"Not a thing," I said quickly. "I'm just happy to see you. The doctor said everything went fine. No surprises."

He closed his eyes for a moment and then opened them again. "I want to keep it."

"Keep what, Adam?"

"My nut."

I opened my mouth and then closed it again. "Um, what?"

"What do you think they did with it? Put it in a jar?"

I was trying to figure out what sort of response would be the most soothing when I heard a distant commotion.

"Oh my God!" squealed a female voice. I froze, listening for sounds of distress. "Oh my God!" came again. But it sounded more like joy than terror. And wasn't that odd for the surgical ward?

I was giving Adam's hand another squeeze when a nurse stuck her head into the room. "Samantha!" She hissed at her colleague. "You know that band Hush Note?"

"Yeah?" her coworker said, looking up.

"One of 'em is out in the waiting room. Get someone to cover for you. Come see."

"Oh, crap," I whispered to myself. Jonas was *here?*

Adam's gaze swam up to my face again. "If they put it in a jar or something, I could bring it home with me."

The voices outside grew louder, and I thought I could hear Jonas arguing with someone.

"Just a second, Adam," I whispered. "I'll be right back." After patting my brother's hand, I dashed into the hallway. I found the origin of the scuffle at the nurse's station, where a group of women surrounded the desk—and Jonas.

"Excuse me!" I elbowed my way into the center of the group. "Jonas, what are you doing here?"

He turned to me, looking flustered. And, damn it, just one look into his green eyes had a wave of longing rolling through me like the tide. It took a few beats of my heart before I could focus again. Belatedly, I noticed he was holding a rather enormous plush horse in his arms.

"You weren't answering your phone, and so I followed the signs to surgery."

Focus, Kira. "I need to get back to Adam."

"Why? Is he all right?"

"Yes, probably. But we sure aren't here for the fun of it."

I could *not* have this conversation in a public place. I turned away, and Jonas followed me to the double doors. After pushing through, an unfamiliar nurse stopped me. "Who are you here for?"

"Adam Cassidy. I'm his sister."

The nurse checked her clipboard. "Okay. And you?" She gave

Jonas an evil stare. Clearly she was not a Hush Note fan. "Are you family?"

"Yes," Jonas said at the same moment that I said, "No."

"Am so!" Jonas complained. "I'm his niece's father."

The nurse rolled her eyes, tired of us already. "You have ten more minutes in that recovery room. Then Mr. Cassidy is relocating to a private room down the hall."

"Thank you." I stalked past her, Jonas hot on my heels.

When I reached Adam's side, he gave me a watery smile. His eyes drifted behind me, to Jonas and the giant stuffy under his arm. "For me? You shouldn't have."

"It's for Vivi's birthday."

"She'll fucking love that," Adam rasped. "She's going to make us pretend it's real, isn't she? I'll have to feed it."

"But not clean up after it," Jonas pointed out.

Two nurses swooped in on Adam, one checking his IV, the other writing on his chart. "We're going to move him now. Room number 227. Okay, Adam? Are you up for a little ride?"

"Whee!" Adam called as the gurney began rolling.

Without a glance at Jonas, I began following my brother down the hall. When we reached room 227, the nurse paused at the door. "Give us a couple of minutes to settle him."

And so we stood there in the hospital corridor: Jonas, me, and a large stuffed pony. Reluctantly, I met his eyes.

"Baby, why?"

"Why *what?*"

He rolled his eyes. "Why won't you talk to me? I've been out of my mind."

I took a minute to study his face. With those warm, clear eyes looking back at me, it was hard to keep my cool. "I just wanted to get through this." I tipped my head toward Adam's room.

"But I can help you, right? With *anything*. Wasn't that the plan?"

I thought it was. Until I realized all over again that you could break my heart. "I thought it would be easier to talk to you when things had settled down."

"Easier for you, maybe. But I'm all alone on that bus, wondering if you guys are okay."

All alone, he'd said. *As if.* That only made me angry.

"Why couldn't you just return one of my calls?"

"I *did*, Jonas. But you were too busy to come to the phone."

His eyes widened. "I'm never too busy for you, unless I'm onstage. When was this?"

I shrugged, miserable. I really didn't want to get into it, especially not here. "We can talk about it later."

"We can talk about it *now*, Kira. I didn't get any calls from you."

"It was Wednesday night. A woman answered your phone, and she said you..." I swallowed. "Look, I'm not talking about this. Not now. Not with Adam looped on drugs and Vivi at a friend's house."

"A woman answered my phone. On Wednesday night?"

"Just... drop it, okay?"

"What did she *say*, sweetness?"

"Don't..." *call me that*, I wanted to say. But I only shook my head, horrified to find that my throat felt hot just remembering that call.

Jonas pulled his phone out of his pocket and tapped at the screen. "I'm sorry to doubt you. I *do* see a call from you at 10:28. It lasted thirty-two seconds."

Thirty-two seconds of utter humiliation. That sounded about right.

He tapped the screen again and held the phone to his ear. Apparently nobody was picking up, because after a few moments, he tried a different number. I wondered when the nurses would finally let me into Adam's room.

"Ethan. Yeah, I made it here. Please tell me that it's pouring in Nashville. *Good.* Listen—is Quinn there? She's not answering my call. I need her, like, right this second." He shifted the stuffed horse to the other arm. "Hey, Quinn. Tell me this—did you answer a call from Kira on Wednesday night?" He made a grunt of irritation. "Girl, it's a yes or no question."

I winced.

"You let *who* answer my phone? *Some woman.* What woman? Fuck—it doesn't matter. *Why* did you let some stranger fuck with Kira when I was out eating barbecue with a bunch of DJs with body odor? And what exactly did that rando tell her I was doing?"

Oh dear. I may have jumped to a few conclusions. But in my defense, that's exactly what the other voice on the phone had wanted.

"She was *vague*, huh. In what way?" He turned to face the wall and proceeded to knock his forehead into it. Twice. "Quinn, seriously, that is some next level bullshit. It's the kind of bullshit you can't stand, and I honestly don't know how you could do this to me."

As he listened to Quinn talk, he pinched his eyes shut in an expression of anger.

"Okay," he said finally. "Here's what I need from you. I'm going to hand the phone to Kira. And you're going to tell her the truth. *All* the truth, Quinn. If you're entirely honest, I won't tell *Us Weekly* that you cried during your nose-piercing. And when I get back to the tour, you can try to explain why you'd do such a thing."

He held out the phone to me. "Jonas, I..."

"Please. Just listen to her. We need to clear this up."

I took the phone and put it to my ear. "Hello?" *Please, Lord, make this conversation last five seconds or less.*

"Look," Quinn's voice was softer than I thought possible. "I don't know why I let that happen. It was a dumbass thing to do. And I'm sorry. You both deserve better, and your kid is seriously cute."

"Thank you," I said curtly.

"Wait—" Quinn said, anticipating the handoff of the phone that I was about to do. "Promise me you won't hurt him."

"What?"

"Jonas is so sweet and lonely that I worry about him. And he never stops talking about you. So please be good to him. He's the best there is."

That stopped me cold for a moment. Was Quinn in love with him? "Okay," I said eventually. "Point taken." Then I offered the phone to Jonas again.

He put it to his ear. "I know you're sorry. Yeah, okay. Just don't *ever* do that again." He signed off and put his phone back in his pocket. Then he set the stuffed horse down, where it stood in the hallway like a dog at attention. Putting one hand on either side of my shoulders, he trapped me against the wall. "I need you to talk to me if you have a question. Don't just hide."

Well, *ouch*. "All right. Fine."

"Maybe I should have been more clear when I saw you last, but there wasn't enough time. You're it for me, sweetness. There won't be anyone else. And Quinn won't be the last person to try to make you wonder about me. I read about myself in the tabloids all the time. According to them, I've been engaged a dozen times. Also, I once had an alien mistress, who gave birth to my half-human child. But the people who say all that shit are people who have unfulfilling lives, and don't know us at all. I need you to remember that."

I stared up at him and tried not to drown in his turquoise gaze.

Jonas cupped my jaw in his palm. "That goes for Quinn, too. She's an angry girl. She has her reasons, but that doesn't mean she's allowed to pull any of her bullshit on you. I'll make sure of it."

"Okay. Were you ever *with* her?" I asked suddenly, sounding just as jealous as I felt.

"No, baby." Jonas closed his eyes for a moment, and then opened them. And when I forced myself to meet his gaze, I saw pain there. "But I was with a lot of people. I was always looking for something and never finding it. And then when I found it, I didn't recognize it, and I walked away. I'm *never* doing that again. If I have to quit this tour to prove it to you, I will."

"You can't do that," I whispered.

He shrugged. "I can do whatever I want. It won't make people happy. It would cost me a fortune and put Nixon and the rest of the band in a big fat lurch. But I don't know any other way to show you that there's only one thing I'm scared of. And that's losing you and Vivi again."

"I'm scared of plenty," I blurted, my eyes watering.

Jonas pulled me into his chest. "I know you are. And I know you have a lot to handle right now. So we'll do this however you need to. But I'm not walking away, Kira. I'll keep telling you, and I'll keep showing you as often as I can."

I let him hold me right there in the hallway. "It's been just Vivi and me and Adam, for a long time."

"I know, sweetness. So you have to get used to me. And I'm trying to help you do that. But first, you have to tell me what's wrong with your brother."

I felt suddenly exhausted. This was the most emotionally draining day in an emotionally draining month. "He has testicular cancer. Or he did until about a half an hour ago. He asked me not to tell anyone, because he's embarrassed. You can do the math on why."

"Oh, shit," Jonas said. "Is the math...two minus one?"

"Yeah." I sighed.

Jonas gave an uncomfortable grunt. "That sounds horrible. You must be so worried."

"It hasn't been an easy week. Let's go and see him now," I whispered.

"Let's," Jonas agreed.

* * *

THE NURSES WERE TRYING to get Adam settled into his room, but he just wouldn't relax.

"Who do you have to blow around here to get your own testicle back?" he wondered at the top of his lungs. "They must have a jar of formaldehyde, right? In the pathology lab? I want to keep it on the shelf of my office. Jonas! Come over here. Can you pull some strings?"

"I would if I could, dude."

"The drugs they have here are really awesome. You should try some."

"Maybe another time."

"Jonas, I only have one nut," Adam confessed.

I wished he would stop talking, because after the drugs wore off he was going to regret saying all of this.

"I knew a drummer who only had one," Jonas said. "Whenever he got drunk he used to tell the story of how he lost one in an accident. He liked to show us the scar."

"Fuck me!" Adam shuddered. "Did you know—" He swiveled his head to look at Jonas. "—most testicular cancer is self-diagnosed? Feel yourself up and live a long life."

"That's good advice, man." He held up a hand and Adam high-fived him.

"I need to know how weird it looks," Adam said. He put one hand over his eyes. "But I'm afraid to look."

"You can look tomorrow," I said gently.

"Hey, Jonas? Can you write me a song called One-nut Wonder? I could use it to pick up guys."

"That would totally work," Jonas agreed, not bothering to hide his smile.

"So, I think I'll sleep now?" Adam said loopily. "Can you take care of Kira? I think she's freaking out." Then Adam's eyes seemed to roll back in his head, and he relaxed onto the pillow.

I let out a shaky breath, my heart quaking. Adam had come through the surgery, but nothing was settled.

"Can I take you home?" Jonas asked.

I shook my head. "I want to stay until he wakes up again. Or at least until five o'clock." I checked my watch. "That's about as long as I dare to impose on the friend who's taking care of Vivi right now."

"Okay." He paced. "What if I picked up Vivi? I could bring her home to your apartment, and feed her some dinner."

"Oh." My heart dipped at the idea of Jonas and Vivi walking the streets of Boston together. Could I really just hand Vivi over to him?

Jonas stepped closer to me. "Hey." He tipped my chin gently toward him. "I'd never let anything happen to your little girl. I can keep her safe. Is she far away from your place?"

My eyes met his, and the familiar warmth I found there gave me a jolt. When he looked at me like that, it was hard to be afraid. But also, it was hard to say no. And that couldn't be good. I cleared my throat. "She's at our friends' house right across the street."

"Ah." He smiled. "Then how is this hard? I can take care of her, Kira. I'm not saying that I'm a natural. But I promise to text you if I have questions. And Vivi is so quick, she'll tell me if I'm fucking up."

I had to smile, because it was true. "No f-bombs, for starters."

He smiled back at me, and that smile could power the Eastern Seaboard. No wonder women threw their underwear at him. "Noted."

With a resigned sigh, I dug my keys out of my pocket. "This is the outer door. And these two are for the apartment. Top and bottom locks. If you guys get hungry, the take-out menus are in a kitchen drawer. Vivi knows where."

"What does she like to eat?"

"Everything. Indian, as long as it's not too spicy. Chinese. Pizza."

"Really? What a fun kid."

"She is," I whispered.

With another smile that practically turned me to a liquid, he picked up the stuffed horse, tucking it under his arm. "What's your friend's name, and which door am I knocking on?"

* * *

WHEN JONAS HAD LEFT, I took a minute to check on Adam. He was sleeping peacefully, his hands relaxed at his sides. His breath made a faint whistle each time he exhaled. I wanted to put a hand through his hair, just touching him to reassure myself that he was okay. But I didn't want to disturb his sleep.

So I sat down on the hard little plastic chair beside his bed and took out my phone. I dialed my friend's number and spoke softly when Kathy answered. "Adam is doing fine," I assured my friend when she asked. "But there's been a little change of plans. Vivi's father is on his way over to pick her up."

A shriek came through the phone. "Say *what?*"

The volume made me wince. "Yeah. He's... back in our lives all of a sudden. I haven't wanted to talk about it until I was sure."

"You know," my friend dropped her voice, probably so that the girls wouldn't hear her. "Vivi told me that she met her daddy, and I'm ashamed to say that I thought it was just a fantasy."

A fantasy was a good word for it. I still wasn't quite sure that he was here for good. "Well, it's true. And in fifteen minutes, when a guy knocks on your door, that's him."

"What does he look like?"

"Well... do you know the band Hush Note?"

"Sure?"

"He looks a lot like the lead singer. Also, he's carrying a big stuffed horse."

There was a brief silence on the line. "He looks like a rock star? No wonder you had a kid at twenty-one. I'll try not to drool."

Good luck with that. "Thank you, by the way," I said. "I really appreciate your help today."

"Any time, Kira. Vivi is a doll. I'm going to go stand in the living room now, looking for a hot guy with a stuffed horse."

"You can't miss him."

* * *

A HALF HOUR LATER, I received a text from Kathy: **WTF?**

A moment later, I received another. **WT everloving F?**

I replied: *I guess you met Jonas. Vivi was happy to leave with him?*

My phone vibrated, and when I answered, Kathy's squeal was high-pitched. "I cannot *believe* how badly you've been holding out on me. *Thanks* for the warning. I just became a babbling idiot when he walked in here. I don't think I even pronounced my own name right after I opened my door to a *rock star*."

"Sorry," I whispered. "I haven't figured out how to talk about him yet."

"Figure it out, girl. Because... Jesus Christ."

"Was..." I cleared my throat. "Did Vivi have any issues with seeing him?"

"Vivi is over the moon. 'My daddy is here!' You should have seen her. Or maybe not, actually. Up till now you were spared the daddy obsession that both my little girls have. And this for a man who can barely take care of himself, let alone his own children. So I guess you're in for the same."

"I guess," I agreed.

"We are *due* for a girls' night out, lady. You have a few stories to tell me."

"But the story isn't all that interesting, Kath. Girl meets boy. Girl throws herself at boy with inadequate birth control. There's a reason I don't talk about him."

On the other end of the line, Kathy gave a deep chuckle. "That's a shame, because I think the two of you would look really cute together. He's never been married, right?"

"And probably never will be," I said quickly.

A groan came from the bed beside me.

"I've got to go. Thanks for your help today. I owe you."

"You don't owe me a thing for the babysitting. You owe me *big* for the lack of detail."

I snorted. "Okay, as soon as things quiet down, we'll find a night to go out."

"I'll hold you to it."

After we disconnected, I looked my brother over. His eyes were still closed, but he had a grimace on his face. I put a hand on his forehead. "Are you okay?"

"Kira," he croaked.

"I'm here. Are you in pain?"

"Some," he said, opening his eyes.

"They set you up with this pump." I showed him the cord. "You just press this button whenever you need a hit of the painkiller."

"Fancy," Adam said, pinching the button. His eyes fluttered closed again. "I hate hospitals."

"I know." I took his hand again.

"Just want to get dressed and go home," he said.

"Tomorrow," I promised.

"Where's Vivi?"

"With Jonas, if you can believe it."

Adam's eyes popped open again. "Oh! He was here, wasn't he?"

"Yeah."

My brother smiled. "You're letting him babysit. That's so adventurous of you."

"I know." I smiled back at him. "It's killing me."

He kept smiling even as his eyes drifted closed. "She'll be fine, Kira. It's... nice. And it's nice that you're here with me. Thank you."

I rested my cheek on the edge of the mattress and held Adam's hand tightly. "You're so welcome, sweetie. Anytime."

I thought he'd fallen asleep. But a minute later, he spoke again. "Please don't move to Seattle right away."

"What? Who's moving?"

"Mr. Hottie is going to take you both. Just don't let it be too soon..." Then Adam fell asleep for real, his mouth going slack.

"I'm not going anywhere," I promised. I had no interest in living in Seattle. And it's not like anyone had asked me to.

TWENTY-FOUR

KIRA

I sat with Adam as long as I dared. He was in and out of sleep. I answered his phone a couple of times, as coworkers called to make sure everything had gone smoothly.

At eight o'clock, though, I kissed his sleeping forehead good-night and headed home.

I splurged on a taxi to get home quickly, but of course there was mad traffic in Back Bay. "What a rookie move," I whispered as we inched along Beacon Street. I shoved my phone in my pocket, willing myself not to text Jonas again like a nervous freak.

At six I'd allowed myself a casual "how's everything going?" text. In reply, I'd received a picture of a smiling Vivi, seated in her dining chair, shoving a piece of what looked like naan bread into her mouth.

It was smart of Jonas to send me that proof-of-life photo, the sort that kidnappers sent with their ransom demands. In truth, my little girl looked happy as a clam. I could only imagine what Vivi negotiated for a dinner order. ***No vegetables, Daddy. Those'll kill me. And what are we having for dessert?***

In the interest of appearing mostly sane, I'd restrained myself from calling or texting again. But now it was past Vivi's bedtime, and she was probably having a meltdown. Jonas was likely at his wits' end, trying to charm her out of a tantrum.

If he was smart, he'd let her watch *Frozen* on his phone.

After thrusting money at the driver, I leapt out of the cab when it stopped on my corner. At the door, I realized I didn't have my keys. Jonas did.

I gave the buzzer the barest of taps, in case Vivi was conked out in the living room.

A moment later the lock released, and I skipped the elevator in favor of dashing up the stairs. When I reached my apartment, the door was ajar, waiting for me. Quietly, I pushed it open and tiptoed inside.

But neither of the two people in the living room was a sleepy four-year-old girl.

"Dad," I said, shock in my voice. "What are *you* doing here?"

In my wildest dreams, I never expected to find my father sitting opposite Jonas, the two of them holding bottles of Sam Adams. My father was watching the baseball game on what must have been Jonas's iPad.

Slowly, my father lifted his eyes from the screen. "What a nice greeting, Kira," he quipped. He took a casual sip of his beer, as if it were the most normal thing in the world to hang out in our living room with my secret lover who was also Vivi's daddy.

I dropped my handbag onto the little entryway table, trying to get a sense of the vibe in the room. The two men looked oddly comfortable, and I didn't know what to make of it. "Dad. You never come to Boston. I thought you hated it here."

My father's expression sagged. "I know I complain about Boston. But today I thought you and Adam might need me."

Jonas had remained silent during this little exchange. I risked a glance at him, and he gave me a wink.

"I'm sorry if I didn't keep you in the loop," I said to my father. "But I didn't know if Adam told you about his surgery or not. If he was keeping a lid on it, I didn't want to blab."

My father set his beer down and faced me. "He emailed me last night to tell me what was going on. He said everything was probably going to go smoothly, but I should call you tonight to check in. Just in case."

"But you drove down," I whispered.

My father smiled. "I did."

"And... I see you've met Jonas."

My father leaned back in his chair and returned his eyes to the baseball game. "Yes, I have. So I guess now would be a good time to ask whether you and your brother have any *more* news to share with me?"

I swallowed hard. "I guess you're all caught up now."

My father snorted.

"I'm going to peek at Vivi," I said, needing a moment to myself. "Did she go to sleep willingly?"

"Of course," my father said, which made Jonas chuckle. "Okay, *willingly* isn't the right word. But she went, eventually. Many storybooks were read." My father glanced toward Jonas. "By both of us."

Well. If one person could be counted on to act normally this week, it was Vivi. But this was the oddest moment in a month full of odd moments.

Kicking off my shoes, I tiptoed down the hall, nudging open the door to Vivi's bedroom. Even before my eyes had adjusted to the dark, I saw that Vivi had gone to sleep with her body smushed against the wall. Most of her narrow bed was occupied by the horse, which lay on its side, its head on the pillow.

Slowly, I eased the horse off the mattress and set it on its plush hooves beside the bed. I pulled the covers up to Vivi's shoulders and then watched my daughter take several slow, sleepy breaths.

From his new spot in front of the bedside table, the plush horse looked like a sentry, guarding Vivi.

All was well, then. Surprisingly well.

In the living room, I could hear my father grousing about some minor Red Sox error. To *Jonas*. As if they'd been watching baseball games together for years.

I can't wait to tell Adam about this, I thought. And I was socked by a new little gust of concern for him. He was all alone in the hospital, disoriented and still in pain. Biting my lip, I walked back into the living room.

Jonas patted the sofa cushion beside him. "Have a seat?"

Feeling antsy, I walked over and perched on the edge of the couch beside him. "She had the horse in bed with her."

"That was part of our negotiation," Jonas said.

I couldn't help but smile. "I wish I could have seen her face when you showed up with that thing."

"Yeah. I'm in good and solid now." He crossed his feet on the coffee table, looking pleased with himself.

"I'll say," my father agreed. "And for God's sake, don't do anything to imply that the horse isn't real. She doesn't like that."

"Don't snub the horse," Jonas added, and then both men laughed.

They *laughed.* Together. How was that even possible?

"What is she going to name it?" I asked.

And now the two men cracked up. My father even dragged his eyes off the Sox to look over at Jonas and smile. "*You* tell her."

"Not a chance."

"What?" I asked, exasperated.

My father grinned. "You know when kids learn a new word, and then they want to use it all the time? You named one of your dolls Cutlass when Mrs. Wetzle got a new Oldsmobile."

Jonas let out a bark of laughter, and my face flushed. "Did Vivi name the horse after a car? Because Subaru isn't so bad."

Jonas and my father laughed again. It was as if the entire world was in on the joke, except for me. If I weren't so baffled, I might be annoyed.

"She called it..." Jonas broke off laughing.

"The horse is..." My father threw his head back on a snort.

"*Testicle!*" they both said, and then howled with laughter again.

I groaned. "Please tell me you're kidding."

"Nope. Sorry," Jonas said, wiping his eyes.

"He's the genius who taught her how to *spell* it," my dad gasped.

"Nooooo." I giggled. Their giddiness was getting to me, too, and there was an edge of hysteria in my laughter. My stomach shook, and I had to lean over and brace my face in my hands.

Still laughing, Jonas put one warm hand on my lower back. "Yeah, I didn't see that coming. I suggested lots of horsier names. Spot. Brownie. Blaze. But she wouldn't go for any of them."

"Figures." I chuckled. But really, after all that had happened, a horse called Testicle wasn't really so bad.

"Did you eat?" Jonas asked.

"No," I admitted.

"I saved you some chicken saagwala and rice."

"That sounds great," I said, popping up off the sofa again.

Jonas rose, putting a hand on my shoulder. "Sit. I'll get it." He walked out of the room toward the kitchen, as if he'd been here for years.

"Well," my father said.

"Well," I repeated.

"It was quite a shock to hear Vivi say, 'This is my daddy.'" My father pressed his lips together, as if a thousand other words might come pouring out if he didn't.

"I'll bet it was." I wouldn't apologize, though. When I'd first told my father I was pregnant, he'd actually threatened to kill whomever was responsible. The scene had played out like a bad movie. In the hit parade of guilt that I'd carried these past few years, keeping the details from my father didn't even make the Billboard Top 100.

He sighed. "She looks just like him, doesn't she?"

"Sure does." I fiddled with the piping on the edge of the sofa cushion. "He's going to be around some. He wants to spend time with her."

At that, my father actually smiled. "And with you, I think."

My face got red, but I didn't say a word. Whatever I decided, it was none of his business. Although it was hard to know how to handle this version of my father—the one who drove down from Maine to see his children. The one who wanted details.

"I do worry about all of you," he said quietly.

"I see that," I whispered. "But you aren't always nice about it."

He shifted in his chair. "I've always been ten steps behind you two. It's terrifying. It's the same way I felt with your mother. I've spent the last ten years terrified that you'd also disappear on me for good."

Whoa. In the first place, I hadn't heard my father mention my mother in more than a decade. And he'd said more about himself just now than he ever had before.

"I want to help, but the two of you never listened to your old dad."

"You've been too hard on Adam," I said immediately. *And me.*

My father flinched. "I know. I still love him, though. Even if I can't protect him from the difficult life he's chosen."

"But he hasn't! He's just... *Adam.*" I wasn't in any shape to make a cohesive argument about Adam's sexuality. Then again, I wasn't going to let my father off the hook. "That's the way he was made. If you can't accept that, you should stay in Maine. I'm not kidding."

He was silent for a long moment. "If I went to the hospital right now, would they throw me out?"

I shook my head. "The night after surgery, one family member is allowed to sit beside him."

"Do you think he'd mind if I was there?"

The question was a more humble one than I expected from him. "I don't think he'd mind at all. All Adam has ever wanted from you was a little support. Sitting with him qualifies. Quietly, of course."

"Okay, then." He stood up. "How do I find his room?"

I hesitated. "The chair there is awful, Dad. You won't be comfortable."

He shrugged. "I'll stay for a couple of hours. Then I'll come back here. If you lend me your keys, I won't wake you or Vivi up."

"Oh. I... Jonas has them."

"Has what?" he asked, coming around the corner with a plate in one hand and a glass in the other.

"My keys." The sight of Jonas moving through my apartment so comfortably was startling. There were so many times when I'd pictured this. I'd craved one more easy night in his company. Just one simple moment, like we'd had all those summers ago.

He handed me the plate, then drew my keys from his pocket.

My father took them, heading for the door. "Leave a light on for me."

"Will do," I croaked.

Even after the door shut on my father, I stared at it, wondering what had just happened.

"Hey. Are you all right?" Jonas set the glass down on the coffee table.

"I guess so." I gave my head a shake and tried to snap out of it.

"Sit down. Eat your dinner." He laughed. "Holy crap, I just sounded like somebody's dad."

"It's true. You did." I sat on the sofa and took a bite of rice. I never allowed Vivi to eat anything on the sofa, so I was breaking my own rule right now. But that's the kind of night that it was. "Thank you for this. And for taking Vivi earlier. Did you have any trouble?"

Jonas grinned. "The only hard part was getting her to stop talking long enough to eat. But once she started eating, a huge amount of food disappeared in a short amount of time."

"That's my girl."

"I cleaned her up as best I could. But she wasn't too interested in having her face wiped."

"Sounds about right."

"And anyway, that's when your dad showed up."

"So what was *that* like?" I took another bite and watched Jonas sit back to talk to me. What a strange little intimate moment this was. Two parents, talking about putting their kid to bed. Just like anyone.

"He's kind of hard to read," Jonas admitted, putting his hands behind his head. I tried not to stare at the way his T-shirt stretched against his chest muscles. "He's got that whole taciturn New Englander thing working. At first I thought he was just trying to place my face, you know? I could tell he was floored when Vivi called me Daddy. But he shook my hand and took it like a man."

"Wow. I'm sorry. I had no idea he was coming."

"It was fine. Maybe it was better that way, you know? He didn't get a chance to chew me out before I could stick a beer in his hand and make nice with his granddaughter. He loves Vivi."

"He does, indeed. So maybe he'll cut you a break because you contributed half her genetic material."

"Maybe."

We lapsed into silence while I finished my plate of food, and Jonas turned off the baseball game. The glass he'd brought me contained a beer. "Thank you for feeding me," I said, setting the plate down on the coffee table.

Jonas reached over and gave my knee a squeeze. "Do you know how many times you fed me? I want to take care of you."

"You do?"

"All the time." His smile was wistful. "Come over here, will you?" He opened his arms.

I hesitated for about two tenths of a second before I did exactly what he asked. I let him fold me into a hug.

"Last time I saw you, I tried to tell you that everything would be easy, but that was wishful thinking. My tour lasts a long time. Next we'll head south, and then we'll finish on the West Coast. Flights get canceled. My best friend is suffering, and I have to figure out whether I can help him."

"Mmm," I said, trying to listen. The feel of Jonas's heartbeat against my own was distracting. It wasn't just sex that I'd been missing—simple affection was a luxury I'd rarely had from a man.

"But you matter to me. So much. It's going to take me a few

months to figure out how I can spend chunks of time with you. So I need you to be patient with me. I need *you*, Kira."

I tucked my face into his neck and took a deep breath of him.

"Say something. Tell me where your head is."

My head was nestled against the soft collar of his T-shirt. "When we're in the same room, it's easy to say yes to you. When you walk out, it's harder."

He ran his fingers through my hair. "Should I go out on the sidewalk and phone you? Because I love you just as much when I'm on the road, Kira. I don't know how to convince you that it's true."

I lifted my head from his shoulder. "Spending time with you has always been..." *Just admit it already.* "Magical, okay? But then you leave again, and I feel like I've been run over by a truck."

He gave me a sexy smile. "Magical. I can work with that. Me and my magic wand..."

I gave him a playful slap on the chest. "Don't laugh at me, okay? I'm trying to answer your question."

His face got serious immediately.

"I think about you out there, doing your thing. All those people screaming your name. And I wonder why you'd want Vivi and I to pin you down. I just don't trust it."

"You don't trust it," he repeated with a wince. "You don't trust *me*."

"That's not what I said..."

He held up a hand. "It's fine, Kira. I've never given you a single reason to trust me. The first thing I ever told you about myself was that I was a jackass who never loved his ex-girlfriend. Then I went away for five years. I had a lot of growing up to do. But I've come a long way."

"So..." I cleared my throat. "I still don't know how it could work. I need to be in Boston. Adam is not okay yet, and I think he's afraid I'll leave him. I could never do that. Not after he's done so much for me."

Jonas gave me a squeeze. "Can I be with you in Boston? I

asked Ethan to look for a real estate agent who works in this neighborhood."

I raised my head. "Really?"

"Really. I'm going to take some time off after my tour. My life gets easier then. Can you wait ten weeks for me?"

I could. And more than that, I wanted to. "All right. We'll have to make time to talk on the phone."

"Do you have a calendar? Like, a paper one?"

"Sure? Just a minute." I went into the kitchen and returned with a wall calendar that Adam had made with a picture of Vivi on every page.

"Aw! Look at this. I need a copy." Jonas pulled out his phone. "Okay. August seventh my tour is over. And I don't have another show date until the twenty-fourth, in Munich."

"Munich?"

"We're headlining a music festival. Even though I told my agent not to book anything more in Europe or Asia, I can't cancel this. But maybe you and Vivi could fly over with me beforehand, and we could go to Euro Disney, or something."

I clicked my pen and made a note on the calendar. "Don't even *breathe* the word Disney near Vivi until the day you are ready to pull up to the gates."

"Point taken," he said.

"Okay, Mr. Magic. What else is on your calendar?"

TWENTY-FIVE

JONAS

I sat with Kira for hours as we worked through the details of our busy lives.

Together, we mapped out the next several months. This time, I was more honest about all the uncertainties in my life. "I have to figure out if Nixon is okay. And when we'll need to get into the studio again." I didn't explain to Kira that Nixon always felt better again when fall arrived, because I really didn't understand it myself.

"Okay," Kira said, setting the calendar down. "That's a lot of flying to Boston."

"I don't mind," I said quickly.

"It's just..." Her eyes lifted to search my face. "How does this work next year? When you can't take any more time off? Your life is in Seattle and ours is here."

I hitched myself closer to her on the couch and pulled her in. "I probably have to record in Seattle, but I can write anywhere. I promise."

Kira started to say something else, but I didn't let her. I leaned forward and took her mouth in a kiss. Just one. And she tasted like heaven. Like an angel.

She *was* an angel. Kira took care of her brother and her

daughter. She'd once taken care of me, and I wanted to return the favor. I needed to start now. Kira was probably exhausted. I broke our kiss. "It's late, and you've had a tough day. We should get some sleep."

She smiled, and I felt it all over. "My father is staying here. I don't quite know where to put you."

This made me grin. "You can't close the barn door after the horse gets out, Kira. I don't think he'll be shocked if I sleep in your bed."

For a moment I thought she'd argue. "I suppose you're right," she said after a pause. "I'll get him set up to stay in Adam's room. I'll leave him a note."

While she did that, I went into Kira's tiny room, where a double bed took up most of the floorspace. It wasn't meant to be a bedroom, that much was obvious. There wasn't even a closet.

I'd mentioned to Kira that I wanted to rent a place in Boston. But I'd rather buy a roomy brownstone and put a little recording studio in it. There would be a big bedroom for the two of us, a room for Vivi, of course, and also a guest room. There would be space enough for everyone. And it needed to be close to Adam, of course.

Did such a place exist? I'd have to find out.

I got ready for bed and climbed under Kira's covers without waiting for an invitation. A few minutes later she appeared in the doorway wearing her black nightgown. Her eyes swept over me, and her lips quirked in amusement.

"What's so funny?"

"You. There."

"You see anything you like?" I wiggled my eyebrows at her.

Kira rolled her door shut—it was a pocket door, the sliding kind—and then she shut off the light and slipped into bed beside me.

"Your room is like a little cabin," I remarked.

"That's the generous description. It's meant to be an office. I gave Vivi the real bedroom, so she'd have somewhere to keep her toys."

"Makes sense," I said, reaching for her. She fit perfectly against me. "The only thing I really don't like about your room is that there's no lock on the door."

"I never needed one before. And my father could come home any minute..."

"I know." I kissed her nose. "Tonight I won't be able to show you how much I've missed you." I kissed her again, though, and Kira was ready. She leaned in, and slowly we tasted each other. I'd been dreaming of this for days. I swept a naughty hand down her body, shamelessly palming her core.

Kira made a sound that could only be described as a stifled whimper. "None of that," she whispered. "Not until you plan to follow through."

"Oh, I'll follow through," I promised. "The next time I see you."

She frowned. "You're right. That's perfectly reasonable." But then she slid a hand over my hip and onto my fabric-covered cock that was already straining against my boxer briefs.

I groaned and pushed her hand away, for which I received an evil giggle. "Point made, sweetness. Now cut that out." I eased her body over mine, arranging us so that she was half-lying on me, but not touching my eager dick. "This is nice, too, you know."

"It is," she agreed, giving my shoulder a little squeeze. "This is pretty awesome."

I kissed her forehead. "Love you, Kira."

She sighed in my arms.

And I was happier than I'd been in a long time, sex or no sex. Although I mentally adjusted my real estate wish list, adding a bolt for the bedroom door. And a big kitchen. "You know, I asked Vivi what she liked to eat for breakfast. And she said you make awesome strawberry pancakes. She said you'd make them for us tomorrow."

"Maybe," Kira hedged. "If there's time before I go to see Adam."

I gave her a little pinch on the ass. "I'll convince you."

"Mm-hmm," she said lazily, and I took another deep breath of her clean, citrus scent.

I was drowsing when I heard the apartment door open and then shut again. At the sound of the deadbolt locking, Kira lifted her head from my shoulder .

Mr. Cassidy was home.

We lay there silently, listening to quiet footsteps move about the apartment as Kira's father got ready for bed.

I turned my head so that my mouth was just beside her ear. At a very low volume, I moaned.

"Stop that!" she hissed.

"If you promise to make the pancakes," I whispered, "then I won't start grunting like a horny pig right now."

Kira clapped a hand over her mouth, her ribcage expanding with laughter.

"Unh, baby," I grunted, thrusting my hips, threatening more noise. She pressed her hand onto *my* mouth this time. Naturally, I moaned beneath her fingers.

"Stop!" she squeaked. "I'll make the freaking pancakes."

I had to roll my face into the pillow to laugh.

"You are so evil," she hissed, but I could feel her laughing, too.

For several minutes, we both had to fight off laughter. Finally it was quiet in the apartment again, and my stomach had stopped shaking. I was still grinning in the dark, though. I wanted more of this—the comfort of lying beside my girl, laughing over some bit of nonsense. "I hope there's real maple syrup," I whispered to the ceiling, trying to get one more rise out of Kira.

But her breathing had evened out. She was sleeping.

It was so peaceful that I closed my eyes and didn't open them again.

Hours later came the unfamiliar sound of a rolling pocket door. There was movement beside the bed. Slowly, I opened my eyes. To my horror, a strange animal stared me right in the face, only inches away. Startled, I sat up in a big hurry, only to realize it was the stuffed horse.

"*Shit,*" I gasped.

"You said a bad word," Vivi said, climbing onto the bed.

"Sorry," I said, catching my breath. "But your horse scared me."

"He likes it when you call him Testicle."

Kira groaned. "What time is it?"

"Time to make the pancakes!" I gave her hip a squeeze.

"With strawberries," Vivi added. "And whipped cream."

"Whipped cream?" I asked.

"No whipped cream," Kira mumbled into the pillow. "I need coffee."

"I can probably figure that out," I said, getting out of the bed. I found my jeans and stepped into them.

"I know where the filters are," Vivi volunteered. "Can I push the button?" She ran out of the room.

I leaned over Kira, kissing the back of her neck. "I like waking up in your bed."

She opened her eyes and smiled at me. And it was better than strawberry pancakes. Or even whipped cream.

* * *

THE MORNING WENT TOO FAST. I drank coffee sitting on the living room floor, listening to Vivi talk about her horse. Fulfilling the promise that I'd extracted with underhanded tactics, Kira made four-grain strawberry pancakes after her father woke up.

Somehow, she even made Vivi's pancake come out in the shape of a heart.

"Make Daddy a heart, too!" Vivi demanded. "They taste better."

I bit back a cheesy comment about getting Kira's heart. "I like the taste of round ones," I said instead. Kira was already slaving in the kitchen because I'd asked her to.

"Here you go," she said, handing me a stack of three

pancakes with butter oozing between them. "Troublemaker," she whispered under her breath.

I took my plate to the table and sat down between Vivi and Mr. Cassidy. I cut a wedge from my pancake stack and put it in my mouth. Then I groaned out loud.

"What?" Vivi demanded.

"So good," I said, swallowing. "Everything your mother ever cooked for me is just so *good.*" I raised my eyes to Kira and then gave her the tiniest eyebrow wiggle.

With a look of warning, she turned quickly back to the skillet.

My phone vibrated, and I unpocketed it to see that Ethan had ordered a car for me for one hour from now.

One more hour. How was I going to walk out of here where everything was wonderful and just *leave* again?

Across the room, Kira's land line rang. She snatched it off the counter. "Adam?" Her face relaxed as she listened to the caller. "Okay, honey. I will. See you then." She hung up.

"How is he?" Kira's father asked.

"He sounds good!" She smiled, lifting pancakes onto a plate for herself. "He said not to rush over there, because he felt okay, and he thought they'd discharge him around eleven."

"My car comes in an hour," I said.

Vivi looked up, a piece of strawberry in her teeth. "Can I go with you?"

"Not this time," I said gently. "I have to go back to work. But I promise I'll be back."

After eating, I made sure to clean up Kira's kitchen as best I could without knowing where everything belonged. I'd lived a wild life for a while now, one where dirty dishes didn't really figure in. But I was ready to wash stacks and stacks of them if it meant more days with Kira and Vivi.

And then I was down to half an hour. I threw my things back into my duffel. The minutes ticking down made me feel edgy. I hated goodbyes. And Vivi felt it, too. She was galloping around, getting a little crazier than Kira wanted her to be.

Kira's father sat on the ottoman and pulled on his shoes. "Vivianne, say goodbye to your dad right now, and I'll take you out to the swings in the park for a while."

She stopped twirling. "Really?"

"Really."

Vivi marched over to stand in front of me. "Bye, Daddy."

I scooped her into my lap. "Bye, sweetie." She smelled like maple syrup and weighed less than seemed possible. "I'm going to call you guys, okay? And you can call me. We can use Skype, too."

"'Kay," Vivi agreed.

I gave her one more squeeze, and then she squirmed out of my grasp. "I'm going to the park now."

"Okay," I said, my throat prickling.

She wiggled into her sandals and went to stand by the door. I quickly shook Mr. Cassidy's hand, and then the two of them went outside.

The door closed with a click.

I let out my breath and turned to Kira. "That was nice of your dad. He made that a little less stressful."

She sat on the arm of the sofa. "It really was. And he isn't known for being Mr. Sensitive. I don't even know what to think."

I reached up and took her hand, pulling her down into my lap. "I still have to say goodbye to you, though."

"Yeah," she said softly, running a hand through my hair.

I grabbed her hips, turning her until she got the hint and straddled me. I leaned back against the couch and smiled. "You don't have to wait a half hour to kiss me goodbye."

"That's not how goodbye kisses work," she whispered.

"It is if they last a half hour," I argued.

She wiggled on my lap, bringing her body closer. "Is that so?" She leaned down and kissed me.

I smiled against her lips, because she smelled like maple syrup, too. "Mmm," I said, deepening the kiss. And maybe good-byes weren't so bad after all. I trapped her bottom lip between my teeth, and Kira melted against me. One kiss turned into another, and then another.

I cupped her ass. "We're alone right now," I whispered between kisses.

"Not for long," she panted. "Fifteen minutes, tops."

"If you feel like I do right now," I said against her lips, "then we only need about five. Put your arms around me, sweetness."

When she did, I stood, lifting her. I carried her into her room, depositing her on the bed. Then I slid the door shut and made very good use of those last fifteen minutes.

TWENTY-SIX

KIRA

My face still felt flushed as I tucked myself back into my clothing. I raked my fingers through my hair.

Jonas had never looked better. Sex-tousled hair looked natural on him, and I didn't want to stop looking at him, ever. I could drink him in all day and never get enough. He jammed his hand into his pocket, bringing his phone out to check the screen. "The car is outside."

Chin up, I coached myself. This was only a temporary separation. "I'll walk you out."

Jonas slung his duffel onto his shoulder and strode through the apartment. I nabbed my keys and followed him out the door.

In the stairwell, Jonas held my hand. "I told Vivi she could call me anytime. My shows mostly start after she's asleep, anyway."

"Okay," I said, opening the exterior door. "Text me if you have downtime, and we'll call." I was watching Jonas's face, because he was so easy on the eyes, when his expression suddenly morphed into anger.

I turned to see a big camera just a few feet from my face.

"Jonas!" the stranger behind the camera called. "What's the pretty girl's name?"

Jonas grabbed my hand. I expected him to pull me back into the building, but he led me to the black car waiting at the curb. He yanked open the door and then pointed, allowing me to duck inside first. Then he slid in after me and slammed the door.

The driver pulled away from the curb. I watched over my shoulder as the photographer snapped a few extra pictures as we drove away. Then he gave up, turning away, heading down the street.

"Turn here," Jonas instructed the driver. His jaw was tight. "And turn again, then pull over."

The car came to a stop, and Jonas scrubbed his face with his hands. "I'm sorry about that."

I truly didn't know what to say. "Is that going to happen a lot?"

"God, I hope not," he said, studying me now. "Ethan told me about a new law that stops them from taking pictures of kids. So that's a good trend. Tonight I'll call my publicist and ask her to work on a strategy."

"Okay," I said quietly.

Jonas threw his head back against the headrest. "Look, I know it sucks. You don't want that in your life. But I hope you want *me* in your life. And I intend to be worth the trouble."

I reached out to take his strong hand in mine—the same one that fingered the chords for all the songs he'd written. The one that caught Vivi when she jumped off the dock in Maine. The one that had washed the batter bowl in my kitchen an hour ago. "I know you're worth the trouble."

A smile began at his lips and spread slowly until it warmed his eyes. "I want to be, Kira. I mean to be worth it." He took my face in both hands, giving me a single kiss.

"Now, now," I said. "No more of that. You have to get to the airport, and I have to get Adam home."

But he gave me one more, still smiling. "I'll call you tonight."

"I know you will. Unless you can't. And then we'll talk tomorrow."

"Okay. One more just for saying that." He kissed me again, and I laughed.

Then I made myself open the door and get out of the car.

He waved at me through the back window as the car pulled away.

TWENTY-SEVEN

JONAS

I sat in the car on the tarmac, watching them fuel up the charter flight I'd booked. I pulled out my phone and called Nixon.

"Hey! Did you get some time with your girls?" my friend asked.

"I sure did. I'm so glad I came up here. Where are you now?"

"On the bus, dude. So I got no idea where the fuck we are."

"What do you see out the window?" I asked, just to give Nixon a hard time.

"The curtain," he answered, and I laughed.

"Thanks for making the effort to figure that out."

"Don't mention it."

There was a silence then, but it wasn't uncomfortable. I could picture Nixon lying on his bunk, passing the time until the next show. "We're going to take a little better care of ourselves from now on, okay, dude?"

"Whatever you say, big man. Did you call to find out if I'm drunk? I'm not. Ask me to recite the alphabet backwards, or some shit."

"Can you?" I challenged. "I'm not sure I can do that sober."

"Okay, maybe not that." We both laughed. "I'm not drunk, though," he said after a minute. "I swear."

"I didn't call to spy on you. I was just thinking about how we used to love touring. But these last couple of years have been rough. The label just keeps adding cities. Next year I'm going to push back on them."

"All right. I won't argue."

"What if we toured only in May and September? Maybe there's somewhere else you'd rather go for the summer. You know, change it up. Keep yourself from hurting."

"Like a rehab place?" Nixon did not keep the scorn out of his voice. "I hate that shit. Yeah, it's easy to stay sober when you're there, but they want to talk to you all fucking day. I'd rather have oral surgery than talk to those fuckers."

"There might be another way," I said thoughtfully.

"Yeah? What's your plan?"

"I'm going to give it some thought, and I'll let you know. Looks like the jet is ready for me. I'll see you in a few hours, okay?"

"Glad you got to see Kira," Nixon said.

"Me too, man. Me too."

TWENTY-EIGHT

KIRA

Two Weeks Later

I checked the mail on the way back from the park. In our lobby mailbox, I found two bills and a large envelope addressed to me. The return address read: *John Jonas Smith, The Purple Bus, Somewhere in Missouri.*

I smiled to myself as I followed Vivi onto the elevator.

I didn't open the envelope right away. I had no idea what was inside, but I savored it nonetheless.

I settled Vivi with a snack at the kitchen table, and then I called my brother. "Hi," I said when he answered his office line. "I know I'm a pest, but I needed to know how you're feeling." Adam had had his first radiation treatment at noon.

"I'm fine, Kira. Really. And I'm leaving the office in half an hour."

"Glad to hear that, honey. I'm making white lasagna for dinner."

"You are a total babe. See you soon."

After I hung up, I got comfortable on the sofa and opened the envelope from Jonas. There were several pages. It seemed he'd written me a letter on copy paper, the lines of text dodging pictures that he'd printed or copied onto each page.

DEAR KIRA,

We just spoke on the phone last night, but there were some things I wanted to show you.

The band had to fly to Seattle for a charity gig, which meant that I got to spend one night in my own apartment. I spent the whole time imagining what it will be like when you and Vivi come out here in October. And look what I pulled out of my desk.

It has that travel-weary look, doesn't it?

I FLIPPED the page to see a picture of the envelope I'd tucked into his guitar case all those years ago. The corners were tattered now. I'd penned his name on the front, with swirly letters that looked feminine and hopeful.

The sight made me groan aloud. I'd spent many hours of my life wishing I'd never even sent that thing.

Mercifully, he did not photograph the actual letter. Because even a glimpse of the envelope reminded me too much of being twenty and clueless. And hopelessly in love with someone who lived on the other side of the country.

I read on.

YOU KNOW I'll always regret that I didn't respond to your letter. I can't change what I did in my knucklehead past. I can, however, sit down and write you now.

And I've included pictures, because a certain short person we both love hasn't learned to read. So here we go.

First up is a picture of my Seattle apartment building. It's fancy but a little cold. I had a decorator handle all the furniture and lamps and crap. So my unit is comfortable, but a little boring. You'll have to trust me, because I decided to send you a photo of the pool instead. See? Vivi will love it.

HE WASN'T WRONG. She'd love the photo and the pool itself and anything else her daddy wanted to tell her.

And so did I. Jonas and I had enjoyed several nice telephone conversations these past two weeks. But holding his letter in my hands was special.

I turned the page to find a pixelated photo of a little European store front.

THIS ONE DIDN'T COME out so well. It's a restaurant in Munich that serves fondue. I was planning our trip to Munich in August, and I remembered that I'd once been to this place, and that it was fun to dip things in cheese. If you and Vivi travel with me, I propose that we'll find <u>at least</u> one unusual restaurant per country. I mean, if you're coming all the way to Germany, you should eat something regional, no?

Wait. Is fondue French, not German? Is that regional enough? Please weigh in.

Now here is a picture of my bunk on the purple bus. Those are my feet at the end of it. And please notice that big empty space on the wall, which really needs a drawing. In marker or crayon. I'm not picky.

Just to be fair, I've enclosed a drawing I did for Vivi of me pushing her on the swings. (Isn't it lucky that I decided to become a musician instead of an artist?) Please see what you can do to get our kid to send me some artwork. Ethan says that the hotels on our itinerary are pretty good about holding mail for us if it gets there before we do.

I peeked at the final sheet of paper, which was indeed a drawing. Of sorts. There were two stick figures in the foreground. One of them used stick-figure hands to push a stick swing. On the swing was a little stick girl with curly hair.

In the background on a bench was one more stick figure. An arrow pointed at its head, and above the arrow was scrawled "Hot Mama!"

And, sure. The drawing was crap, but the compliment made me purr.

I'LL SIGN off for now, Kira. But I miss you both, and I think about you all the time.

I wish you were here on this bus with me right now.

I wish eight weeks would hurry up.

And mostly I hope you'll forgive me for never having written you a letter before now. I plan to write many more of them. This one is a down payment.

You're it for me, Kira. No matter where I go, I'll always come back to you.

You're my purple kitty.

Love you so much,

Jonas

OH MY.

I sat with the letter in my lap for a long time. It was a much different letter than I'd wanted to get from him all those years ago, but so much better in its own way. These weren't the fruitless yearnings of two young people who had no idea what to do with the connection they'd found. Instead, they were the heartfelt words of a man who was ready to love me for good.

It was more than enough.

I put the drawing aside for Vivi. Then I got up and went to my desk, taking out a piece of stationery. With the pen in my hand, I considered what sort of letter I would write.

Dear Jonas, it should begin. *I loved your letter. And I love you. You did not mention whether or not your apartment has a kitchen. Or a cupcake pan. Because if I had those things, I could make you some very macho cupcakes. Please advise...*

I smiled to myself. It would be a very different letter than I had written last time. And he would not need to carry it around the world, because he'd have me with him, instead. As it should be.

Still smiling, I called Vivi. "Sweetie!"

A minute later, my daughter appeared in the doorway, her turquoise eyes squinting with a question. "What?"

"Do you think you can draw Purple Kitty?"

"'Course." She shrugged. "Why?"

"Daddy would like it."

Vivi considered this for a moment. "I gotta find my purple crayon." She spun on her heel and marched off again.

Chuckling, I watched her go, then turned back to my own letter.

EPILOGUE

ONE YEAR LATER

Kira

I hung three wet towels over the rails of the new deck. With Vivi and Adam out of the house for a little while, I had a few moments to myself to prepare for the onslaught of our guests. It was hot for June, and the deck boards warmed my feet as I crossed to the sliding glass doors.

Inside, I did a scan of the living area. Things were still a bit unfinished—the window trim around the new skylights had yet to be painted, and a sawdust smell lingered from the renovations. But Jonas had only purchased the B&B a few months ago, and it was really quite surprising how much the contractors he'd hired had accomplished already.

I fluffed the pillows on the brand-new sofas, then headed into the kitchen where the real work had been done. Mrs. Wetzle's old kitchen had been gutted and then filled with surfaces and appliances that seemed too fancy for Nest Lake, Maine.

In fact, the purchase of a summer place seemed awfully extravagant. But Jonas had retooled his summer schedule in a way that allowed us to spend some blocks of time here. Like, this week we'd have four days together, with the band members as our guests. After, the band would play a couple of New England cities and then take more than a month's break. This summer's tour had been concentrated into a few short bursts, with lots of time for family.

Even so, I thought the purchase of Mrs. Wetzle's home was indulgent, especially when my father's house was practically across the street.

"I want it to be *our* place, so I can have industry people visit if I need to." He'd chuckled as he'd added, "But I'm going to send them the directions before they agree to come. You know —fly to Maine and drive an hour and a half. If they still think the meeting is worthwhile after they figure that out, then they're free to come."

"You are a very clever man," I had said, patting him on the chest. "But it hardly seems worth all the money you're putting into it."

"Sweetness, Nest Lake is my favorite place *in the world*. And the B&B is for sale at a dirt-cheap price. Would you rather I dropped five million on Maui?"

"Heck no."

"So you see what a practical man I am?"

At first we'd had quite a few arguments about money, until Jonas had laid it all out one afternoon. "I have a lot of it," he'd said. "And I never had anyone to spend it on before. I didn't blow it on a lot of bling like some guys, okay? And Kira, I'm in a hurry to enjoy it a little. You can't take it with you."

"I know," I'd conceded.

Jonas had also bought an apartment in a fancy Boston high rise. He'd wanted a house, but the apartment building had doormen and security, twenty-four seven. It also had an underground parking garage, which foiled the paparazzi. Vivi and I had moved in with him in January, after Adam had been finished with radiation, and Jonas had been finished with all his overseas obligations.

Since I'd been able to go to school full time this year, I'd finally finished my degree. Then—and this felt a little weird—I didn't bother looking for a job. Not yet, anyway.

"Get a job if you want a job," Jonas had said when we'd talked about it. "But don't get one for money. Vivi is only five, and you can't get these years back. So if staying home with her is what you'd prefer, then do it. Or, if you want to work, we'll hire a nanny."

"That would cost nearly as much as I'd make," I'd pointed out.

Jonas had just shrugged. "Do what makes you happy. Because money isn't an issue right now."

It was the first time in my life that was true.

Walking into each of Mrs. Wetzle's guest rooms, I checked one last time to see that everything was in order.

Hopefully I'd soon stop thinking of this place as Mrs. Wetzle's.

In March, Vivi and I had driven up to get the deed and the keys. It had been just the two of us, because Jonas had been touring Australia.

Mrs. Wetzle had cried at the closing, even though it was her idea to sell the house and move into an upscale retirement community in Portland. "I'll miss the place," she'd said, dabbing at her eyes.

"We'll take good care of it," I'd promised.

"I hope your musician comes back to you," she'd added.

"He'll be back on Tuesday," I'd said in what was probably a testy voice.

"Well. I sure hope so. Musicians are special, but they don't stick around. My Harry was a pianist. He loved me, but he loved the big life more." She blew her nose. "He left me when I was thirty-two. I never loved another man."

Just like that, all the irritation drained out of me. I'd always thought her dislike of musicians was a character flaw, like her bad cooking. It never occurred to me that it was personal. "I'm so sorry to hear that," I'd said, chastened.

"At least you got a baby out of it," Mrs. Wetzle went on. "I was alone all these years."

Just when you think you know a person.

A few minutes later, the keys to the B&B had been in my purse, and the property lawyer had finished collating the documents. I'd wished the older woman luck, and I'd gone back across the street to see how many cookies Vivi had conned out of her grandfather.

The following week, a pack of contractors had descended on the place, transforming it into a nearly unrecognizable space. The room Jonas had rented six years ago used to have a separate entrance. It had been reconfigured to be a first-floor bedroom, just off the open-plan great room.

"I don't care particularly where everyone sleeps this weekend," Jonas had told me over the phone this morning. "But that room is *ours*."

"Really?" I'd asked. "Back to the scene of the crime?"

"Hell, yes. That was the hottest night of my life. Nobody else gets that room. Ever."

Of course, the bedroom looked completely different now. The new bed sat against the opposite wall from where it had been before. The old carpeting was gone, revealing pretty oak floors. Yet outside the windows the lilac shrubs still grew. They were blooming now, filling the room with their heady scent.

The place was familiar, yet totally different. So was I, for that matter.

I wandered upstairs, looking into each bedroom in turn. Most had queen-sized beds in them, but one bedroom had two sets of bunk beds instead.

"We have to have four children to make that worthwhile," Jonas had joked. "I don't want you to complain that four beds is too extravagant."

"You crack yourself up," I'd quipped. Though he often told me that he wanted more children. Usually when we were both naked.

Satisfied by my inspection, I wandered back downstairs into

the scene-of-the-crime room and sat on the bed. There was a brand-new magazine waiting there for me—I'd bought it to celebrate the end of exams, which had finished only a week ago. But makeup tips and celeb gossip just couldn't hold my attention, not when Jonas was about to show up. We hadn't seen each other in three weeks, and I was feeling almost more impatient than Vivi for Jonas to arrive.

Finally, after what seemed like hours, I heard the sound of bus tires on gravel.

Grinning like an idiot, I forced myself not to dash around like a kid on Christmas. Calmly, I walked through the house to the back door. Slipping on a pair of flip-flops, I stepped out onto the long front porch.

The bus doors swung open, and Jonas jumped down first, a huge smile on his face. "Yeah, baby! I'm back." He jogged toward me, and then we were holding each other tightly. I buried my face in his neck, and he whispered in my ear. "Missed you, sweetness."

"I missed you, too."

He stepped back and grinned at me. "How does the house look? Show me everything."

"Shouldn't I greet..." I pointed at the bus.

He shrugged. "They'll understand. Besides, I think Nix and Quinn were asleep when we pulled up." He tugged my hand and led me inside. "Wow," he said right away. "The new living room looks great."

"It really does."

"The old one reminded me of a Depression-era movie."

"Why did you buy it if it reminded you of the Depression?"

Jonas squeezed my hip. "Location, location, location."

I giggled at the sheer ridiculousness of that idea. "In the dictionary under 'middle of nowhere' there's probably a picture of Nest Lake, Maine."

"It might be nowhere, but it's *our* nowhere. I want to see the kitchen." Jonas ducked behind the new wall of glass blocks and whistled. "Nice."

"I know. It really is."

Jonas looked around. "Where's the Vivster?"

"Well, she spent most of the day asking, 'When is daddy coming? When is daddy coming?' So I sent her out for a bike ride with Adam. They'll be back soon."

"Awesome. I brought her a birthday present."

"Jonas! You already sent her a pile of them."

"Yeah, but this one is *in person.*"

"Hi, Kira!" a voice boomed behind me.

I spun around. "Ethan!"

He caught me in a hug. "I went shopping outside of Portland. If it's okay with you, we'll grill some steaks tonight."

"That sounds great. What can I make to go with them? It's too early in the season for corn on the cob."

"We'll bake some potatoes. I've got it handled."

"Do we have any beer yet?" Jonas asked, heading for the Sub-Zero.

I smiled at him. "Would I host your band without beer?"

"So where's Adam?" Ethan asked.

"Well, he spent the day asking me when you were getting here. So I let Vivi take him out for a bike ride."

At that, Jonas snorted into the refrigerator. He came out with three bottles of Shipyard ale.

"None for me," I said quickly.

"No?" Jonas shrugged, putting one back.

I felt a flush hit my neck. I'd been savoring my little secret for the last few hours. But if I didn't tell him soon, he was going to know something was up.

Ethan took a beer. "I'll divvy up the rooms," he said before heading back outside.

The moment he left, Jonas set his beer down on the countertop and grabbed me. Surprised, I made a very sexy noise, something like "ooorff!"

"Sorry," Jonas mumbled into my neck. His fingers stroked my back, coming to rest on my ass. With a yank, he pulled my body against his. "How many times do you think I can get you naked between now and Tuesday morning?" he asked, kissing his way across my hairline. "We have a little work to do, you and me. Vivi needs a baby sister."

I pulled back. "Well, there's a problem with that."

Concern crossed his face. "A problem? Wait... do you have your period?"

His look of horror was so genuine that I had to bite back a smile. "Just... follow me." I turned and walked into our bedroom, with Jonas on my heels. I shut the door behind us.

"Is something the matter?"

I shook my head. "It's just that you can't get me pregnant this weekend."

"Why not?"

From my back pocket, I pulled the pregnancy test I'd taken earlier in the afternoon. "I already am."

First I saw amazement in his eyes, and then sheer joy. "That..." He grabbed me for a kiss. "Is..." I got another one. "Amazing." And then he began to laugh. "How long have you been sitting on this news?"

"I'm a week late, but I waited to take the test until about an hour ago. I was going to wait until you were here, but the suspense..."

I had to stop talking, because Jonas picked me up and carried me over to the bed. "This doesn't change my plans for the weekend very much," he said, running a hand up my bare leg. "We'll have pregnant sex instead of baby-making sex." He lifted my T-shirt and began kissing my stomach.

"There's nothing to see, Jonas. Give it a few months."

"Shh..." he said. "I'm busy here."

The wet, open-mouthed kisses on my lower stomach began to have the most glorious effect on me. I shifted my hips on the bed.

"You like that, don't you?" Jonas whispered. He rolled back the waistband of my shorts, his kisses teasing me with their proximity.

"Jonas..." I whimpered. "Lock the door."

He disappeared for a few seconds to do just that, and then came back to yank my shorts down my hips, my panties with them. "I needed you before," he said, kissing his way up the inside of my bare thigh. "But now I'm desperate to celebrate." Then, with no more preamble, he dropped his wicked mouth to my pussy and kissed me right where it counts.

Sex with Jonas had only gotten better now that we lived together. I let out a loud moan.

"Mmm," he echoed, the hum of his lips vibrating against me.

"Jonas, I need you," I begged. "And we don't have a lot of time."

Instead of answering, he flattened his tongue between my legs and just held it there.

"Please," I cried. It had been too long since I'd held him in my arms. And he was still too far away.

But he only teased me with his tongue. "Bossy" he whispered between kisses.

"Hurry," I urged, writhing with need.

Finally, I heard a zipper give way. And then he crawled up my body, resting his hips against mine. The temptation of having him so close to where I needed him made me flex against the bed. "Kira," he whispered. "Is it safe to do this?"

Instead of answering, I grabbed his shoulders and pushed him over to the side. Scrambling, I climbed on top as he settled on his back. Then, one knee on either side of him, I leaned down, my hands pressing his forearms against the bed, and impaled myself on him.

The look on his face was a gorgeous mixture of lust and surprise. "Jesus, Kira."

Usually, I let him take the lead. I'd certainly never thrown him down quite like that and jumped on his erection.

There was no time for embarrassment. Who knew how many minutes we had until someone called us? This ache demanded attention, and the feel of him immobilized beneath me was too beautiful to ignore. With his hands still trapped, I began to move.

"Oh, fuck," Jonas panted. His eyes were unfocused, his breath sawing in and out. "Fuck, that's good. And... what is that amazing scent?" He inhaled deeply.

"Lilacs," I breathed. There was a hedge right outside the window, and the room was heavy with their perfume. We were making love in Maine, the breeze tickling the window curtains. Right where it all began...

I shifted on his body, stirring my hips against his. There had never been a more beautiful moment in my life. Or maybe they were all beautiful. My soul was too crowded with pleasure to know for sure.

Jonas's wrists jerked as he struggled to lift his torso, angling for a better look at my body. But I kept a tight grip on his arms. The smile on his face told me exactly how much he enjoyed this. I quickened my rhythm, watching his face until his head flopped back with abandon. "Use me, sweetness. Just like that." Tightening his jaw, he punched his hips against me.

And then I couldn't hold off any longer. "Oh," I moaned. It was coming. And it was going to be good.

Jonas chose that moment to overpower me, slipping his wrists free, grabbing my shoulders, tugging me down onto his body. "Mouth, baby," he demanded.

I dropped onto him for a wet, sliding kiss that brought me right over the edge. His hips jerked beneath me, and then our moans slid together, winding around our tangled tongues, riding out our bliss until there was nothing left but rapid breathing.

We lay there for a sweaty minute or two until Jonas broke the silence. "Damn," he said, giving me a squeeze. "Can we get married now?"

My heart skipped a beat, because it was the first time Jonas had ever said the "M" word to me, and it had sounded like a joke. I laughed to cover my discomfort. "Sounds like you gave the idea a whole lot of thought first."

He untangled himself from me, and I was sorry to see him go. Even sorrier when I heard him fumbling with the pair of khaki shorts he'd dropped on the floor only minutes before.

Yet Jonas didn't put them on. Instead, he came back to the bed, sitting beside me and fumbling into one of the pockets. He cast the shorts aside again, and I didn't understand why. Until I saw his outstretched hand, and the pretty little blue box that sat upon it.

"I *have* been thinking about it," he said. "And I got this for you."

With a shaking hand, I reached for the box. Cracking it open, I found a beautiful diamond solitaire inside—the stone was square in shape, simple. And just *beautiful*.

"Marry me, Kira," Jonas whispered.

"Oh my God! I love it." I looked into his eyes, which were even more beautiful than the ring. "But you never bring up marriage."

He grinned. "I would have asked you months ago. But I waited a year, because I wanted you to trust me. I didn't want you to feel rushed."

"I wouldn't have turned you down."

"I don't know, lady. You still haven't said yes." His eyes teased me.

"Yes!"

With a whoop, he wrapped his arms around me. "Can we tell Vivi about the baby?"

"No way. It's too early. But we can talk about the wedding. And then we can plan it to happen immediately, so I won't look like a whale bride."

"Well. I suppose I can live with that." He kissed my neck.

I heard voices on the other side of the door, so I reluctantly got up and began to reassemble my clothing. I tossed Jonas's shorts at him. "Put these on. We have to pretend to be respectable."

He gave me a lazy smile. "Why start now?"

"Good point." Half-dressed, I climbed back onto the bed to kiss him again. And again. And many more times after that.

THE END

ACKNOWLEDGMENTS

A special thank you to Claudia, Jenn and Michelle for reading early and catching the last few errors. Thank you to Edie for your tireless editing.

Thank you to Sarah Hansen for your beautiful work.

Thank you to Tim Paige and Erin Mallon for your stellar performances on the audio book!

Made in the USA
Las Vegas, NV
29 September 2022

56186202R00154